DEAD SPOTS

MELISSA F. OLSON

47N RTH

Text copyright © 2012 Melissa F. Olson
All rights reserved.
Printed in the United States of America.
No part of this book may be reproduced, or stored in a retrieval system, or
transmitted in any form or by any means, electronic, mechanical, photocopying,
recording, or otherwise, without
express written permission of the publisher.

Published by 47North
P.O. Box 400818
Las Vegas, NV 89140

ISBN-13: 9781612185590
ISBN-10: 1612185592

For Mom and Dad, who rolled their eyes, shook their heads—and then backed me up every time.

Prologue

Jared loved trees.

His little sister was the better climber, to his disgust, but at twelve, she lacked Jared's reverence for the trees, his respect. Emily would shimmy up, crow her victory, and skitter down again, laughing and breathless. It was Jared who loved to sit and listen to the wind, to find the perfect nook and watch the leaves move.

After their mother died, Jared and Emily took to the trees, escaping their house each hot summer night to sneak into the park at the end of their block. They stayed as late as they could to avoid having to hear their father cry and hiccup into his Jim Beam. Sometimes he brought women home—cheap, disposable women with acrylic nails and vacant eyes—and this was too much, too far. It was better in the park, where they could climb the trees. After the sun set, the mothers packed up their children and the joggers ran home. A listless park employee came to chain and lock the gate, and Jared could pretend they were out of the city and truly alone. Emily curled up at the bottom of a tree to read a book in the harsh streetlight, brushing at the ants. Jared would nestle into the branches above, humming so his sister wouldn't be afraid.

One night at the end of September, Emily fell asleep, and Jared could listen to the wind and the quiet all by himself. He squinted at the branches, trying to see shapes and patterns, and wished again that the LA smog didn't cover all the stars, that he could just pick up and go somewhere clear. Somewhere with trees. He was supposed to have his learner's permit by now, but his father couldn't sober up enough to help him get it. Jared thought about his mother, who hadn't been a saint but had tried hard, and his father, who was so weak and pitiful that Jared already felt as though he himself were the adult. He was turning this thought over in his head as he too drifted off to sleep.

When Jared opened his eyes, hours had gone by, and he almost fell out of the tree in his shock. He opened his mouth to yell for Emily, but closed it again when he heard the voices below. He squinted downward but couldn't make out the figures surrounding the tree. Had they been discovered? How much trouble would they get in? Jared suddenly had a child's impulse to hide, to leave Emily to take the blame, but after a quick flash of guilt, he began to creep slowly toward the lower branches. He relaxed an inch when he made out the two ordinary-looking young people talking to his sister. Just checking on her, probably. Before he could call down, though, one of them moved suddenly, and Jared heard Emily's scream, shattering the air. He suddenly couldn't move, couldn't go help, even as he saw the second figure join the first: gently, reverently, biting down into Emily's neck.

Chapter 1

At 2:00 a.m., Eli's ceiling fan made a sluggish *whug-whug-whug* noise and stopped moving. I know because I was staring at it.

It had been an unusually warm September in Los Angeles, and the temperature in Eli's bedroom had to be pushing eighty. I threw off the sheets and muttered something along the lines of "stupid fan," which made Eli stir beside me, rolling over and throwing an arm across my waist. He smelled like the sea, from surfing, and in the weak light from the streetlamps outside the window, his deep tan glowed against my pale skin. He nuzzled into my hair, and I was saved from having to awkwardly disentangle when my cell phone started playing a muted rendition of "Black Magic Woman." Work. Thank God. I gently lifted Eli's arm and rolled out of the bed, hurrying over to my jeans, which had somehow gotten thrown over the mirror on top of his dresser. Huh. Luckily, my cell phone had clung to the pocket, and I grabbed it and flipped it open. Yes, my phone still flips. It is also not smart.

Kirsten's voice was cheerful and apologetic, as usual, directing me to a vacant house in Calabasas where a young realtor and her two friends had been playing with love spells. I picked up the men's wallet I keep in my front pocket and pulled on the jeans and purple top I'd worn to the bar. Then I grabbed my keys and my knee-high boots and tiptoed out. I didn't leave a note. He would figure it out when I got to the door, anyway.

Whenever I'm not around, Eli has to go back to being a were-wolf.

I hadn't felt drunk when I followed Eli's pickup truck back to his place, but it still took me a few tries to find my van, which I guess is what happens when you drive after two glasses of whiskey. On the way to Calabasas, I used the stoplights to put on my boots and pull back the tangled mass of my long near-black hair. Even in LA, the streets were nearly deserted, and I had that creepy sensation that city people get when there's no one around, like maybe everyone else in the world has died or left without your knowledge. Before I had to go too far into that pleasant line of thinking, though, the lady in my GPS announced that I'd arrived at my destination.

I pulled into the driveway of a raincloud-gray McMansion, and the witches—I use that term loosely—opened the garage door and waved for me to pull the van right in. They were nearly identical: all blonde, all scared, and all wearing some slight variation of light, sleeveless sweaters and what my mother used to call slacks. I would not have been able to pick them out of a lineup.

"Ms. Bernard?" said the blonde on the right, stepping forward. "I'm Sarah-Ann Harris. Thank you so much for coming."

"Not a problem," I said briskly. I slid open the van's side door and grabbed my work duffel. "Tell me what's happening."

Sarah-Ann Harris glanced at her two friends, who looked away. "Um, well, we were trying this spell, you know, because Hillary's boyfriend keeps cheating, and we wanted him to fall in love with her alone for forever?" She headed into the house, walking backward like a tour guide, and I followed her, with the generic blondes trailing behind us like a limp parade. Because they're such a diverse collection of talents, I never know what I'm going to get on any given witch case, but the silent line of expensive highlights was a little unnerving. "There was this sacrifice part—"

"Chicken or dove?" I interrupted.

"Um, dove. But then we couldn't go through with killing it because Ashley's in PETA." she babbled. Hillary and Ashley? Seriously? Worst witch names ever.

"And we were gonna just set it free, and then something happened..."

We rounded a corner, entering a spacious dining/living area with no furniture. I eyed the polished hardwood floors first and decided I didn't need to bother with surgical booties. At the far end, glass double doors opened onto a three-seasons porch where I could see candles and books spread on the floor. As we came closer, I spotted a panicked little gray dove hopping frantically about in the doorway, and it took me a second to figure out what the big deal was. "Is its *head* on backward?" That was a new one, even for me.

"Yeah, um, I'm not sure what happened. We think maybe the pages got stuck in the spell book? And we did some kind of healing spell instead, only it didn't heal?" Sarah-Ann said. "So, like, if you go near it, the dove's head will go back, right?" She looked like she was about to cry. God.

"No," I said grimly. I strode across the room, my boot heels striking the polished wooden floors like a timpani drum, dropped my bag, and bent down to pick up the terrified little thing. It cuddled into my chest for a moment, looking at my face with its backward-facing eyes. I took a deep breath and snapped its neck with my other hand. Ick. But at least its head was now facing the correct direction. When I looked up, Sarah-Ann and the clones were staring at me like I'd just stabbed a preschooler.

"But," Sarah-Ann said in the reasonable, patronizing voice of a woman who's used to getting the window booth, "we called for you. Kirsten said to call when something went wrong, and we did."

I crouched in front of my duffel and retrieved a ziplock baggie the size of a shoebox, talking as I worked. "Ongoing spells undo themselves around me, and you couldn't perform any kind of magic within about ten feet of me. But the dove wasn't really under a spell anymore, it was physically changed." With the little body secured in the ziplock and the ziplock stowed in my bag, I turned back to the women, handing each of them one of Kirsten's cards. "Sarah-Ann, I know you have this number, but here it is again, just in case. Kirsten will be expecting each of you to call her tomorrow morning to discuss what happened tonight. If she asks her questions and is satisfied with your answers, that'll be the end of the matter. Do not make her track you down."

They each nodded at me, frightened, and I took another deep breath, trying to stay professional. "Now, will there be anything else? Do you guys need help clearing up your spell materials?" They shook their heads in unison, still looking stunned, and I gave them a nod in return. "Then I'll see myself out. Have a good evening." I turned on my heel and marched out to the van, putting the little dead bird in the freezer compartment in the back. In the morning, I'd take it to Artie, my furnace guy. If it had been a human body, I'd have gone right away, but a dead dove wasn't worth sneaking onto his property at 3:00 a.m.

Back in the van, I leaned my head against the steering wheel for a second. It irritated me that they had expected me to fix the dove, or maybe it just irritated me that I couldn't. I'm a null, which means I can cancel out magic within a radius, but I have limits, too. As I sat up and turned the ignition, my cell phone rang again, and I checked the caller ID. Dashiell. Great. A vampire was just what my night needed. I flipped it open. "Bernard."

"Scarlett," Dashiell began, drawing out the *a* as usual. "There is a situation in La Brea Park. I will meet you at the entrance in fifteen minutes."

"Uh, okay. I'm in Calabasas now, on a Kirsten case, but I'll be there as fast—" I realized that I was talking to myself and shut the phone, glancing at the clock. *Shit.* Even with no traffic on the freeway, there was no way I could get to the entrance of La Brea

Park in fifteen minutes; it was impossible. And Dashiell was coming himself, in person? He might be the most powerful creature in Los Angeles, but like most vampires, Dashiell stays the hell away from me if at all possible, not wanting to age even a few minutes.

It had to be really bad.

I briefly considered speeding, but only in that way you think about something you know you'll never do. That's one of the rules: don't get pulled over. My van is checked weekly to make sure all the lights are working and the gas and oil tanks are filled, and it undergoes a full inspection and detailing twice a year. If the cops pulled me over right now, all they would find was a dead dove, but even that would be bad. I had no idea whether they'd be able to figure out that I'd broken its neck backward, but even something small like that could get the rumor snowball rolling, or at best, tarnish my reputation with the supernatural community. In my business, there's no such thing as an overreaction.

I drove south on the 405 highway as fast as I dared, three miles over the speed limit, but I was still another fifteen minutes late to meet Dashiell. La Brea Park closes at sunset, so the actual entrance driving to get into the park was chained and locked. As I pulled up to the gate, he materialized out of the shadows, a forty-ish-looking vampire in impeccable black pants and a deep-green cashmere T-shirt. His dark-brown hair was a little mussed, and his blandly handsome face looked dangerously angry. I was definitely in trouble.

I parked the van at the curb and rolled my window down, turning the engine off. Dash took a few steps toward me, but stayed well out of my ten-foot radius.

"You are late," he stage-whispered. "Our situation has grown more complicated."

No point in groveling. "I'm sorry. Tell me what's happening."

"I got a text message from a private number and came to see for myself," he said shortly. "There are three bodies ahead; they have been torn apart. There is blood, so I do not think it was the vampires. Perhaps one of Will's people." Vampires, as a rule, don't waste blood. Will is the head of the local werewolf pack. The werewolves in Los Angeles occasionally run around in the parks that close at sunset. LA is one of the rare cities where the Old World creatures share territory more or less in peace, though when push comes to shove, Dashiell is in charge. Witches and werewolves aren't immortal, after all. It's an uneasy peace, darkened by preceding centuries of tension, and it works best when everyone sticks to their own kind. Usually the vampires take care of vampire business, and the wolves take care of wolf business, but there is some overlap, especially when the perpetrator is unknown.

"What's the complication?"

"A jogger ran through here two minutes ago, and she saw the bodies. You have only a few minutes before the police arrive." He pointed toward a nearby clump of trees. "Go." And just like that, he vanished.

I grabbed my duffel and sprinted toward the trees, fumbling to pull out a flashlight as I went. In cases where there's a time crunch, you have to prioritize, and priority one would be the bodies. There would still be evidence without bodies, but the police couldn't do much with a few bloodstains outdoors in a public park. I raced through the trees, trying to avoid roots and rocks, and stopped dead a quarter mile in, where I found a small clearing that had been painted red.

Chapter 2

I stared. I've seen dead bodies before, of course, and plenty of blood, but this was...very different. At first it just looked like meat, like one of those movies where the monster is blown to bits and the pink pieces fall down everywhere. Except, this time, the monster was actually people. I counted heads and came up with three. Their bodies had been carved open at the stomach, and the insides were pulled outside. All four limbs had also been separated from each body, though there was way too much blood for me to determine which had come first, the evisceration or the dismemberment. The limbs sat in a pile in the center of the clearing, with the body cavities and body insides stretched around them like petals on a flower. It was almost a *pattern*, and I suddenly thought of the squares on a patchwork quilt. The smell of blood—and other things—was overpowering, even to my human nose, and I realized that the blood was *everywhere*. Splattered on the scrubby little plants, the tree trunks. I saw enough spilled blood to wonder if the killer had deliberately hit every artery. Maybe he had. Fear suddenly wobbled in my stomach. I tried taking a woozy step forward, but the shock made it feel as if I were slogging through gelatin.

That was my first big mistake: I hesitated. My kind of crime scene cleanup is all about moving quickly—not only are you generally in a hurry, but you never want to take too much time to think about what you're looking at. This, however, was the worst scene

I'd ever been to, and I probably stared for a full minute, though I wasn't exactly aware of the time passing. Finally, without taking my eyes off the carnage, I slid a hand into my duffel's outside pocket and pulled out a heavy garbage bag, the thickest Hefty has ever made.

I had just pulled apart the bag's folds, ready to snap it open, when a cop ran into the clearing from the opposite side. Suddenly, my head cleared and time sped back up.

"Police!" he hollered, gun pointed at my chest. "Show me your hands!" I let the garbage bag flutter to the ground and obediently raised my hands to shoulder height. He was young, around thirty, and Latino—and very handsome, even for LA. Under his leather jacket, I saw that his badge swung on a chain at his neck, just like the cops in movies. His gun barrel never strayed from me as he glanced about the scene and then swore in Spanish, his face paling to a sickly gray.

"Did you do this?" he demanded bluntly, and I just shook my head.

"Are you the only one?" I said stupidly, my tongue still thick.

"The rest are coming. Don't you move." He began to circle around the gore, stepping carefully on the scrubby grass. "Easy, now."

He reached slowly for the handcuffs on his belt, and I realized for the first time the kind of trouble I was in. Even if I could convince the police that I wasn't the murderer, I would be on their radar forever. My reputation for discretion would be ruined, if it wasn't already, and I would probably lose my job. I took an automatic step backward, and then three things happened at once: I heard the first sirens, the cop opened his mouth to scream at me, and the werewolf burst into the clearing between us.

It was a male gray wolf, thin but still unmistakably, unnaturally huge, and it ran at an angle pointing straight toward the bodies, probably smelling the meat. The cop swung his gun toward the new threat, looking frightened, and the wolf saw this and tried to reverse directions. But it was too late: with its last few steps, it skidded just a little too close to me. I felt it cross the edge of my whatever, my blankness, and then the change happened in midair. A wolf had taken the leap, and a man crashed to the ground, naked and tumbling. He fell facing slightly away from me, and I saw the cop actually drop his gun with the shock of it.

This time I didn't hesitate. I turned on my heel and raced back to the van. I threw open the driver's side door and tossed my bag onto the passenger seat, trying to think over the sound of the police sirens. I started the van and threw it into drive, but instead of turning back toward home, I took the first left, across from the park entrance, and found myself in a small middle-class subdivision. Gotta love LA, where you can cross any street and be in a whole different town. The houses had bars on the first-story windows but not the second, which meant it was a decent, if not completely secure, neighborhood. I took two more quick turns and parked the van on the street near a house that still had its lights on. I turned off the motor and squashed myself down onto the floor in front of my seat. It wasn't perfect, but I didn't think I'd be able to get all the way to the highway before the cops came flying by. I tucked my hair under a dark baseball cap, opened the door, and darted around the van to slap on the big logo magnet I have that says *Hunt Bros. Cleaning Service.* Fake, but since my tax returns say that I am a professional housecleaner, I figured I could always piece together a story if needed. Any eagle-eyed insomniac neighbors wouldn't have much to go on, just a cleaning service van parked outside a house where people were still awake. I just hoped that the cop at the crime scene hadn't seen what kind of car I drove. I sent Dash a text message, shielding the phone's glow with one cupped hand, and crammed myself down between the two front bucket seats to wait it out.

My mind was churning, questions ping-ponging around the inside of my head. What on earth would have done what I'd seen in the clearing? In five years doing crime scenes, I'd never encountered that kind of brutality. With modern technology and modern cautiousness, it's rare that I even get a complete dead human body anymore. That's the thing about LA: it might be the second-biggest city in the country, but in the Old World, it has about the prominence of Tucson. This town is a pretty undesirable place for the supernatural to live: there's not enough space for the wolves, who can't afford to be stuck in traffic on full moon nights, and the city is too young and too spacey for the vampires. There are probably more witches than anything else, but so many of them are a joke, and most of the rest don't play with the really dangerous magics. Sometimes one of the werewolves will lose a limb in a fight, or the witches will hex something wrong like that poor dove, but neither faction has many actual casualties anymore. Even the vampires, who regularly feed on humans, have had centuries to learn how to feed without crossing that line to where the victim will die. I'm occasionally called in when the new vamps accidentally kill, but even then, it's all very obvious. Hungry vampire equals dead human.

But what the hell would have done what I'd just seen? Thinking about the scene in the clearing, I realized that I'd never really had a chance: even if the cops had taken a little longer to get there, there was no way in hell I would have been able to clean up that... mess. It would have taken one person hours just to collect all the body parts. What could I have done?

When thirty minutes had passed, I scooted up into my seat and stepped out to get my logo magnet. Then I tossed my baseball cap on the passenger seat and carefully steered the van farther into the subdivision. It took me a while to find my way back to a major street, but I finally pulled onto Pico and followed it west. When I was sure I knew my way home, I took a deep breath and called Dashiell.

"What happened?" he demanded, before I'd said hello.

"It was too late. There was a cop on scene before I could do much. He saw one of the wolves, Dashiell."

"He *what?*" I explained about the werewolf in the clearing. "Who is this cop?" he barked angrily, as though I had personally invited the guy along as my date.

"Uh...I didn't get a name."

As a rule, vampires do not sigh in seething annoyance, but Dashiell made a special exception for me. "This would not have happened if you had simply arrived on time, Scarlett."

"I know it's bad. I just couldn't make it there." I bit down on any further excuses, not bothering to point out that I wouldn't have had the time to clean up that mess anyway. I'd known Dashiell long enough to know that he was not a big fan of apologies. Apologizing is weak, and weakness tends to make vampires think of prey.

"Scarlett, now is not a good time," he said. I automatically glanced at the clock on the dashboard. I keep track of the dawn, for obvious reasons, and it was only twenty minutes away. That was going to hurt us: if I can't get to a crime scene for some reason, Dashiell has to throw his weight and money around to get things buried, and now he wouldn't be able to do so until after sunset. Why hadn't I thought of that earlier? "You will come to the estate tonight at eleven thirty to discuss this further."

I chewed on my lip, deciding what to say. Screw it. "Dashiell, could you please just tell me if you're gonna try to kill me?"

He actually laughed, but it was a dry, grave chuckle that made me shiver. "Scarlett, I am very displeased. But if I wanted you dead, I wouldn't invite you politely. And there would be no *trying.*" The line went dead.

I tossed the phone into the baseball cap on the seat next to me. This was very bad. I'd skated by for eight months with only a handful of incidents each week. Of course it figured that the one time I got two scenes in one night, it would be the most gruesome murder I'd ever seen. That kind of killing was going to get a lot of attention—enough that I suspected even Dashiell wouldn't be able to keep a lid on it. He would be furious with me, and that was not good for either my professional reputation or my personal safety. He might not be able to bite me, but despite our ability to extinguish magic, nulls like me aren't invulnerable. We're just as fragile as any other human being, and all Dashiell really had to do was buy a gun or have one of his personal goons beat me to death. I heard myself chortle, an edge of hysteria escaping my throat. *Who would they get*, I thought, *to clean up my body?*

It was ten minutes to dawn when I dragged myself through the back door of the compact West Hollywood house that I share with my housemate and landlady, Molly. Who, I should mention, is also a vampire.

"You're home!" she squealed, rushing toward me at much-faster-than-human speed. She had on designer sweatpants and a Paul Frank T-shirt with a picture of an angry-looking kitten biting a dog. Molly looks about twenty, with shoulder-length hair (currently red) and the body of a high school tennis star, but she's really a hundred and twenty-something years old, born in Wales the same summer that Jack the Ripper was terrorizing the East End of London. She was turned into a vampire at the age of seventeen. I've never heard the full story on how it happened, but I get the impression that it wasn't accidental—that was right around the time when skirmishes between the vampires and the witches led to the vampires becoming much more thoughtful about who they let into their undead club. They went after a lot of poor, pretty girls, like Molly had been.

Molly doesn't hate what she is, exactly. Unlike some vampires who deliberately try to spend time with me, she doesn't really want to be human—ugh, humans, am I right? She just doesn't want to look like a teenager anymore, which is understandable. Seventeen was pretty much an adult in her own time, but in the twenty-first century, she couldn't even buy a lottery ticket. So a few years ago, she offered me a deal, through Dashiell: in exchange for spending as much time around her as possible, I could have the spare bedroom in her house practically for free. Since my weird little ability doesn't cost me anything, or even tire me out, I thought that sounded like a pretty good deal. Molly and I have sort of become friends, too, though sometimes I can't believe she's older than me, let alone older than, say, automobiles or World War I.

As she stepped into my radius, she did the little halting gasp that vampires always take when they're around me—it's the feeling of going from immortal back to mortal, and a vampire once told me it's like waking up from a coma, only to find you have been beaten nearly to death. Molly's skin lost its luminous glow, and she jerked as her heart restarted. She wiggled her jaw absentmindedly, poking her tongue at her teeth. Vampires don't actually have *fang* fangs, but their canine teeth have evolved to be much sharper than a regular human's. It has to feel weird to have your teeth get more and less pointy when I'm around. Then Molly went back to smiling beatifically at me, wringing her hands from a few feet away. Molly is a hugger—I know, who's ever heard of a hugging vampire? —and though I have finally trained her not to touch me, she does tend to hover two feet away.

"*While You Were Sleeping* is on, and Peter Gallagher just fell on the tracks. Want to watch with me?"

"Thanks, but I think I'll pass." *Again*, I thought. Molly's favorite technological advancement is movies, and she's been there for every step: from their birth through the spread of theaters, home video, then DVD, and now Blu-ray and 3-D. When they bring back Smell-o-Vision, she'll be the first in line at Best Buy. She adores film, which is probably why she bought the West Hollywood house to begin with—supposedly, Marilyn Monroe once threw up in the downstairs bathroom during a party. I would have a lot more respect for this passion if her absolute favorite genre wasn't romantic comedy.

"I'm just going to go up to my room, I think. Maybe read a little and go to bed. Are you working tonight?" I asked.

"Nah, I'm good," she said happily. Molly doesn't really have to work—I've learned that vampires always seem to have a mysterious source of income, the result of being alive long enough to acquire, say, gold doubloons or fist-sized jewels—but she has a low-key part-time job transcribing interviews and meeting notes online. At home, she can type at lightning speed, having no trouble finishing in moments what would take me an hour. But she likes to go to coffee shops and work in the middle of people.

I'm guessing this is also where she gets her victims, but she and I don't really talk about that. Vampires need to feed anywhere from every night to every four or five days, depending on how active they are and how much they take. Older vampires, like Molly, have the practice and control to feed a little bit from a victim, then take their memory of the event away completely, which is called "pressing their minds." Most of the time, the victims are left feeling a tad weak and fluttery, as if they've just made out with a stranger. No harm, no foul, right? The messing-with-memory thing gives me the creeps, and I am very grateful that Molly is old enough to control herself—and also that she could never feed from me personally.

"Okay!" Molly crossed the living room and pulled the blackout drapes, then settled herself in the easy chair on the back wall by the window. It's the farthest seat from the TV, but after some experimentation, we had discovered that it was directly under my bedroom. Molly never misses a chance to age, especially this close to dawn. Vampires die when the sun comes up, but in my radius, Molly can stay up and finish her movie. Of course, that meant she'd die when I left the radius again to come downstairs, but we're both used to lots of transitioning back and forth. It happens. I sometimes wonder what Molly's ideal age is—twenty-two? twenty-eight? thirty-five?—but I haven't got the guts to ask. Whenever she gets there, I'll have nowhere to live.

I stripped off my work clothes, pulled on the ancient XL Chicago Bears jersey I inherited from my father, and crawled into bed. But the adrenaline hadn't yet faded enough for me to sleep. I stared at the ceiling, thinking about my all-time worst crime scenes. Once, a witch had burned to death—I know, the irony—when a spell had gone wrong. There had been a dead child once, too; that had given me months of nightmares. But both times had been accidents, witch magic or vampire feeding gone too far. This was deliberate. It had looked like the battlefield in one of those medieval war movies. Barbaric. I pulled the blankets tighter. At this point, it takes quite a bit to rattle me, but that scene had done it. I closed my eyes, willing sleep to come.

It took a long, long time.

Chapter 3

As he knelt in the clearing, Officer Jesse Cruz really wished he could just go back to a couple of weeks ago.

It had only been nine days since his promotion, to plainclothes officer third grade, and there were times when he imagined he could still feel the starchy itch of his uniform collar, the poky little Officer Friendly pin he used to wear to all the schools. His first week at the new precinct had featured a lot of cracks about his looks and his Officer Friendly gig, and Jesse had been shy enough as a kid that he had never really learned how to make friends by teasing back. But his mother was an old-school Mexicana, convinced that the greatest troubles of the world could be fixed with food bribes, and apparently Jesse had inherited this viewpoint. At 2:30 a.m. on a Tuesday morning, he had been standing in a twenty-four-hour bakery picking out donuts for the rest of the night shift. He had felt awkward in his leather jacket, unable to shake the feeling that everyone in the bakery knew he was a cop. And being a cop buying donuts...Well, it's embarrassing.

Not that trying to buy friends with baked goods isn't kind of embarrassing in itself, he had thought as he walked back out to the unmarked car. Jesse was buckling his seat belt—Officer Friendly always does—when he had heard the call come over the radio, the code for a multiple homicide. Jesse listened as the dispatcher described a clearing in La Brea Park, and he felt a thrill in his stomach when he realized just how close he was already. He started up the car, sticking the little domed flasher on the roof with one hand, and felt a shiver of excitement as he sped out of the parking lot. Maybe he'd even be the first one there.

The second that he would replay, over and over, was the moment when he'd actually dropped his gun. The girl with the bright-green eyes had startled him, and obviously the body... parts...in the clearing were beyond gruesome, but he was doing okay at that point, he'd thought. Then Jesse caught movement out of the corner of his eye and glanced over in time to see the giant dog bound toward them. He'd felt a pang of regret as he clicked off the safety—Jesse loved dogs—but before his finger could even tighten on the trigger everything had changed.

Not a dog. A naked man.

Working on autopilot, he had swooped down and picked up the service weapon, aiming for the guy's chest, but the guy had remained motionless, curled up on the ground. *Let's try this again,* Jesse had thought, loopy with shock, as he rose and began to circle around the blood again, toward the naked man. "Police! Don't move!" he'd shouted, keeping a few feet away as he got far enough around to see the guy's face. It was a normal human face, sort of wispy and pinched-looking, and if the guy hadn't been stark naked, Jesse almost might have convinced himself that he hadn't just seen a giant husky change into a person. No way had he seen a giant husky change into a person, right?

The guy —who was actually kind of little and scrawny when you saw him up close—finally opened his eyes and started to pull himself to a sitting position. "Stop!" Jesse had ordered, and the smaller man sort of shook himself and met Jesse's eyes. Then his gaze darted around the clearing, and when he looked back to Jesse, there was an almost mischievous grin spreading across his face. Before Jesse could open his mouth to speak again, the guy pulled himself into a ball and rolled forward, a look of intense concentration on his face. Jesse stared, completely speechless, as limbs started to move under the man's skin, as if they were stretching in two directions. His skin started to sprout tiny hairs, but before Jesse's eyes could even adjust to this development, the dog—*not a dog*, Jesse thought numbly, *a wolf*—was back. It had taken maybe twenty seconds.

The animal shook its fur, panting a little, and without a glance back at Jesse, it turned and raced off into the darkness. Jesse had fallen back to his knees, and for the first time, he really looked at the carnage in front of him. *What the hell?*

That was how the next cops on the scene found him—Officer Friendly on his knees in the bloody mud, looking stunned. And for the first time, he wanted nothing more than to go back in time and undo his promotion. Officer Friendly never had to deal with wolves that were sometimes naked guys.

When the first-response team joined Jesse at the scene, they attributed his stunned, wide-eyed look to shock and the gruesome arrangement of the bodies. If they could even be called "bodies" at this point. It was a perfectly reasonable response, and nobody even hassled him much over it, to his surprise. Jesse figured that even the most hardened veterans hadn't seen anything like this before; everyone looked subdued and shocky. A couple of the rookies had run into the woods to vomit, though Jesse had managed to keep his coffee down. He was glad he hadn't gotten the chance to eat any donuts.

When asked to describe his arrival at the scene, Jesse heard his own voice telling the story without any mention of the girl with the green eyes or the naked...man. Lying about witnesses and withholding information were pretty much fireable offenses for a cop, but it was over and done with before he'd stopped to really weigh the consequences. He couldn't describe the woman without describing the man—Jesse still wasn't using the word *werewolf*, even in his own head—and he couldn't describe the man without explaining how everyone had gotten away from him. So Jesse kept his mouth shut, stuck to the sidelines, and watched the bustle and activity all around him.

He didn't realize he was waiting for his moment until it came: a few seconds when the photographer was setting out equipment and the medical examiner arrived, when everyone else was occupied with paperwork and conversations and tasks. Jesse saw his chance and swooped down to pick up the black plastic garbage bag, tucking it smoothly into his jacket pocket. He immediately felt awful. He'd already lied to his fellow officers and concealed two possible witnesses, and now he was hiding evidence. This was not what he would call being a real cop. For a moment, Jesse considered walking over to the detective in charge and confessing everything. But he didn't want to get locked away with an army of shrinks.

Besides, Jesse knew that the girl he'd seen wasn't the actual killer—the forensics people on-site had already speculated that it must have been a really big, seriously muscled guy, and she was maybe five foot seven on a good day, not much over a hundred pounds. And whoever had killed those people would have been *drenched* in blood. Still, she had to be important to the case somehow, and if he couldn't make her part of the official investigation, he decided that it was his responsibility to follow up with her on his own.

When the detective in charge finally dismissed him, Jesse headed back to the precinct, and straight to the lab.

Jesse had first met Gloria "Glory" Sherman, the lead forensic pathology technician, at an event for the public high schools in the county. Glory had given a speech on career opportunities in forensic science, and Jesse was there as Officer Friendly. They'd struck up a friendship, and once, he'd even brought Glory and her two kids to see the film set where his mother, a makeup artist, was working. Jesse liked Glory's no-nonsense kindness, so he made a point to say hello and deliver the occasional Starbucks. There are some people you just want on your side.

"Hey, Glory, you here?" he called, scanning the cluttered tables and shelves. Suddenly, she popped up into view, stretching to her full five feet one inch. Her face looked stressed and thin, and she'd jammed her glasses on top of her head so she could rub her eyes. "Were you, like, taking a nap on the floor?"

"Funny. Just cleaning up a spilled beaker."

"Blood?"

She smiled. "Apple juice. What's up?"

Jesse entered the lab and pulled the garbage bag out of his jacket pocket, handing it over. "How long would it take you to lift a print off this?"

She pulled on new surgical gloves and took the bag over to the three hundred–watt bulb on her desk lamp, sliding the glasses back down onto her nose. "Well, they're latent, obviously, but pretty strong. Even with your elimination prints, it shouldn't take long. But I'm backed up with this park thing." She raked her fingers through silvery-blonde hair, looking tired.

"Has that evidence come in already?"

"No, it's still being processed—"

"Then could you maybe just do this quick first? Please?" He gave her his best pleading look, and she sighed.

"What is it, exactly?"

"It's a...personal project."

She looked skeptical. "What, like your neighbor is a litterbug, something like that?"

"Something like that, but, Glory, I swear I wouldn't bring this to you if it wasn't important. Really."

Glory checked her watch, and Jesse could see her relenting. "I'll give you an hour, while they finish compiling all the evidence from the park. If I haven't gotten a match by then, you're going to have to wait."

"Thank you!" He bent at the waist to kiss her cheek, which just caused her to grumble.

"You owe me. You're going to take Rob and Natalie to the batting cages next Saturday."

"It's a deal," he promised, leaning against a lab table. Everything in the room was solid and purposeful, and being there helped ground him again, made the memory of the werewolf seem like some kind of hallucinogenic side effect of the shock. *But it wasn't,* his brain insisted. Jesse ignored it.

Thirty-seven minutes later, Glory called his extension. Jesse rushed down to the basement lab, where Glory was already checking in new evidence from the park, a pleased grin on her face. "I've got your girl," she said smugly. She handed over a printout with a mug shot at the top. The girl was a few years younger, but it was her. Her green eyes and pretty face glared out from under that pile of dark hair, daring the photographer to do something.

"Scarlett Kaylie Bernard, now twenty-three. She was arrested last year for arson, burning down a shed in the suburbs. The DA didn't press charges, which is a little weird—usually they at least plead out Anyway, that's her." She gave him a suspicious look. "Now tell me I didn't just use department resources to look into your blind date."

"No, no, it's definitely important," he assured her. He thanked Glory and headed back to his desk to think about his next move.

Chapter 4

My dreams were full of blood—splattered over trees and twisted, ripped limbs. This time I was in the middle of the clearing, not just on the edges, and the blood was all around me, 360 degrees of it. It crept toward me, threatening to ooze its way up my legs and onto my clothes, all the way to my face and down my throat. I woke up shivering, the blankets tangled in my legs.

I spent most of the day sleeping, watching TV, and avoiding my cell phone. Dashiell, Kirsten, and Will all had specialized ringtones, so it was easy enough to ignore everything else. When I finally checked the little screen late that afternoon, Eli had called three times, probably wondering where I was. Whoops. I had sort of forgotten all about him. I'd also missed a call from my brother, Jack. That was a surprise—Jack and I don't talk much. He still lives in Esperanza, the little town ninety minutes east of LA where we both grew up. Jack wanted to be a doctor, but when our parents died he couldn't swing medical school, so now he works as a laboratory technician at Esperanza's only clinic. We avoid each other by unspoken mutual agreement—him because he feels guilty about not taking care of me when Mom and Dad died, and me because, well, I was responsible for their deaths.

So why would he be calling me? I decided I would put off finding out. I'm brave like that.

Just before sunset, I pulled on my gym clothes and took off for my daily four-mile run. I can't be attacked by supernatural forces, but I can sure as hell be chased, and I bruise and break bones just like any other human. I'm just not a gun-carrying, karate-knowing, kick-ass kind of girl, so I lift weights a couple of times a week, and I run every day. Not that I'm one of those go-getter Nike kind of runners, either. I actually kind of hate it, but it's the only real responsibility I have.

Molly "woke" up when the sun went down at six thirty, and we ordered Chinese and watched reruns of *Friends* for a few hours. Molly gets a huge kick out of things like eating, going to the bathroom, and just generally pretending we live in a bubbly sitcom universe where nobody is undead. I get that, and I was definitely in the mood to hang out in bubbly sitcom land for a while.

At ten, I went upstairs to shower and change. When I came back down, damp hair darkening the back of my shirt, Molly eyed my jeans and green T-shirt with what could only be described as a foreboding disdain. "That's what you're wearing? You're not going to change?"

"Molls, I thought you liked me the way I was." When she didn't smile, I looked down at myself. "What? The T-shirt's from Banana Republic."

"Scarlett"—she sighed and shook her head—"he's the most powerful person in the city, for crying out loud. At least find pants without holes. And brush your hair."

I looked down and spotted the small hole worn in the knee of my jeans. Whoops. "Spielberg's got more power," I grumbled, but I went back up to my room and dug out a pair of khakis. After a moment's thought, I also swapped my Chuck Taylors—one of the most popular shoe brands on the market, which helps when I have to leave footprints—for my good boots. I tugged the elastic band out of my messy ponytail and picked up my brush from the nightstand. When it was finally neat, I twisted it up into a smooth ballerina bun and secured it with a rubber band and bobby pins, turning my head back and forth to check my handiwork in the mirror. *Good enough.* Sometimes I consider chopping my hair down to a nice manageable three inches, but I would miss it too much. It's less useful and more confidence-boosting, like Superman's cape.

Besides, it's just like my mother's hair.

By eleven, my stomach was doing nervous backflips, the way it always does when I butt heads with Dashiell. To be fair, though, I should have seen all this coming quite some time ago. I'd gotten overconfident with eight months of nonemergencies, and then I'd let this smack me down hard. Of course Dashiell was upset. I took my Taser off the charger (although it really only works on vampires while they're close enough to me to be human, it makes me feel better to bring it along when I can), picked up my keys and wallet, and stuffed everything into the various pockets of my olive-green canvas jacket, which looks like something an investigative journalist would wear in a political thriller. Molly calls it my "coat-o'-nine pockets." Then I went through the back door and into the autumn night.

As LA neighborhoods go, West Hollywood is fairly benign after dark. Molly's house is the unchanging oasis in an area that has developed around it for decades, crowding her in with restaurants and bars that have gone through various stages of hipness. At this point, there are only four other residences on Molly's street, and the neighborhood is mostly frequented by a middle-aged, upper-middle-class crowd that goes to bed before eleven.

I went through the teeny backyard in about six steps and closed the decorative gate behind me (vampires don't worry too much about security), breathing in the cool, congested LA air. It smelled pleasantly of concrete and hamburgers and car exhaust. Molly's property has a single-spot carport next to the back door where she parks her Prius. I have to pay a small fortune to keep my van in the big parking garage down the street. The garage was mostly empty by the time I got there, and I kept my head down and walked quickly and purposefully down the wide, empty pavement to my van on the lower level. When I glanced up, though, I realized that someone was leaning against my hood. My hand went toward the pocket with the Taser. As I got closer, though, he pushed himself off and turned to face me, hands tense and ready at his sides. I recognized the handsome cop from the clearing.

I paused, standing twenty feet away. I briefly entertained the thought of Tasing him and running. Then I shrugged to myself and kept going. If he had the van, he knew who I was. Where was I gonna go?

"You're under arrest," he said briskly, as I walked up.

I snorted. "Bullshit."

"Excuse me?"

"You're not here to arrest me. You came alone, you waited for me to come to you, and you haven't even identified yourself. Besides, you know damn well that I didn't kill those people."

"How do I know that?"

I sighed. "Is this, like, a cop test? Because it was done by someone a lot stronger than me. Because I had no weapon, and I wasn't covered in blood. That much carnage, there's no way the killer could stay clean."

"There's still plenty I could arrest you for. Obstruction of justice, accessory after the fact, tampering with a body..."

"Ha. You found me how? Prints? I was in the park earlier that day, and I forgot a garbage bag. The worst thing you've got on me is littering. Besides, I have at least three people who'll swear I was somewhere else." That wasn't completely true, but if push came to shove Dashiell could probably arrange something.

He stepped closer now, into my personal bubble. He smelled like Giorgio Armani cologne and oranges, and his caramel skin was reddening.

"At any rate," I continued, "that's not why you're here."

He loomed over me, trying to intimidate, but I didn't take a step, didn't even lean back. I was on my way to see the cardinal vampire of Los Angeles, who was very angry with me. The B-team cop didn't exactly have me shaking in my boots.

"So why am I here?"

"You're here," I said right back, tilting my head up to meet his eyes, "to ask me if you really saw a werewolf last night."

He broke first, turning away. Probably he was a little embarrassed. "Look," he said, leaning back against the van again and holding out empty hands, "can we start over? My name is Jesse Cruz. I'm a police officer with the Southwest Homicide Division of the LAPD. And you are?"

"You already know who I am." He made a little head motion at me, indicating that I should play the game, and I rolled my eyes. "I'm Scarlett Bernard. I'm a freelance housecleaner."

He reached out his hand, and I reluctantly shook it.

"I'm guessing that you don't actually clean any houses," he said.

I just shrugged.

"Look, can we go somewhere and talk? Obviously I have a lot of questions."

"There's somewhere I have to be right now."

"No problem," he said. "I'll ride along."

"That's not happening," I said shortly.

"You know, I may not be about to arrest you, but I can certainly make your life harder. Like following you to your next engagement."

Oh. Crap. For a moment, I considered trying to lose him, like in the movies, but he was trained in evasive driving and I wasn't. I checked my watch. "I need to make a call first."

"Fine."

I pulled out my cell and gave him a pointed look, but he just shook his head. Not going anywhere. Rolling my eyes again, I tossed him my keys and climbed into the van before he could object. He frowned at me through the window, but didn't open the door.

I dialed Dashiell, who picked up on the second ring. "It's Scarlett. I'm going to be a little late." In a low voice, I explained about the cop.

Dashiell hissed into the phone. "What does he know for sure?" he demanded.

I thought about it, watching as Cruz paced a short route back and forth in front of the van. "At this point, it would probably be difficult to convince him that there's no such thing as werewolves."

"That's it? Nothing about vampires?"

"No. Although, one often follows the other, at least according to the movies. Can you press his mind?"

There was silence on the line for a moment. "No. Too much time has passed. That technique exists to erase a few minutes or a simple memory of a person. He has been walking around with this knowledge for nearly twenty-four hours. I can't take it away without causing telltale damage."

"What do you want me to do?" I asked. I was trying to be helpful, so as not to remind him that this was technically all my fault.

"I will get someone to take care of him."

My breath caught in my throat, and I felt very unfamiliar pangs of conscience poking at me. I know I spend most of my time concealing other people's crimes, including murders, but I had never actually known about someone's death in advance. Besides, I was the one who'd been too slow to get to the crime scene, *and* I was the one who'd been stupid and left the garbage bag. This guy was just doing his job. I thought about his face when that werewolf had changed. Without really meaning to, I imagined him having a family—kids, even. I looked back up at Cruz, but I couldn't see his left hand to look for a wedding ring. "But this kind of thing has happened before, right?" I argued. "And then you just pay him off or whatever?"

There was a growl of warning in his voice now. "It has happened, but each time, it has been so much simpler to just remove the obstacle. Besides, I am not convinced that your policeman will be willing to work with us."

To my own surprise, I heard myself pushing. "Dash, I know that I'm not your favorite person right now, but I'm respectfully asking for you to let me try to fix this. I think I can get through to this guy. Let me tell him the history. If that doesn't work, you can always kill him later."

Dashiell was quiet again, and I waited, glancing out the window at the cop in question, who was glaring at me with his arms folded across his chest.

Finally, Dashiell said, "All right, Scarlett. I'll let you follow your instincts on this matter, but I still need you here. And if Officer Cruz tells even one person about the Old World, I won't be killing just *him*. That's not a threat, Scarlett. It's a promise." And he hung up the phone.

I leaned forward and rested my head against the wheel. Not. Good.

Cruz opened the passenger door next to me, and I jumped. "Well?" he said. "Let's go."

I shook my head. "I have permission to fill you in on some stuff, but you can't go with me tonight."

He held up my keys, letting them jingle. "You sure about that?"

Crud. *Way to think ahead, Scarlett.* I held out my hand. "Give me the keys."

He shook his head, looking mulish. "I'm risking my job just by letting you walk around free. I'm not leaving until I get some answers."

It probably wouldn't be a great idea to Tase the nice police officer. I ran through my other options—get out of the van and run, call the powerful angry vampire to reschedule, or just take the damned cop with me. While I was thinking, Cruz rolled up his jacket sleeve and looked pointedly at a silver Fossil watch.

"Fine," I sighed. "Here's the deal. You can come with me, and we'll talk on the way, but when we get there, you will stay in the car."

"Yeah, sure," he said casually.

Crap, crap, crap. I started the van and pulled out of the garage, heading west toward the 101 freeway entrance on Sunset. I felt Cruz staring at me the whole time.

"Okay," I finally said, "what do you want to know?"

"That guy was a...a..."

"Werewolf," I supplied. I couldn't blame him for the hesitation. Pop culture has built this whole supernatural thing up to the point where it's practically a cliché. Even the werewolves think it sounds silly to say *werewolves.* "Yes. I haven't met him, I don't think, but he must be part of the local pack."

"There's a *pack?*" He was already beginning to sound dazed.

"Yes. Our pack is small in proportion to the city's population, but this isn't the most werewolf-friendly town, as you might imagine. Better than New York, though."

"Okay...I'm assuming if werewolves are real, there's other stuff, too."

"Yeah," I said.

"How does it all work?"

"Dude, I don't know. It just does."

His voice was skeptical. "Please don't make me threaten you again. It's just kind of tacky."

I sighed. How had Olivia first explained this to me? "Fine. Back up a second. The first thing you need to know is that there's magic in the world. Not bunnies-being-pulled-out-of-top-hats magic—I mean like this completely wild, powerful force. The second thing is that Darwin got a lot of stuff right. Thanks to evolution, every species in the world is part of an enormous family tree, the fossil record. It would take up, like, the side of a mountain, but in theory, you could map it all out. Are you still with me?"

"Yes."

"Okay. At certain points on that enormous family tree, when a species branched into two, it was actually branching into three. So, there would be the first branch, the second branch, and the magical branch."

"You're talking about speciation," Jesse said.

I pointed at him. "Yeah, that's the word I can never remember. Anyway, it didn't happen all the time, and nobody really knows why it chose certain species to branch out, but that's magic for you." Even the smartest people in the Old World barely understand the surface of it. "At the beginning of the world, there was an imbalance—the energy of the world contained too much magic, not enough non-magic. Then those creatures who were built entirely of magical energy—spirits, mostly—began to die away, and magic started to settle down."

I was half expecting him to fight me on it, but he just looked at me patiently, so I went on. "Okay. At some point, evolution led to man, but there was a whatchamacallit, a magical speciation. There were humans, and then there were also humans who had the ability to manipulate the magic itself. Conduits."

"Like what? Wizards?" His voice was skeptical.

"Don't give me the face. I'm just telling you what was told to me. Those conduits were powerful—almost too powerful. Some of them decided the power was too much, and they made a point to use as little of it as they could. Eventually, their magic...diminished and changed. Those people eventually were called witches. Wait, shit, that's my exit." I jerked the van onto the Pasadena Highway.

"And the other conduits?" he prompted.

"I'm getting to it. You have to understand that these were spectacularly powerful beings. Magic was part of their blood itself. And the remaining conduits divided into factions. There was a group of them who kept craving more and more power, and they eventually discovered that they could use magic to steal power by stealing one another's blood. Something to do with blood symbolizing life force in spells. Then they all got afraid of getting killed by each other, so they started to experiment with the line between life and death."

His eyes narrowed. "Bernard, please tell me you're not talking about vampires."

"I wish I could," I said, sighing. "But you're right—that group eventually evolved into your basic modern vampire." He looked stricken and a tiny bit exhilarated, as though I'd just confirmed the existence of Batman. "But there was a second group of conduits, and they rejected the greedy ones and took to the wilderness, using their magic to transform into eagles and bears and wolves, predators who loved to run and fly and hunt...Look, we're gonna be there in like ten minutes; how much magical history do you really want here?"

"I want all of it," he said stubbornly.

"Argh. Fine. The shape-shifters, the ones who loved the wild, found that the more things they shifted into, the more magic they had to use, and the harder it became to return to humanity. Pretty soon, it started to hurt them to be men and women again. They tried rejecting the magic, living just as humans, but that was even worse. So they cast a great spell, restricting themselves to a dual nature. They picked wolves."

"Why wolves?"

I shrugged. I had some personal theories about pack bonding and loneliness, but hell, he could make his own guesses. "I don't know why; I'm sure there was a reason. The point is, afterward, both groups—the wolves and the vampires—they adapted to what they needed, like any other species, but both reproduced through blood contact. If any werewolf blood touches a human, infection. If any human swallows vampire blood, infection. Then there's this whole history of tension between everyone, which I'm skipping for time"—he started to protest, but I waved him off—"and because you still haven't gotten to the big question."

"Huh?" I felt his eyes on my face. "What big question?"

I glanced across at Cruz and smiled. Okay, so I was enjoying this a little. Sue me. "What am *I*?"

"Oh. Oh, yeah. I mean, you're not, like, a vampire? God, that feels like such a stupid thing to say."

"No, I'm not a vampire. Kind of the opposite, actually."

"What's the opposite of a vampire?"

"I'm a null."

"You're annulled? What?" he asked, confusion in his voice.

"No, no, two words. A. Null." I spelled it. "It's what people like me are called, although there are only a handful of us. I'm sort of a blank space, I guess. A dead spot in the supernatural world. There's something around me—an energy or field of some kind—and when someone from the supernatural community enters it, they lose whatever was supernatural about them. Think of it like a bubble that I live in. I'm the center, and the bubble moves as I move."

After the vampires and werewolves refused to help the witches in their time of need, after the witches discovered that magic hadn't just adhered itself to humans but also to silver and a whole class of plants, after the many battles that resulted, evolution took another step and came up with nulls. Theoretically, I think we were supposed to restore balance. It sort of worked. Nulls are the wrecking ball of the supernatural world: we swing in and out of situations, creating damage and chaos. But sometimes in a really useful way.

Cruz was silent, and I looked over at him again. He was staring straight ahead, different reactions flying across his face. I almost felt sorry for him—when this had all been explained to me, my parents had just died and I was half in shock anyway. The concept of magic actually made about as much sense as living in a world without my mom and dad.

"But you're...human, right?" he finally asked.

I shrugged. "For the most part."

"How big is the bubble?"

"I've never gotten out a tape measure. Maybe ten feet? If I get really, really upset, it expands. And whatever was magical in that range is lost until it leaves the bubble again. A vampire, who was originally descended from humans, becomes a human again, with all the vulnerabilities. A werewolf becomes a human again, too. The magical part of speciation just disappears. Get it?"

"Yeah, I guess. So that animal in the clearing last night—"

"The werewolf," I supplied.

"Yeah, okay. It was a wolf, and then it got too close to you, and that's why it changed back?"

I nodded. "Yes." The wolves actually love changing because of me rather than by themselves, because with me, it's instantaneous. When they change back and forth naturally, it's very painful and takes a few minutes. "And I bet after I left, it became a wolf again and ran off. Am I right?"

"Yeah." A thought occurred to him. "Wait, it could have hurt me! How could you leave me alone with it?"

I shrugged. That hadn't really occurred to me. "I was trying to get out of there. Besides, you had a gun. Shooting the wolf wouldn't kill it, but it'd definitely back off. Probably. You were fine." He still looked indignant, but he'd get over it. I pulled off the freeway. "We're almost there, Cruz. You gonna stand by your word?"

"Sure I am. I'll wait in the car. I want to think about all this and maybe ask some more questions." He set his jaw stubbornly. "But then you and I are going to make a new deal. You're going to help me solve this murder. Be my guide."

My turn to be shocked. "Who am I, Jiminy Cricket? You don't even know for sure that those killings were related to the Old World."

"Maybe not. But you do. After all, you were there." I felt his gaze on me without looking over. "Why *were* you there?"

I changed the subject. "What do I get out of this?"

He smiled smugly. "I won't arrest you, and I won't tell a soul about you or your world. When the case is solved, you just go back to your life."

I thought this over. I could point out that telling anyone about the Old World would end up getting him killed, but I didn't think it'd be such a good idea to threaten him. At the same time, though, I don't work for free, and running around town playing detective sounded like a lot of work. It could even interfere with my TV schedule.

On the other hand, if he really set his heart on it, Officer Cruz could really put the big suck on my life. Having a cop follow me around forever would pretty much guarantee that I'd lose all my freelancing gigs, not to mention my retainer.

This is what I get for saving his goddamned life. "Fine. Deal."

Chapter 5

It was nearly midnight when I finally pulled into Dash's driveway. Dashiell and his wife, Beatrice, owned a gorgeous Spanish-style mansion in the richest part of Old Pasadena. I know that movies and TV shows always depict vampires as these suave, debonair seducers, and Dashiell is probably the vampire I know who is closest to that persona—rich, kind of mysterious, definitely suavish. He's got the sophisticated killer thing down pat, which I suppose you'd need to run a big city, even a dumpy (supernaturally speaking) city like LA. In my experience, though, most of the vampires are more like Molly—frozen in time, trying to cling to the person they were while alive. If they can even remember that person.

But if any of them give me hope, it's Beatrice. She's one of my favorite vampires—both a gracious hostess and the only vamp I've ever met who seems sympathetic to my strange situation. Once, at the lavish Midsummer's Eve party that Dash throws for the supernatural community, she found me sitting by myself in the backyard, playing with the fringe on my dress and wondering what had possessed me to come. "Oh dear, you don't really fit in anywhere, do you?" she'd said, getting close enough to pat my shoulder. She'd taken my hand, pulled me up, and said, "Come on, I'll introduce you to some fascinating vampires who will be *thrilled* to be in your presence." Even then, I'd liked that she didn't treat me as either something scary or a hired-help cockroach, which are the two vibes I usually get from the undead.

I got buzzed through the gate—yes, most of the things that would actually attack Dashiell could get past the gate easily, but maybe it had come with the house—and drove up to the circular parking area, while Cruz let out a whistle at the sight of the house. I had to admit, it was a view worth admiring. The house is pure Spanish elegance, with long, regal columns and flower boxes at every window. Beatrice loves geraniums and tends to favor the bloodred color for some reason. I parked the van on the imported Spanish tiles, next to three or four other cars. I frowned. Dashiell always has underlings around, but it seemed excessive even for him.

I turned in my seat to look at Cruz. "Look, I know this probably seems really...whatever... but you need to stay in the car, okay?" I said again, searching his face. "It's important."

"Why?"

"Because when you're with me, you're safe from all things Old World. But when you're away from me, they can...do things."

"Like what? Fly?" he asked, eyes big.

I couldn't help but grin. "No, not that I've ever heard of. Or change into bats or mist, that's all nonsense. They evolved like any other species; it's just that they evolved ways of controlling their prey—like they can mess around with your head. Make you do things, or forget that they just fed on you. It's hard for them to get humans to do anything truly against their nature, like going on a killing spree or falling permanently in love, but they can still do tons of damage."

"You're serious," he said skeptically, but there was real fear in his voice. Finally.

"Yes. You should be fine if you stay here and keep quiet," I said. I had my hand on the door handle, but he was still giving me that distrustful look. I refrained from smacking him. "Cruz, look at it this way: if you were a bloodthirsty creature of the night, don't you think you would enjoy stumbling across a police officer to be your very own puppet?"

"Oh."

"Yeah, 'oh.' If for some reason you get confronted, be polite and submissive, and do not make eye contact under any circumstances. Just ask for me. Got it?"

"Got it," he said, suddenly meek.

"Okay." I took a deep breath and stepped outside the car, leaning back in to hand the keys to Cruz. "Lock the doors when I'm gone, and don't open them for anyone, okay?"

He nodded soberly, and I closed the car door.

It's my habit, when calling on vampires, to do an abbreviated version of "ding-dong-ditch." I walked up to Dashiell's front door, rang the bell, and then turned and dashed into the middle of the yard, moving so the door was well outside my radius. It was undignified as hell, but I've learned that it's a good idea to give vampires the option of staying away from me if I can swing it. Better to look silly for a minute than to piss someone off by forcing them to age. Beatrice opened the front door, looked around, and spotted me in the shadows. "Scarlett," she called pleasantly, smiling at me, "you may come closer. It is all right."

Beatrice gave me a brief, light embrace and ushered me through the house into the courtyard, her stiletto heels clicking smartly on the marble tiles. She wore a tight, pale-yellow dress that set off her olive skin and waterfall of dark hair. I suddenly wished I'd dressed better. Next to Beatrice...Well, to be fair, most people would look scrubby next to Beatrice. She has this exotic-grace thing going on, vampire or not.

Dashiell's mansion is shaped like a circle, with a surprisingly large outdoor area in the center the size of a baseball infield. Beatrice had it neatly tiled, with walls that were covered in long, climbing flowers and subtle lighting that was augmented by the classiest-looking tiki torches I had ever seen. There was a banquet-sized table in the center where Dash conducted most of his Old World business. I had a vague sense that Dash had plenty of legitimate business interests as well, but I didn't really know anything about that. Nobody hires me for my business skills.

I paused by the courtyard door, looking at Dashiell for where to sit. He was parked in his usual spot at the head of the long oval table, down the courtyard to my left. When necessary, Dashiell will get close to me, but he prefers to keep his distance. I think it's more about vulnerability than vanity—Dashiell is very old and very powerful, with plenty of enemies. I suspect that being reduced to human again makes him feel as if there's a target on his back. Sure enough, Dash tilted his head to indicate that I was to sit down to my right, keeping him out of my range. I sat.

"Scarlett," he called across the distance, "what is happening with the young policeman?"

I wondered, not for the first time, where Dashiell came from originally. His English is excellent, but the formal way he speaks reminds me of someone who started out with another language entirely. I always think he looks a little Italian, but *Dashiell* is French—of course, that could just be a name he picked. Someday, when he wasn't irritated with me, I would ask.

Or not.

"He's willing to cooperate," I said in a normal voice. Vampire hearing is excellent, of course. Heightened strength and speed and all that. It had taken me a few tries to get used to this kind of conversation, but I mostly had it down. "He's agreed to keep his mouth shut in exchange for me helping him with this case."

"You?" Dashiell said with an indulgent little smile, as if I were a toddler who had just offered to drive his car. "What can you contribute to a police investigation?"

I spent a second wondering whether I'd just been insulted and decided that it didn't really matter. "He thinks that there are supernatural elements at work here, and I can be sort of his...

liaison, I guess. I'm the only person he knows who is connected to the Old World."

He went still, thinking this over. When vampires go still, it is scary, since they don't need to actually breathe or blink. "Very well," he decided, finally. "I did not get very close to the victims." Something like embarrassment flickered across his face, and I realized for the first time that Dashiell hadn't approached the scene because of all the blood. As I've said, vampires gain control with age, and Dash's control is stellar. That much blood, though, would have tested even his strength. No wonder he was touchy about the whole situation. "But I would like to know more about this strange killing as well. And this way you can keep an eye on Officer Cruz. I do not love the idea of having you as a spy," he continued, with an annoyed little emphasis on the word *you*, "but I suppose it cannot be helped. We will discuss the fate of the policeman further when your collaboration is finished."

Fine. Message received. I was an idiot, and Cruz's life would depend on how he handled himself during his investigation. But if that were the case, why had he let Cruz live in the first place? It wasn't because he was a cop, because if vampires know how to do anything, it's make a murder look like an accident. It couldn't actually be because I'd asked him...could it?

Nah.

"Now, to other business," he said and waved through the window at Beatrice, who was in the kitchen.

She nodded and left the room for a moment, and when she came through the patio door, Will was with her. I brightened a little. The werewolves, as a rule, like me a lot better than the vampires do, probably because I calm the sense of unrest that comes with being a shape-shifter. It also helps that I pose no immediate threat to them.

My spirits dropped again a second later, however, when I saw the next person through the door. Wolf packs are usually led by a mated pair, the *alphas*, who function like parents, and then there are a whole bunch of intermediate wolves who are like their kids. Ordinarily, the two alphas would go almost everywhere together, but Will hasn't found a mate yet, so instead, his pack has a *beta*, a platonic second-in-command who accompanies him on "official" visits like this. Unfortunately, in Will's pack, the beta happens to be Eli, who trailed Will onto the patio. His ice-blue eyes—the color of a husky puppy's—met mine and flickered with the recognition you only get from people who've seen you naked. I tried not to squish down farther in my seat.

Along with his second-in-command, Will had brought his *sigma*. Even though the pack hierarchy is sort of vague in the middle, everyone does know who the weakest member of the pack is. In a healthy werewolf pack, the sigma is the absolute lowest member of the food chain—why they're called sigmas and not omegas is beyond me, but they probably have their reasons. Unlike regular wolves or even dogs, though, werewolves value this person. The sigma is the member most in need of the pack's protection, and he or she becomes like a favorite younger sibling. Kind of like the Tiny Tim of the wolf pack.

In Will's pack, the sigma is Caroline Brooks, a petite, competent pixie who also happens to be Will's personal secretary and office manager at the bar he owns. Bringing Caroline along meant two things: first, it indicated that Will was there on business, requiring her aid, and second, it was a quiet gesture that he was not afraid of Dashiell. Protecting the sigma is vital in werewolf packs, and bringing her along meant that Will didn't see Dashiell as a threat. Or that Will was powerful enough to bring his weakest member into the heart of the vampire world and keep her safe. I wondered how Caroline felt about being used for symbolism.

The three of them gave Dash a casual, but respectful, greeting as they came through the door. Will came over and ruffled my hair, which I tolerated even though I'd have to redo it later. Except for all the muscle, Will looks like the average suburban dad in any sitcom. He looks to be in his late thirties, but werewolves age more slowly than humans, so who knows. He treats me with fond detachment, like an entertaining but ultimately expendable younger cousin. Caroline bent to give me a hug, whispering, "It'll be okay," into my ear. Eli didn't say anything, just looked at me with his sad puppy eyes.

Okay, fine. I probably should have left a note.

The wolves trooped down the courtyard to Dashiell, where Will took the seat to Dashiell's right. Then Eli sat on his right, and Caroline took the chair beside him. I suddenly felt as if I were on trial.

"I didn't know you were coming," I said to Will.

He shrugged, raising his voice so I could hear. "It was a last-minute thing. But this affects all of us, so I thought I'd show in person."

"What about Kirsten?" I asked, a little bluntly.

Dashiell and Will exchanged an amused look without answering me. They think that Kirsten is kind of a joke. They do business with her, but neither of them is all that impressed by witches. I personally think underestimating Kirsten is a mistake, but nobody asks me. I'm just the janitor.

I decided to take the initiative. "Okay, look, I know this is about last night. I know I screwed up. But I'm handling things with this cop."

"We know," Dashiell said. "But Will and I have discussed it, and we feel that the time has come for you to take on...help."

Will's voice was gentler. "She's been dead for almost six months, Scarlett. And she wasn't able to work for a long time before that."

He was referring to my mentor, Olivia. She was the only other null I'd met, and had trained me on crime scene cleanup. Then she and I were partners for four years before cancer took her life. You can be completely bulletproof when it comes to spells and vampire bites, but not even nulls get a free pass from the big C.

Supernaturally insignificant or not, LA is at least a two-person area for cleanup, and every single person on the patio knew that I should have swallowed my feelings and found a replacement for Olivia the day I took over from her. At the time, though, I'd just been through a horrible shock. Besides, I was in no place to trust a new partner, after what I'd been through with the first one. Everything I'd had, really, was because of Olivia.

And everything I had lost, too.

I set my jaw stubbornly. I get crabby when I'm clearly in the wrong. "You can't just put an ad for a null on Craigslist. There are, what, five or six of us in the world? We don't exactly have an employment office."

"We know," Will said patiently. "But in all likelihood, there are more of you than that. It's just hard for nulls to find out what they are." This is true. Most likely, plenty of nulls live and die without discovering their ability. "Besides," Will continued, "you don't absolutely have to be a null to do the work that you do."

Crap. There went my best excuse.

"It just helps. And it's safer."

"So here is what we'll do," Dashiell said. "I have put out some feelers, trying to track down another null. If that proves too difficult, we will perhaps try one of the witches." Vampires can't really do my job, since a) they get distracted by blood, and b) they're dead during the day. I do get the occasional daytime crime scene. "In the meantime, though, Will has graciously offered one of his wolves to help you. You will begin training him immediately."

"One of the wolves? That's not a good..." I started, but then swallowed it. *These two are my bosses*, I reminded myself. I didn't really have a choice here, and protesting would just make me look whiny and unprofessional. *Olivia wouldn't have liked that*, I thought sourly. I looked over at Will. "Who is it?" I felt a fleeting hope that he had nominated Caroline.

But Will and Caroline both glanced over to Eli. Oh, no. *Shit, shit, shit.* My one-night stand—well, okay, three-night stand—could not be my apprentice. "I'm not sure that's the best idea," I said carefully, without looking at Eli. Nobody needed to know that we'd slept together. I was not about to turn this into a supernatural telenovela.

"Is there a problem with Eli that we should know about?" Will asked pleasantly.

"No—"

"Then I think he's the perfect candidate. Obviously his schedule can be flexible." Since, you know, Will is his boss.

"But will he be all right around dead bodies?" I asked, trying not to sound desperate. "He'll be working by himself eventually, and I'm told the smell can be very distracting."

"Eli used to be a paramedic," Will replied easily. This was news to me, though I'd never really considered Eli's life before he changed. "He says he'll be fine."

Was this Eli's suggestion? Did Will already know about Eli and me? Maybe. Will didn't miss much. But he might have just not cared, or maybe he was playing a deeper game here, trying to get me to actively participate in the search for nulls. Crafty Will. He looks like a church deacon, but I've long suspected he could be ruthless if he needed to. I was definitely going to have to get to the bottom of who had put Eli's hat in the ring, but that could wait. For now I just had to suck it up.

"Sounds good," I managed, and the mood in the courtyard relaxed just a little.

The meeting broke up, and everybody started to leave. I was about to head back to the van and Cruz, who I'd almost forgotten about, but I had an idea. I pulled Will aside—not that it mattered, because everyone on the property who was ten feet away could hear like a bat, with the exception of Cruz and me—and asked him if he had any pictures of the wolves in human form.

"Pictures?" he asked blankly, tilting his head to one side. "Maybe we do. Why do you ask?"

I told him about the bodies, the wolf in the clearing, and the cop. I didn't mention that he was out in my van at the moment, because Will might feel obligated to inform Dashiell. "I never saw the guy properly, but I think Cruz did. If I could show him some pictures, we could figure out who it was, see if he saw or smelled anything there."

I could see Will's metaphorical hackles going up. "Are you suggesting that one of my wolves may be responsible for this?"

I shook my head. "No. Definitely not. Or at least, not this wolf. If one of the wolves did kill those people, he'd have no reason to leave and then come back to the scene. I honestly think that this wolf was just running in the park, smelled the bodies, and came to see what it was. I just want to ask if there's anything else he noticed."

"But you're also pretty much asking to out this wolf to a police officer," Will objected. "And me along with him."

"Will, you didn't see what happened. It was...It was awful. And a lot of things depend on finding out who did it."

He sighed, relenting. "I think I have some pictures at the bar from the Fourth of July picnic. You can bring your cop by to look at them."

"Can we do it tonight? Now?"

Will checked his watch and gave me a weary, indulgent smile. "Fine. I'll meet you over there."

I thanked him and tried to head out, but just as I closed the front door behind me, it opened again and Eli stepped out. It felt strange to have people keep popping in and out of my radius, but I'd grown used to it.

"What happened to you?" he asked bluntly. I knew what he meant.

I hugged my arms around me. The September heat wave had broken sometime that day, and the fall night had grown chilly. "I got a call. I had to work."

"You couldn't have woken me up? Left a note?" His face was hard, and he was fidgeting.

"Look, Eli—" I began, but he cut me off.

"I get it. You don't have to do the whole 'just friends' talk."

I didn't say anything.

"And I want you to know, none of this"—he gestured toward the house, to the meeting we'd just left—"was my idea."

There was a long, awkward pause, and then he suddenly burst into an earsplitting grin.

"What?"

"Nothing. I'm sorry, I just always forget how nice it feels to be around you. How...restful."

I rolled my eyes. This is exactly why Eli and I will never go anywhere. The remnants of the very powerful magic—the Original magic that led to conduits evolving into shape-shifters and shape-shifters evolving into werewolves—just never leaves the wolves. As I understand it, werewolves constantly have to fight to keep their control, like an itchy humming that's always in the back of their minds. (Ironically, real wolves have a similar problem—what was once described to me as "genetically coded predatory behavior.") They can't help themselves; the magic makes them feel a continuous pressure to be hunting, killing, feeding. *Maybe that's why the shifters chose to become werewolves*, I thought suddenly. Huh.

Some wolves have a harder time than others, and Eli really struggles with his inner animal. When he's around me, though, he is a de facto human again, and all that goes away. If he were an alcoholic, I would be the thing that made him never want another drink. Or maybe I'd be the thing that let him stay permanently drunk.

Some girls would probably get off on that kind of thing, but whenever this happened, with any of the wolves or the vampires, I just felt vaguely used. I didn't mind when it was Molly because I was getting paid for my services, and because she's sort of become my friend. But I didn't want the guy I was...seeing...to be in it for those kinds of perks.

"Listen," I said brusquely, "you're working for me now—for *me*, not for Will or Dashiell. You're not a spy or a partner; you're my apprentice, at least temporarily. Got it?"

"Got it."

"Good. Keep your phone on. The next time I get a call might be later tonight, or tomorrow during the day, or not for another week. But when I call, you need to answer, wherever you are."

He grinned, and even I could appreciate the irony. Two hours ago, I would have ducked all calls from Eli. Now I was ordering him to pick up the phone from me. Life is funny.

"Okay. Good night, then." I turned on my heel and marched down the sidewalk to the driveway. So there.

Chapter 6

There were only two cars left in the driveway—Eli's battered pickup truck and my van. I didn't see any sign of Officer Cruz at first, but when I got closer, I realized he'd squashed himself down between the seats. I opened the driver's side door, causing him to jump.

"Oh, hi," he said nervously, looking embarrassed. "I wasn't hiding."

I climbed in and slammed the door. "What were you doing, then?"

"One of the guys who came out of there, he was with this girl, and she turned into a...a wolf," he said, still a little shaky. The werewolves have to change at the full moon, but most of them are also strong enough to change a few times in between. "They were just playing, you know, goofing around like you do with a dog, but I thought it'd be easier if they didn't see me."

"Good call," I said mildly and saw him cracking his knuckles, one by one, as he gazed intently out the window. I sighed. I had already turned the key in the ignition, but now I shut off the van.

"What?" he asked, finally looking up to meet my eyes.

"Get in your goddamned seat and buckle up. Everyone else has left. We're fine." Looking embarrassed, he climbed back into the passenger seat and clicked his safety belt. I looked him over again. "Are we gonna have a problem?" I asked. "Are you gonna wig out and run to CNN or something?"

"What? No," he said, his focus now entirely on me. He sounded indignant enough that I started the van and began backing into the turnaround so we could go forward down the driveway. As we pulled back onto the street, Cruz finally said, "It's just...When we were in the park, everything was already so heightened—the bodies, the blood, the fact that I was there alone with the suspect. No offense," he added. "It's not like I'd convinced myself that it was all my imagination, it was just..." In the corner of my eye, I saw his hands waving helplessly.

"Adrenaline," I supplied.

"Yeah."

I glanced over. Cruz looked calm now, like he was thinking through his words.

"But this time it was so casual and everyday. Like it was... normal."

"It *was* normal," I pointed out. I felt his eyes on me. When I got to a red light and looked over, he was grinning.

"Yeah," he said in wonder. "Yeah, I guess it was."

Hair of the Dog—yes, I know, the most obvious bar name ever—is located in one of the funky little stretches of Pico on the West Side. It was after 1:00 a.m. when we arrived, but Will's place is always busy. Ordinary humans like his microbrews, and the werewolves tend to hang around long past bar close. They're a pack, of course, but they also tend to stick together just like anyone who shares a common malady.

We came in the front door, and the bartender, an African American werewolf in her late twenties, looked up and nodded at me. I threaded my way toward the bar, Cruz lagging behind me as he tried to study the decor. I'd explained where we were going and why, but it hadn't really prepared him for the bar's effect: Will had set the place up to be sort of an overtly kitschy love letter to dogs and wolves. There are posters, cheap calendars, historic articles, *Dog Fancy* magazine spreads, etc. covering every inch of the brick walls. If you look really closely, you can even see a couple pictures of Will's pack, disguised in wolf form. It's a small space, so the effect is sort of like a den, I guess.

"Isn't this a bit...on the nose?" Cruz murmured at my back.

"Yeah. It's excessive. But Will's a fan of the 'hiding in plain sight' approach." To those in the know, it's ironic and funny. To outsiders, well, lots of bars have themes.

At the bar, I asked for Will and learned that we'd beaten him, probably only by a few minutes. I ordered a Diet Coke and, playing a hunch, got a regular for Cruz. I carried the sodas to a battered wooden table that was as far as I could get from the rest of the bar patrons and settled down, with Cruz across from me.

After a long pull of the Coke, he began to study the people around us. "Bernard," he said in a low voice, "why are half the people in this room staring at you?"

I glanced around. He was right. I was getting a lot of stares from the crowd. Most of them seemed curious but neutral, a few were a little pissed, and more than a few had the same pleased look of relief I'd gotten from Eli. When I closed my eyes and concentrated, I could feel all of them humming in my radius. I opened my eyes again. "Because right before we came in, half the people in this room weren't human. Now they all are."

"But they're...you know. In people form."

"It doesn't matter. They never stop feeling the wolf. It pulls at them, like the vampires are pulled toward blood."

"Really?"

I nodded, a little solemn, and explained about the magic residue. I'm really, really glad I don't have to worry about ever becoming a werewolf. "Some of them love the feeling, but most have kind of a hard time." I played with my straw, trying for inconspicuous.

"Do you see the man from the park? I warn you, he may be wearing clothes now."

Cruz smiled and glanced around, but shook his head. "No."

"Damn. It would have been nice if it were just that easy."

"Do you come here a lot?"

"I try not to. My being here, it messes with people. Some of them don't mind—hell, a lot of them like it—but I try not to interfere." Also, I tend to do stupid things like get drunk and go home with bartenders when I'm not really supposed to be drinking at all, since I'm continuously on call for crime scene cleanup. Sometimes, though, I get sick of being around normal people, who have absolutely no concept of my life.

Cruz just nodded, and I looked over at him, suddenly feeling a little girly rush of something like shyness. He was so good-looking—that perfect skin, warm eyes, full lips, muscle tone—I just kind of had to marvel at it. He looked a little flushed and excited but seemed to be handling all of this pretty well, all things considered.

"Don't you have people you should be reporting to right now?" I asked him. "Aren't you on the park case?"

"Technically, I was off duty at eight p.m., and I'm not due in again until eight a.m. I'm on my own time right now."

Damn. So much for sending him off to his boss. "What kind of things are you guys investigating?"

He stared at me for a moment, then shrugged, probably figuring the same thing I had: we were in this together. "Today we were mostly trying to identify the victims, see what they had in common. That kind of thing can lead to a common link." He hesitated. "Before, you mentioned the possibility that this wasn't related to the Old World at all. Do you really think that could be true? Honestly."

If I lied and said it looked human, would he leave me alone? But before I could respond, the bartender called my name and tilted her head toward Will's office. I nodded my thanks. Before I could think about it too carefully, I said, "It's possible, but I doubt it. The wolves run in that park, and there was so much blood everywhere, and it looked so ritualistic...It looked like a lot of other supernatural crime scenes I've seen."

He stared at me, and I realized my mistake.

"You've seen a lot of crime scenes?"

Aw, crap. The thing is, I'm not all that great with subterfuge or politics—I'm not really a five-moves-ahead kind of girl. I caught the bartender's eye again and held up one finger, rolling my eyes a little to suggest that the delay was Cruz's fault.

"Okay. I need to explain what I do for a living," I began.

As I talked, his face got more and more stormy. When I finished, Cruz was quiet for a long moment, digesting. "Let me see if I understand this," he said at last. "You destroy evidence for a living."

"That's one way to see it, I guess."

"But don't you know how much damage you're doing?" he protested, sounding heated. "These people belong in jail. You're not only destroying any chance for the justice system to work, you're actively incriminating yourself."

"Keep your voice down," I warned, and he took a breath, looking around. "We sort of have our own justice system. And in that system, everyone can tell if you're lying, and smell where you've been, or do a spell that recreates the whole scene. Physical evidence just isn't important. For that, the only thing that matters is getting rid of it before it draws attention in your world."

He rolled his eyes. "Do you hear yourself? 'My world' and 'your world'? What is that? You're a human, too."

I shrugged. "Not exactly. Besides, think about the practicalities. How is the modern justice system going to contain someone who turns furry for three days a month? Or who needs blood to survive? Where's the prison cell that can hold a powerful witch?

If regular humans decided to try to police the Old World...A lot of people would die." I didn't mention that I'd also be out of a job.

He thought about that for a long moment. "They still have to come out," he decided. "That's the only way to make sure everyone is held accountable for their actions. There will be a panic for a while, but then the government will change, and the laws, and the system will adapt."

The first time I'd been taken to meet Dashiell, I'd been too young and stupid to be properly afraid of him, and we'd had practically this same conversation. Confident in the soundness of my argument, and with all the wisdom of my eighteen years, I had told the cardinal vampire of the city that surely the vampires' exposure had to be *inevitable* as technology advanced; cell phone cameras, CCTV, ATM videos, and so on had to make it tough to stay under the radar. Wouldn't it be easier to just come out, get in front of the story?

He'd allowed me to blather on about it for a while, then held up a patient hand. "Miss Bernard," he'd asked calmly, "have you ever heard of the lions of Tsavo?"

"Uh, no."

"In 1898, the British Empire was trying to build a simple railway bridge over a river in Kenya," he began. "But in March, two lions began attacking the camp, eating the workers. They'd developed a taste for human flesh, you see, and for nine months, those two lions terrorized the region. There is some disagreement on the numbers, but they killed and ate at least forty, and possibly closer to a hundred and fifty people in that time."

"So?" I'd said, not carefully enough.

"Lions don't usually hunt humans. This was very strange behavior, and they were very strange lions. But the humans didn't abandon the area. They didn't move the bridge, or send in a bunch of scientists to capture and study the two lions. They hunted them down and killed them. For being *predators*. For simply following their natures."

"That was a long time ago, Dashiell. Times have changed."

He shook his head. "In many ways, yes, but not in the way that humans react instinctively to a threat. They *hunt it down and kill it*. Look at the Americans and terrorists." He had said *Americans* as though we weren't sitting in beautiful Southern California at that very instant. "The witches can mostly pass for human, but the wolves and the vampires have very distinct weaknesses—the full moon and the daylight. We can be hunted so easily." His eyes had met mine then, and glittered with meaning.

"You're trying to tell me something," I'd said, not getting it.

He leaned back in his chair, spreading his hands expansively. "Nulls appeared when the balance between magic and the natural world had shifted toward magic. But when the balance swung back, when the population of magical creatures began to drop, and then to drop further and further, nulls continued to be born. Why do you suppose that is?"

I'd shrugged. "Maybe evolution is phasing magic out entirely."

"That is one theory," he'd allowed. "But there's another."

"What is that?"

"That nulls will help us hide from human detection. That your kind will protect us."

And the way that he'd looked at me, in that exact moment... Well, it taught me to be afraid of him.

"You're thinking like a cop," I told Jesse, emerging from my reverie and taking a sip of my soda. "All law and order, but that's not how the Old World works. Self-preservation is everything to these people. If they were discovered, they would either try to take control of humans or be hunted to extinction. Probably both."

"So they should just get away with killing people?" he protested.

"No, just…Look, right now, the only thing that unites the entire Old World is the fear of being exposed. It kind of works as its own justice system right there."

Cruz thought that over for a moment, but then shook his head. "Okay, look, I need to think about that a little more. I'm still not sure that I shouldn't just arrest you right now."

"Good luck with *that* trial." I checked my watch. "It's getting late. Let's go talk to Will."

I grabbed his hand without thinking. It was warm and dry, and I dropped it almost immediately. What was *wrong* with me tonight? He followed me past the tables and through the EMPLOYEES ONLY door, where the bar's din dropped down to a much more manageable level. Will was waiting for us in the hall outside the office that he shared with Caroline. I introduced the two of them, a little awkwardly.

"Will, this is Officer Jesse Cruz, and Cruz, this is Will Carling. He, um, owns this bar."

The two men shook hands, and then Will said, "Come on in. I'll show you those pictures."

We followed him into the office, and he went behind his big oak desk and took out an oversized envelope full of photos, handing it to Cruz. I sat in one of the visitor chairs and looked at the walls, trying not to fidget. For someone who is technically a creature of the night, Will's life often seems more normal than mine. The walls in his office were lined with pictures of the Little League team Will coached, a huge fish he'd caught, his mom and siblings. I wondered if his family knew what he was, if it bothered them. I felt a brief flare of jealousy, missing my own past as a normal person.

"Him," Cruz said, and I jerked back to attention. He was holding up a photo of Will with Caroline and some of the other wolves, pointing to a slender, wispy man in the back. "This is him."

Will took the picture and looked closely. "That's Ronnie. He's new to the pack, transferred last year from…Phoenix, I think." He looked up and shrugged at us. "I don't actually know him all that well, but he works at a comic book shop not too far from here, a mile or so east on Pico."

"Last name?" Cruz said, suddenly all business. He'd gotten out a little pen and pad. They looked brand-new.

"Pocoa, I think. Something close to that. But Scarlett said you weren't arresting him." He looked pointedly back and forth from me to Cruz, who nodded.

"This part of the investigation is out of the public record. It's just me. We'll ask Ronnie if he knows anything, and if he can help, great, if not, that'll be it," Cruz said, then added firmly, "Of course, if he's involved somehow, I'll have to pursue it." I had to admire Cruz a little bit for that one. Of course, he'd never seen Will turn into a wolf and snarl at an underling.

Will stood up. "Sounds reasonable to me." He reached over and shook Cruz's hand, indicating that the meeting was over. Good. I was tired.

I drove us back to my parking garage. Cruz was quiet beside me, and I wondered for a second if he'd fallen asleep. Then he spoke.

"My mom worked on a vampire movie once."

"Your mom works in the movies?"

"My whole family does. My dad's a composer; my mom's a script supervisor. My older brother Noah is a stuntman."

"Noah Cruz?"

He grinned. "It was part of the deal. My mom's Mexican, and my dad's Caucasian, but she really, really wanted to pass on her family's surname, and he didn't care. So their deal was that she'd keep her last name and give it to us, and he got to pick Anglo first names. So, Noah and Jesse." He looked over. "What about you?"

"What about me?"

"Why the name Scarlett?"

Oh. I was a little thrown, having not realized we were on an adorable-family-story basis. "Uh, I was named after Scarlett O'Hara, but my mom always told everyone it was the book, not the film. She corrected everybody, and it was kind of a family joke after a while. I've never even seen the movie."

"Do your parents know about, you know, what you can do? All of this?"

"They died," I said matter-of-factly, "before I knew myself."

"Oh. I'm sorry," he said sheepishly. "Um…Do you have any brothers or sisters?"

I hesitated. I've always kept Jack's existence far away from my work, but Cruz wasn't really a part of my work, and he could probably find it in some police database anyway. "A brother, Jack. He's older. He doesn't know."

"Do you see him much?"

I shrugged an *I don't want to talk about it* kind of shrug, and we were quiet for the rest of the drive, which was just fine with me. I pulled into the parking garage at two forty-five, feeling gritty with tiredness. "So, tomorrow," he said, one hand on the door latch, "will you come with me to check out this Ronnie guy?"

I leaned back in the seat, feeling even more tired than a moment ago. "Do I have to? Can't you just go without me?"

"I'm guessing werewolves aren't just strong and fast when they're in wolf form, am I right?"

"Yes," I said reluctantly.

"Then I'd like you to come with me. For protection."

His smile was so warm and charming that I couldn't help but smile back. Dammit. Stupid powers of hotness.

"Fine. Pick me up at one."

"That late?" He sounded disappointed.

"I need sleep, Cruz. You can work your own end of the case without me."

He shrugged, unbuckling, and made a move to open the van door.

"Wait," I said, and reached out to snag his wrist.

He turned back, eyebrows raised, and I blushed and let go. Was I really this out of practice with dealing with attractive young men while sober? *Get it together, Scarlett.*

"Look," I began, "I know we talked about this, and I know you already made it a whole day without telling anyone about the Old World—"

"How do you know that?" Cruz interrupted.

Because you're still alive, I thought, but I didn't think a cop would appreciate that particular wording. "Because," I said carefully, "if you'd run around telling people, I can guarantee it would have gotten back to Dashiell by now." While he was still thinking that over, I added, "But do I need to be worried about you going back on our deal? You can't tell *anyone*, you know, not family or your best friend or your dentist…"

Cruz rolled his eyes and held up a hand. "I'm not a child, Scarlett. I understand the stakes here." I must not have looked very convinced, because he met my gaze and held it, giving me a small nod. "Really."

I let out a breath. "Okay. Good night."

Chapter 7

Jesse Cruz couldn't remember the last time he'd been this tired. There had been no point in trying to sleep after Scarlett had dropped him off, since he was working the day shift on Wednesday and only had two hours before he needed to be at work. So Jesse decided to go have breakfast at his parents' house. He reasoned that free food and his mother's customary interrogation would go a long way toward helping him stay awake and thinking.

Overall, he thought he was handling the Old World thing pretty well, although maybe that was partly just shock and exhaustion. Part of him felt as if he were in a movie, and any minute the credits would roll and he'd go back to his normal, supernatural-free life. Films were filled with all manner of supernatural, and though he was a cop now, Jesse had been a child of the cinema. It was hard not to be, growing up in Hollywood with film-production parents. When Jesse was seven, he had seen the original *Dracula* at a friend's Halloween party and became instantly terrified of vampires. He'd hidden garlic cloves in the pockets of most of his clothes, and started sneaking his parents' empty wine bottles out of the recycling bin and setting them up around his room, figuring that since Dracula didn't drink wine, he probably wouldn't like seeing the bottles everywhere. They also served as a nice early-warning system, creating a terrible racket every time someone entered his room and knocked down the stack behind the door.

After about a week of that, his mother had gotten fed up and taken Jesse on a visit to the set of a vampire movie, the third in a popular series. She'd shown him all the different tools that the crew used to make regular actors look like vampires, and the makeup artist had even given Jesse a set of old fangs to keep. He still had them somewhere. After that, young Jesse's fears about vampires had dissolved, but he still remembered that feeling of wonder and terror, knowing there was something out in the night that wanted to get you. And now...He kept waiting for the makeup person to come out and show him the fake fangs, but it hadn't happened yet. *And there was something sort of...exciting about that*, he thought. The world had gotten a lot scarier, but it had gotten a lot more interesting, too.

Jesse's parents' home in Los Feliz was big and sprawling. His mom and dad had taken a basic ranch house and built on to it every ten years or so until it reminded Jesse of a hospital—new additions and corridors that made it hard to find anything. The house was hardly sterile, though—his mother had overdecorated it to the point of suffocation, which Jesse, his father, and his older brother tended to smile about.

When he pulled into the driveway, Carmen Cruz was outside the house watering the mums and dahlias that crowded the porch. Max, his parents' pit bull mix, was prancing—there was no other word for it—in circles around her, trying to catch the falling water in his mouth. As Jesse pulled up, Max went on high alert, immediately charging the newcomer with affection that bordered on assault.

"Hey, buddy," Jesse said happily, crouching down to let Max lick his face. "Long time no see."

"*Hijo*, you were here last weekend," Carmen said, coming up for a kiss. She was short and stocky, with good looks that hadn't faded with age. Last year, she'd finally cut off all her long hair, and Jesse still missed seeing it when he looked at her.

"True, but in dog time, that's like years and years." He kissed her cheek.

"Ah, I see. Am I to assume that this unannounced visit will involve me cooking you breakfast?"

"Only if you want to. I can always hit the McDonald's drive-through," he said mischievously, happy to be in the familiar rhythm of teasing her. It was about as far as he could get from werewolves and dead bodies in the dark.

"God forbid! All right, follow me. Max, come." She slapped her leg at Max, who was eyeing the flowers as though he might lick the moisture right off them. "There's water in the house, silly dog."

In the kitchen, his mother stirred up some *híjoles caramba*, Mexican omelet, while Jesse sat at the counter and drank coffee. He hated the taste of all coffee, but he'd been pretending to enjoy his mother's for years and had no good reason to give up the charade.

For a moment, he wanted to blurt out the story of the last few days—the werewolves, the girl, the whole thing—but he swallowed it. It was exciting to know that vampires were out there, but he still didn't want to piss them off or involve his mother. Instead, he asked, "Is Dad working this morning?" trying not to wince at each sip of his coffee. While her back was turned, he dumped in a few more spoonfuls of sugar.

"Yes, he had an early meeting, but my call time isn't until ten-thirty today, which is why I am here puttering around," Carmen replied, "accidentally" dropping a piece of sausage in front of Max.

"*Mamá*, you know if you feed him like that, he's going to expect to get scraps all the time."

"That's why I make it look like an accident," she said, as though Jesse might be a little dim-witted. He smiled. Her face became very serious. "I saw on the news about the murders in La Brea Park. That is in your district, yes?"

"Yes. I'm assigned to the case. Just a grunt, though."

Carmen made her guilt-inducing clucking sound. "Oh, *hijo,* why you must do this work I will never understand. Your brother said the television show he is working on is looking for a new police consultant. Maybe—"

"Mom," Jesse cut in, "I don't want to have this discussion again. I'm a cop. It's what I do." She sighed theatrically, sliding the finished omelet across the counter toward him and grabbing a fork out of the drawer to accompany it. "I know, I know. It's just that your father and I worry so much. We should never have let you watch so much *Matlock.*"

Ordinarily, Jesse would have laughed and reassured her by emphasizing his low status on any case, but he was suddenly playing on a different level, and there were more risks. The thought was sobering.

His mother cleaned up the kitchen and played with Max while Jesse finished eating. He looked around the sunny room, with its Mexican paintings and vases of flowers, and felt a great swell of gratitude for his family. He thought about Scarlett Bernard, who had such a sadness about her.

"*Hijo,* you have a dreamy look on your face," Carmen said, with mock reproach. Then her eyes lit up. "Is there, perhaps, a girl?"

He rolled his eyes. "Jeez, *Mamá,* you're terrible."

"That is a yes!" she crowed, raising her hands triumphantly.

He couldn't help but smile at her. "It's not like that. I did meet a girl yesterday, a witness, but there isn't anything between us."

His mother waited, raising her dark eyebrows.

"Okay, there is something about her," he admitted. "I've met a lot of women in LA, and she's...different."

"I see," she said, her voice mischievous.

Jesse ignored this. "Thank you for breakfast, *Mamá,*" he said, wiping his mouth and rising to hug her. "I gotta get to the station and catch some bad guys."

"*Sí*, but take care, *mijo*, okay? Be careful with my little boy."

Jesse rolled his eyes good-naturedly and left his parents' house feeling like he'd just gotten eight hours of sleep.

An hour later, however, he was back at the precinct and fading quickly. Despite the coffee he'd had earlier, Jesse was chugging Coke like there was no tomorrow, the acidy taste churning in his stomach. He tried to remember the last time he'd pulled an all-nighter, but it had been years ago. Ages.

Jesse spent the morning making phone calls, trying to identify the three victims. Now that the bodies had been reassembled, it was easier to identify them as a female in her late twenties, a Caucasian male in his early thirties, and an African American male in his midforties. Their clothing, when it was pieced together, had been unremarkable: T-shirts and jeans from the mall, a blazer from Brooks Brothers, a pair of Nikes. The Caucasian male had painted his fingernails black and ripped his designer jeans, but that wasn't a particularly helpful identifier in Los Angeles. To Jesse's surprise, none of them had been carrying any kind of ID, not to mention a purse or briefcase. The victims' fingerprints weren't on record anywhere, and no one had reported them missing.

The coroner's report had been released, but it left more questions than answers. All three victims had been shot first, one by one, in both legs. The shots themselves weren't fatal, but the injuries would have incapacitated the victims so that the killer could take his time with them. Cause of death was technically blood loss: the two main arteries—femoral and jugular—had been severed on all three bodies, and the victims had bled out. The blood work analyst theorized that each of them had belly-crawled away from one side of the clearing, as if to escape their attacker. Postmortem, the bodies had been dismembered and eviscerated, the blood shaken out of the limbs and the intestines spread around the clearing. It was grisly and horrifying, and Jesse was grateful that at least that part had been done postmortem.

The details were important but didn't really help to point in any particular direction. As it stood, the investigators were spinning their wheels. Who were the victims? Why were all three missing their identification? Did they go to the park willingly, or were they forced there from somewhere else? And how had they gotten to the park in the first place? LA was a driving city; everyone used a car to go anywhere. But no abandoned cars were found in the vicinity of the park, so Jesse had called cab companies and bus depots, trying to find anyone who remembered driving the three victims. No one had seen three people like that together, but there were plenty of young women and middle-aged men in cabs that night. One of the uniforms would be going around later with retouched photos of the victims' faces.

At noon, Jesse went to see his supervisor, Captain Miranda Williams. A thick-waisted woman in her early fifties with a large hooked nose, Williams was the opposite of every police captain in the movies his family made. She was maternal, concerned, determined, and loyal. Jesse liked her a lot and was happy that he'd been assigned to her division—even if she didn't seem that happy about it herself. Williams, like the other detectives in the unit, still seemed skeptical that Jesse had anything going on between the ears. Yesterday that had weighed on his mind, but a lot had changed since then. He had other concerns.

Williams was putting the phone down as Jesse knocked on the doorframe and entered. She gestured for him to take a seat. Jesse thought she looked as tired as he felt.

"Please tell me you have new information, Cruz. The press is starting a frenzy over this case. They're calling it the new Black Dahlia, and you know how well that turned out for the department."

"Yes, ma'am. And unfortunately, I don't have any news. But I did have an idea."

"Go ahead."

"La Brea Park isn't all that far from the airport. If the three of them were taken from LAX, it might explain why three such different people were all killed together. Like a random thing."

"Uh-huh." She seemed unconvinced.

"I thought I could take the pictures of the deceased over to LAX, show them to some baggage people, the guys who run the security cameras. If they were coming from somewhere, we could get ID that way."

Williams thought it over and finally shrugged. "I think it's a pretty big stretch, but at this point, we're willing to consider anything. Go ahead. Just call me if you find anything, and get a report back to me before the end of the day, all right?"

"Yes, ma'am," Jesse said.

He knew he'd actually have to do the wild-goose chase at the airport—these things had a way of coming back to haunt you if you didn't follow through—but he could squeeze in a couple hours of his own investigation in the meantime. He drove to Scarlett's, feeling a little nervous. At least it was broad daylight.

Chapter 8

Tuesday night was another rough one. When I finally made it into bed, I found myself trapped in a mental loop, thinking about the murder and Eli and my job. The freelance gigs I get are good—I occasionally attend important pack meetings where there might be extra tension, or chaperone vampires in the business world when they can't avoid a daytime meeting, stuff like that. But I need the steady income of my crime scene job. If not for that, I had absolutely no idea how I'd make a living. I didn't make it through a single semester of college, and I had no skills or non-supernatural job experience. I didn't think McDonald's would care if, one time, I hid three severed limbs, a pool of blood, and a dead hundred-year-old desert tortoise in twenty-five minutes. No, I needed to keep my job, whatever it took, if I wanted to keep eating.

When the alarm went off at eleven thirty, I woke up stiff and cranky, still wearing my clothes from the night before. I dragged myself out for a run, showered, and pulled on yesterday's jeans and a dark-brown T-shirt. No need to dress up for the geeks. I impatiently tugged a brush through my long hair and pulled it up in a clip while it was still damp. I checked the mirror. Good enough.

Molly was still in the armchair in the living room when I came downstairs. She'd probably fallen asleep as a human and died when I'd gone for my run. When I got close enough, she yawned and stretched, then looked around in confusion. When she saw me, she smiled.

"You want coffee?" I asked. Molly likes to be awake during the day, if I can manage it. Going out in the sun completely delights her. Those kinds of perks are the reason why Dashiell has ordered his vampire minions to stay away from me. His protection is part of our deal, which is yet another reason why I don't want to lose my job.

"Yep." Molly swung her legs off the arm of the chair and followed me into the kitchen, careful to keep close to me. She sat down at the little breakfast counter, watching as I brewed the coffee. "So...I heard you're in kind of a mess."

"How did you hear about that?" I asked, though I shouldn't have been surprised.

Molly just shrugged. "You know, the vampire rumor mill." She hesitated for a second. "Do you want to talk about it?"

That surprised me, too. Most of the time, Molly prefers to act as if she and I are best gal pals in one of her romantic comedies. She's always all perky and sort of surface. I wasn't expecting a *Do you want to talk about it?* conversation.

In fact, maybe it wasn't an idle question.

I pulled two mugs from the shelf above the sink and poured a dark stream of coffee into each one, stalling for time. Had Dashiell ordered her to ask me questions? I wasn't stupid; I knew Molly reported to Dashiell about me. I just figured there wasn't usually much to report, as long as I kept anything too personal from Molly. She had no idea that I had a brother, for example. If the impossible happened and I got a real boyfriend, someone I really loved, I'd keep that from her, too.

"Not really," I said carefully. "I think it's going to be okay."

"Do you know—" she began, but then we both jumped as someone knocked hard on the door. "Whoa, jeez. I can't get used to how humans sneak up on each other."

That's not really what knocking on a door means, but I didn't bother saying so. "That must be Cruz," I said, trying not to sound too relieved. "Where do you want me to drop you off?"

"Uh, my room is good." I walked her up there and then skidded down the stairs, suddenly very excited to get out of the house.

Cruz and I were both quiet on the drive to Pico. He looked tired and worn-out, and I wondered how much sleep he'd gotten in the past couple of nights. I felt a sudden, very unwelcome pang of guilt. Because of my screwup with the park murders, I had almost set this guy up to be killed. Did that make him my responsibility? Should I be checking in on his emotional welfare? I considered how my mother would have answered that question, and then Olivia. Then I decided I didn't care. Cruz had dug his own grave on this one. No pun intended.

The comic book shop, which was adorably called Nerdvana, was on a block with two dry cleaners and a day care center. Drop off your kids, read some comics! We couldn't find a meter within a block or two, and Cruz shot down my suggestion that he use his special cop powers to secure illegal parking, so we ended up having to park a few long blocks away and walk back to the store. As we came in, I noticed a little sign above the door that said, *No Cylons, replicants, or shoplifters allowed.*

It was going to be that kind of day.

I stepped inside, Cruz at my heels. The store was one big rectangle, with bookshelves of comics lining the walls and four scarred and faded tables arranged in the open floor space. A glass counter with a cash register took up the back wall. It was 1:40 on a weekday, but each table held seven or eight guys and a huge stack of cards, with more cards spread around the tabletops in careful patterns. I could see a few cards with pictures of little weapons and elves and stuff. When I walked in the room, every single guy froze, staring at me with a combination of shame and resentment, as though I'd just walked into the men's locker room and found them all jerking each other off. Great. I tried to look nonthreatening, and after a long moment, they all returned to playing, but the mood was subdued. Scarlett Bernard, professional buzzkill.

I took a few steps over to the wall, examining the comic titles, and then felt the brush against my radius that meant werewolf. I glanced up and locked gazes with Ronnie Pocoa, now fully clothed and bringing a few fresh decks of cards out from the back area behind the counter. Under the store's bright lights, I realized he was a towhead, with ruddy cheeks and pockmarks dotting his face. Ronnie had to be in his early thirties, but had that baby-faced look of the perpetually timid. Or the perpetually victimized. You see that a lot with the wolves. Cruz stepped up beside me, and Ronnie looked from his face to mine, turning white. Then, to my surprise, he dropped the cards, turned around, and bolted from the room.

Cruz and I exchanged one of those quick *What the...?* looks, and without any advance coordination, he turned and ran out the front door, while I followed Ronnie through the back, trying to keep him within my radius. I was fairly fast, but if he got his werewolf strength and speed back, I'd never see him again. He knocked down piles of boxes and games behind him, trying to trip me up, but I stumbled my way around them. Ronnie raced through a door and into a narrow storeroom where a desk and file cabinet had been haphazardly assembled. I caught him just before he got to an emergency exit door on the far side of the room, grabbing the back of his T-shirt and rearing us both backward. We collapsed in a pile on the floor, and I scooted far enough to kick the exit door open, letting Cruz inside. All three of us were panting. Cruz leaned down to rest his hands on his knees. "What the hell...was that?" I gasped.

"Don't kill me!" Ronnie screeched. "I won't tell nobody!"

Cruz and I exchanged another look. I climbed to my feet, reaching a hand down to Ronnie. He stared at me, terrified, and I made an impatient *come on* motion. "Ronnie, I don't know what you've heard, but I'm not going to kill you. This guy"—I nodded at Cruz—"is a cop. It would be seriously stupid for me to kill you in front of a cop. Do you think I'm that stupid, Ronnie?"

"No."

"Awesome. Can we sit somewhere and talk?"

"Uh...I guess."

Ronnie led us back into the main storeroom, pushing some of the overturned boxes around to create makeshift chairs. He seated himself closest to the door, which I ignored. Let him feel like he had an edge. I glanced at Cruz, indicating that he should take over. Interrogations aren't really my thing.

"Ronnie, I'm Officer Cruz, with the LAPD. I'm not going to arrest you—yet. I just want to know what you saw the other night. Or...um...smelled."

Ronnie's eyes darted nervously back and forth between us. "So...he knows? About us?"

"Yes," I assured him. "It's okay." His eyes didn't leave my face, so I added, "Will knows all about it."

He nodded then, turning back to Cruz. "Um...Well, I was running in the park," he said uncertainly. "We do that sometimes, to stretch out. We go when the park's closed, and we don't hurt nobody."

Cruz glanced at me with a question on his face.

"Their bodies have to change at the full moon," I explained. "But most of them are strong enough to change a few other times during the month if they want to. It calms them."

"Yeah. It helps." Ronnie straightened up in his seat, a little more confident. "Anyway, I smelled blood, and it was *strong*. I had to go see what it was. And then I got close, and I felt something go by me, not too far." He nodded at me. "It was you."

"Right, after you came into the clearing," I said.

"No, no." He was shaking his head. "Before I got to the clearing. I was on my way, and I felt you go by, and I smelled the nothingness."

"I smell?" I said, confused.

"No, you, like...You don't smell, and everything else does. You're a space in the smell."

Huh. No one had told me.

"So, Ronnie," Cruz broke in, "let me see if I understand this. You were on your way to the clearing, and you passed someone you thought was Scarlett, going in the other direction?"

"Yeah."

"And then you came into the clearing, and you saw her and me."

"Yeah...wait," Ronnie said, wrinkling his forehead. "I didn't think about that. I felt you going back the other way."

"That's not possible, Ronnie."

"Yeah...So I guess it couldn't have been you, right? Because I saw you right after that, and you were back in the clearing." He gave a relieved laugh, relaxing down on his seat. "Christ, when I saw you come in the store, I thought you were here to kill me, too."

"Wait, you actually thought I did *that*?" I blame sleep deprivation, but it actually took me that long to figure out what he'd meant.

"Well, yeah. We all know about you. I've been near you before at the bar. Who else would feel like that?"

Cruz and I locked eyes, and I suddenly felt very cold.

"Another null," I said softly.

Chapter 9

The day I met Olivia was the day of my mom and dad's funeral.

I hadn't trusted my ability to drive, so I'd taken the train to Esperanza, feeling as if I were the main character in a movie that had suddenly switched genres. A week earlier, I'd been in a fun coming-of-age-in-college story. Suddenly, I was in a tragedy.

Jack picked me up at the station. He was obviously trying to look strong, but his eyes matched his scraggly red hair. At a little over six feet, my brother didn't exactly tower over me, but he seemed huge and awkward as I walked up, unsure if he should go for a hug or a cheek peck or just take my overnight bag and march off. I dropped the bag and stepped into his arms. I'm all for feminism, but there's something primal and comforting about being engulfed by someone bigger than you. When I pulled away, there were wet spots on his dark-blue button-down. I must have looked embarrassed, because he gave a little *it's nothing* shrug and picked up my bag.

I can't remember anything about the funeral home or the service, or how I got to the cemetery. It was like one minute I was leaving the station with Jack, then there was a blur of tears, and then we were looking down at the coffins as they were lowered into the earth. I kept thinking they weren't just holes in the ground, they were holes in the world. Like once there was a space that was occupied by my mom and dad, and then that space had been violently punched out, leaving a raw hole with ragged edges. *The whole world must be full of scars*, I thought dizzily. I was only eighteen.

Then a pretty woman picked her way across the grass in very high heels and handed me an old-fashioned linen handkerchief. She was in her mid-forties, with long chestnut hair and elegant makeup. Her blue eyes looked sharp enough to cut through you, and she had a five-inch scar running across her collarbone, which was exposed by a gray dress that was simple, but extremely expensive-looking, and tailored to her lean, angular frame. She was neither pretty nor ugly, but sort of haunting. Someone you'd remember.

"Thank you," I said. I remembered that I was supposed to be playing some sort of role. A hostess. "Um, did you know my parents well?"

She glanced around. Jack had carried a couple of pots of flowers to the car, and the gravediggers kept their respectful distance. We were alone. "I'm afraid I didn't know them at all," she said. "But I'm sure they were lovely."

I stared at her, confused. "I'm sorry...Are you a friend of Jack's or something?"

She smiled serenely. "No, Scarlett. I'm a friend of yours. Or I'd like to be."

On another day, I might have called for help right then, but I just kept looking at her, befuddled. Was she from a church or something?

"You see," she went on, "there are very, very few of us. I think we should stick together, don't you?"

Very, very few. Five or six in the world.

Had Olivia just been full of shit? I wondered as Cruz and I walked back toward his car. It certainly wouldn't be the only thing she'd lied about. But, no, that didn't fit—Dashiell and Will had talked about the rarity of nulls, too, and I sort of suspected that if Dashiell had another null option, he wouldn't be using me. If

Olivia was right about us being rare, though, how was it possible that there was another null in the clearing?

"Scarlett?" Cruz asked, breaking into my thoughts. "What does this mean?"

I blinked. "Um...Well, for starters, it means we've been looking at the wrong victim pool."

"Why?"

"Because if a null was there, then someone wanted to kill something from the Old World. It's hard to kill both werewolves and vampires, even witches if they see you coming. But if you could turn them into humans first..."

He nodded. "If the werewolves run in that park, it could have been three of them."

I thought about all the blood at the scene, spilled intentionally all over the clearing. "No. They were vampires. Or at least one of them was a vampire."

"So can we go ask the...uh...vampire boss?"

I checked my watch. It was only three, which meant there were a good four hours until sunset. "We can, but he's dead right now."

Cruz didn't laugh. "Can't you just go near him, and he'll come back to life and talk to us?"

I stopped and turned to look at him. "Whoa. We can't just burst in there. You really think the cardinal vampire in LA doesn't have daytime security? What would our story be? 'Hi, it's Scarlett, mind if I make your boss completely vulnerable for a few minutes? Along with this guy I brought who, by the way, has a gun?' And that's before we even find out what *Dashiell* would do if I stormed in there and made him vulnerable."

He held up his hands in surrender. "Okay, okay. Well, we can start by tracking down the null, right? There are how many of you?"

"That I know of? A handful," I said. I started walking again. "But who knows how many there are total. The theory is that there are some nulls who never find out what they are." I explained the difficulty in discovering new nulls. "If the null lives in a city with a low Old World population, they might live and die without ever knowing. There's another argument that says that doesn't happen, because nulls evolved to be born near Old World populations, but that's all theoretical."

"How many do you know about?"

I counted in my head. "Six. But we're all really spread out, geographically. There's one in New York, two in Europe, one in Japan, one in Russia, and me. That's it." From the corner of my eye, I saw his eyebrows furrow and his mouth open. I held up both palms in a *stop* gesture. "No, I have no idea why. We just seem to be born spread out like that. The Old World doesn't spend a lot of time trying to solve those kinds of questions—at least not with modern scientific methods—so nobody has many answers." To her credit, Olivia had at least tried to make connections between the nulls, spending most of one summer working on an online network between us. I'd corresponded with a couple of people at one point, the ones who spoke good English, but I hadn't heard from anyone in more than eight months. Since she'd died.

"Well, can we find those nulls? Find out where they were the other night?"

"Yeah, sure," I said. "But do you really want to spend time trying to track down international alibis when there could theoretically be unknown nulls right here in the US?"

He looked unhappy. "It's a cop thing. I have to cover all the bases, even the unlikeliest ones. Can you get me a list of names and phone numbers?"

"I only have e-mail addresses. But it'd be better coming from me."

He thought that over for a moment. "Okay." He shook his head. "Man, this stuff is weird."

"Tell me about it."

We were back at Cruz's car. Cruz checked his watch. "Scarlett, look...I have to get to the airport, solidify my alibi for this afternoon. Could you maybe find your own way home?"

Molly's place was only a couple of miles north, but it was still annoying. "Fine," I grumbled.

"Great," he said, undeterred. "I'll come and get you when I'm done with my shift."

"Call first. Where are we going?"

"To cover some more bases. I want you to think about places where these Old World...um...people, hang out. Like that bar. And I want to show their pictures around, see if we can ID anybody. Then we'll go see the vampire boss after dark."

I groaned. "That's not going to go over well."

He shrugged, unrelenting. "That's how it is sometimes."

I swallowed another lecture about taking vampires seriously and being respectful—scratch that, *afraid*—of Dashiell. Maybe later.

I considered walking back to Molly's, but ended up splurging on an overpriced cab. As soon as I got there, though, I realized there wasn't anything I needed to be doing. I toyed with the idea of tackling my laundry or starting to work on the search for a new assistant, but I didn't have the energy for either. Instead, I decided to wake up Molly. If she was going to question me or spy on me or whatever, I wanted to get it over with.

As I walked into her room, Molly gasped, her eyes flying open. Sometimes it's like that. "Hey," she said, running a hand through the tangles in her red hair. Vampire hair and fingernails grow. I don't know why the magic works like that, but it does. Which is good for Molly, because she gets bored with her hair every three months or so. "You're home! Ooh, it's only three thirty, that's so awesome. Want to go shopping? I was thinking I needed a new laptop bag."

She seemed back to her usual peppy self, and I let out a breath I didn't know I had been holding. I decided I didn't really want to spend the day brooding about the possibility of another null being in town. "That sounds fine, if that's what you want to do."

"Really?" she squealed. "Let me just get dressed." I had to stay in the room in order for this to happen, so I politely turned my back. She thinks that's hilarious and told me so again.

I've seen a couple of reality TV shows where people—usually couples—are tied together and forced to stay within a few feet of each other. In real life, without the additional help of a rope (I've considered it, but even in LA, I think it'd look too weird), this is surprisingly hard to keep up. It's so easy to forget and go off to the bathroom or wander a few feet away to look at something or answer your cell phone. By now, though, Molly and I had it down to an art form. We only screwed up once, early in our relationship, when we got separated in a crowd at the farmers' market. Luckily, we were indoors, so when she collapsed, we just told everybody that she'd fainted. Close call.

We went to Westside Pavilion, and I followed Molly around Nordstrom's for a while, ignoring her pleas to pick out a new wardrobe for me. Molly thinks my T-shirt-and-jeans look is gauche and trashy, and is constantly trying to use me as her own personal Barbie doll. I once pointed out that she wears T-shirts all the time, but she airily told me that her shirts and jeans were expensive, so it was okay. I don't think there's anything okay about paying $200 for jeans, but I'm crazy like that.

This is an argument we have a lot.

Molly eventually bought a pair of turquoise flats, which cost more than a community college education, and we went to the Apple store so she could get the laptop bag. Then we settled down in the cafeteria with Jamba Juices.

Molly took a big slurp, not disguising her enjoyment. "So what's going on with you and the dog?" she asked cheerfully.

"Nice," I said. Will and Dashiell seem to get along pretty well, or at least they've developed a good working relationship, but there's not a lot of love lost between most vampires and werewolves, a conflict that the movies have actually gotten right. Both groups prefer each other to the damned witches, though, and I don't blame them. "Nothing is going on, because nothing happened."

"Really? Your mouth says no, but your eyes say yes." Her own eyes sparkled, and I relaxed a little. It was as though the serious moment from that morning had never happened. Maybe I had just been paranoid about that after all. Maybe Molly had just been trying to be a good friend or something.

"You watch too much TV."

"That may be true," Molly said, "but that doesn't mean I'm wrong. Are you into him?"

"Nah," I said. I explained about my suspicion that Eli just likes me for the calm I can give him, trying to be delicate so she wouldn't think I was accusing her of the same. I made sure to downplay my connection to Eli, though, just in case she was reporting to Dashiell. Then I told her about Eli being chosen as my new "partner," and she wrinkled her nose in sympathy.

"That sucks," she said.

"Yeah."

We were quiet for a while, and then Molly asked me about the investigation. "My friend Frederic says you've been running around with this cop, digging into Old World business. Are you sure that's a good idea?"

There it was. Looks like I hadn't been paranoid after all. Her tone had been trying for lightness, but she wasn't used to having to operate human emotions, and the intensity had leaked through.

I shrugged. "They can't really hurt me."

"Of course they can," she said sensibly. "Being up against a normal human doesn't mean you can't get hurt; it just means they'll have to use run-of-the-mill ways to kill you."

"Gee, I'd hate to have a boring death."

"I'm not kidding, Scarlett." Her face was open and solemn, and she suddenly looked much older. Wise and sad.

I sighed. "I know you're not. But at this point, I don't have much choice. If I don't help Cruz, he says he'll talk about Old World business. Which means he'll die."

"Since when do you care about one human death?" Molly asked, not unkindly.

I looked up at her, shocked. Had I really gotten that casual about dead bodies? I mean, sure, I need a certain distance to be able to do the work, but I couldn't be that bad. Molly just saw me as uncaring because she was that way herself.

Right?

"It would be my fault," I said finally. "He only knows about the Old World because he saw the werewolf at La Brea Park, and he never would have if it wasn't for me."

Her brow furrowed. "So what? It's one guy."

Was this how I came off, too? This was something to think about later. "Look, if I help the cop, he might find whatever's doing this faster. And catching this thing will help me in the long run," I said, giving up. "Fewer crime scenes to clean up later."

"Hmm, stopping the crime scene before it happens. Interesting idea," she said, nodding as though I'd finally made sense. The moment passed.

"So," she began again, with a small wicked grin, "what does this cop look like?"

Before I could answer her, my phone rang "Werewolves of London."

Will.

Molly, who had programmed the phone for me, cracked up. I glared at her and answered the phone. At least I'd talked her out of her first choice, "Who Let the Dogs Out."

"Scarlett. I have a problem." "Problem" is code for "job."

"Where?"

He gave me the cross streets for a wild area near Laurel Canyon Park.

"I'm on the way."

"Thank you. Oh, and, Scarlett? I took the liberty of calling Eli for you." There was a smile in his voice. Oh yeah. He definitely knew about Eli and me. Stupid wolves.

I hung up the phone and checked my watch again. Five thirty. It was rush hour, so I'd be pressed to get to the job at all. There was no way I'd have time to drop Molly off, too.

"Molls, you want to go on a job with me?"

"Sure!" She bounced in her chair. "I never get to come!"

"Let's go."

Chapter 10

The GPS led us to a grassy area near the Laurel Canyon dog park, which I had visited once with a high school friend, a long time ago. It's the biggest dog park in the city, with a special area for little dogs, a water fountain that doubles as a doggy splash zone, and a bunch of small, scrubby hills for rolling up and down. It's basically doggy heaven. We had hit traffic on the way, of course, and Eli was already there when I pulled up, along with a sheepish-looking young man I'd seen before at Hair of the Dog, and Caroline Brooks. It looked as if they were standing in the middle of nowhere, but even my human nose could pick up dog smells through the open van windows, and I could see a bit of chain-link fencing peeking out from the bushes. I figured we must be right behind the dog area.

I parked behind Eli's battered pickup and got out, waiting for Molly to crawl across the seat and follow me out the driver's side door so I wouldn't lose her. I suspect that she could get out of most cars on the passenger side without leaving my radius, but neither of us was willing to risk it, especially outdoors on a sunny day. As we walked up, all three werewolves' faces shifted, the way Old World faces always shift around me: Eli and Caroline instantly looked more relaxed, and the young man looked...sort of disappointed. He was average height and very skinny, with a long, bulbous nose.

I immediately thought of Ichabod Crane. He was wearing only tattered Hulk-style sweatpants and a mournful expression.

I pulled on surgical gloves as I walked—no more mistakes this time—lugging my work duffel.

"Hey, Scarlett," Caroline said sunnily. "Sorry to drag you up here."

"No worries. Tell me what's happening," I said. Molly stayed close behind me.

Eli said, "Scarlett Bernard, meet Travis Hochrest. Travis has had a little accident."

"What, you peed on the rug?" Molly said, smirking.

I shot her a look.

"Sorry!" she whispered.

"Guys, this is Molly," I said, stepping aside so they could see her. "She's...also helping me out today. Travis, why don't you show me what you need to show me?"

"Right. Um, it's this way, if you want to just follow me." He led us off into the scrub, and I spotted a faint trail. Fifty feet in, we saw five little corpses all in a row, covered in feathers and flies. Chickens.

Everyone turned to stare at Travis. I raised my eyebrows.

"Okay," he began nervously. "So, I'm a pretty small wolf, and I actually look a lot like a dog. People mistake me for a husky mix all the time, so I come to the dog park sometimes to play with the other dogs. It's fun; they all defer to me right away, and then I get to be like their king..." Caroline gave him a gentle smile that clearly said *get to the point.*

"Caroline came with me to pretend to be my owner, you know. She was at the picnic tables, and I was running around. And I smelled these guys." He nodded toward the chickens. "There are some homes around here; I guess maybe they escaped? Anyway, I couldn't resist." His eyes were pleading for forgiveness. "I jumped the fence, and well..."

"Why not just leave the bodies? Wouldn't everyone figure that it was just one of the dogs from the park?" Molly asked.

Caroline answered for Travis. "Will has drilled all of the wolves to call, even when you think something could be explained away."

"Probably, you're exactly right, Molly, but there's still a one in a thousand chance that the owner of the chickens gets mad and has the bodies examined," I said. "You never know who has money and power in this town. A werewolf in wolf form will still show up as a wolf on a DNA test, and then everyone in the neighborhood will start looking for wolves, talking about wolves...It's not worth the risk, even if it's only a teeny-tiny one."

Molly nodded in understanding.

"You did exactly the right thing," I said to Travis, who beamed in relief and happiness. You could practically see his tail wagging. "You guys can go now."

Without another word, he took off back toward the parking lot on the other side of the park.

Caroline rolled her eyes at me good-naturedly and gave me a quick hug before she followed. "Have fun," she whispered mischievously.

Goddammit. Could they, like, smell it on Eli and me?

"So what do we do now?" said Eli, looking my way.

Oh, right, I was supposed to be training. I pulled out more of my industrial-sized ziplock baggies and told him to gather what was left of the birds. Then I took the bags back to the freezer compartment in the van, pulling out a sack of dirt, Molly sticking to my heels like a shadow. "I want to try something. Let's see if we can use your nose to help," I said to Eli. He was starting to look kind of interested. I handed him another baggie, and then Molly and I backed off, far enough to keep the whole area out of my radius. "Okay," I called to Eli, "now smell for the blood, and wherever you find some on any of the plants or tree bark, pull it and put it in the bag. He followed my instructions, and I watched him very carefully.

This wasn't just about him helping; I also wanted to make sure he could do the work without me around. Werewolves are much more into meat than blood, but even the blood would smell good to him. Eli did fine, though, not even twitching his nose.

"How come it smells so bad?" Molly whispered as we watched Eli.

"That's what blood and bodies smell like to us," I told her. "It probably used to smell like that to you, too. You've just forgotten."

"Oh."

When Eli had all the foliage collected, I ripped open the bag of dirt and started sprinkling it on the part of the ground that had been covered in blood. Then I handed the bag to Eli and backed off again. He sniffed a little, sprinkling in a few spots that I had missed. Then he walked over to Molly and me, and the three of us looked at the scene. You might have thought someone had walked through there, breaking some branches, but nothing else was even a little bit visible.

"Sunset's at seven fourteen," Molly said to me. I glanced up, realizing that the light had been fading around me. "What time is it now?"

I checked my watch. "Five after seven."

"And you still have to show Eli what to do with the chickens, right?"

"Yeah, I guess." I had forgotten that I should probably take Eli along to Artie's. I had gotten used to doing this alone.

"Okay, well, why don't you give me your keys," Molly said to Eli, her eyes sparkling, "and I'll drive your car back to our place? Scar can bring you back there after you're done." She held out her hand to Eli, smiling sweetly, and he automatically reached into his pocket, looking at me uncertainly.

When I didn't say anything, he shrugged and handed her the keys.

"Great!" she chirped, pleased with herself. Vampires can be such jerks.

We spent the next eight minutes loading up my supplies, and at quarter after, Molly took a few experimental steps away from my radius. I felt her pull away from my area, and then suddenly she was vampire. Her skin glowed, and she reached up to stretch. Just to show off, she raced at full vamp speed to the door of Eli's car, faster than I could follow with my eyes. "See you at home!" she called back to us, and I couldn't help but smile. Then I looked over at Eli. Alone with the sex buddy/bartender/apprentice. Awesome.

He was staring after Molly with a look of curiosity. "Vampires really like what they are, huh?"

It occurred to me for the first time that he probably hadn't spent much time around vampires, aside from the formal meetings with Will. "Some of them do. Just like some of you guys like being wolves."

He looked over at me sharply. "None of us like being wolves, Scarlett. The pack is...like a support group for people who are all living with the same illness."

"Even the kid with the chickens?" I said, smart mouth fully mobilized.

"We try to have fun with it. You make the best of what you're given, Scarlett. You should know that by now."

Touché.

Artie Erickson runs an art studio in the Valley, teaching pottery and watercolors to bored housewives and _trés_-bohemian grad students. (I know, "Artie" teaches "art." It's hilarious, let's move on.) His building also has an enormous furnace, left over from the prior owner. The students do glassblowing there, and because it's easier to keep the furnace running than to keep lighting it over and over, Artie also charges local businesses for its use. He had a deal with Olivia, and when she died, I made sure we could still do business together. He's an okay guy, if a little snooty. Art people can be like that.

I don't know how much Artie knows about the Old World or what I do, but I'm pretty sure he doesn't really want to know. The whole studio is gated, and the furnace is around the back through a short hallway. I tell Artie I'm coming; he unlocks the back gate and leaves the back door open. Then he sends me a bill for "waste disposal," which I pass along to the appropriate Old World party. Technically, the entire thing, except for what I put in the furnace, is completely legal.

I explained the plan to Eli on our way.

"So do you even see the guy?" he asked me as we pulled into the parking lot.

"Not usually. Artie's got a pretty good system. I doubt we're the only ones who use his services for...questionable materials." I shrugged, not taking my eyes off the road. "It's a tough market for art teachers."

"Oh."

I jumped out of the van to open up the gate and then got back in to drive through. Most of Artie's classes and events take place during the day, so the parking lot was deserted, lit by a few weak streetlamps and the building's emergency lights. We drove around to the back of the building, where I backed the van up to the enormous double doors leading to the furnace area and turned off the engine. Eli helped me unload the dead birds from the cooler compartment in the back of the van, including the poor backward-headed dove I'd completely forgotten about. Way to go, Scarlett. I flicked on the light switch inside the door and led Eli down the hall toward the furnace room. It was hot just stepping in the door, and Eli flinched at the heat. I handed him my own ziplock bags of dead birds and went up to the iron furnace doors, which were big enough to wheel a piano through. I picked up a nearby industrial-strength oven mitt and pulled open one of the furnace doors, gasping at the heat, and nodded to Eli, who threw in the baggies. Then I slammed the door, and both of us speed-walked out of the room, pausing in the hallway to catch our breaths.

I pulled my sticky shirt away from my chest, flushed with heat. "That," he panted, "was a really big furnace."

Eli followed me back outside, and I clicked the little doorknob lock behind us. I was buckling my seat belt when Eli spoke up.

"Look, Scarlett, we should talk..." he began, his hands twisting in his lap.

I froze. "This isn't a great time, Eli."

"Yeah, well, it's never a great time with you, is it? But we should talk about what happened the other night—what's been happening."

I waited, silent.

Eli stared at me and then scrubbed at his face with the heel of his hands. "Look," he blurted, "do you want to, like, grab something to eat sometime? Maybe have a real conversation in which neither of us is drunk?"

My mouth may have dropped open a little. "You mean like...a date?"

"Yes. An actual date."

"I can't," I said immediately.

"You can't, or you don't want to?"

"I don't know. Pick one." There was hostility in my voice, and I wondered where it had come from. Why can I never say the right thing?

"Argh!" he grunted, looking frustrated. Scarlett Bernard, frustrator of men. His fingers flexed, and I realized he was angry. "You know, Scar, I get that you got a raw deal. What happened to you was awful. Will still feels guilty that he didn't see it coming, or warn you, or whatever. But just because she turned out to be—"

"Shut up," I said too sharply, then regretted it. "You don't know anything about that, so just drop it."

"Tell me, then. Talk to me like I'm a real person and not just a penis that delivers your whiskey."

"Why?" I asked, unable to look at him. I stared at the steering wheel instead. "What's the point? You can't change any of it."

"Maybe not. But I'd still like a shot at making you laugh."

I did look at him then, startled. His light-blue eyes were calm and direct—no bullshit. I sighed and reached down to turn on the engine. "Look, Eli, if you don't want to sleep with me anymore, fine. But—"

To be honest, I'm not sure what I was about to say. I never got a chance to find out, though, because at that exact moment, the driver's side door was wrenched open, and a large head poked into the car. "Ladies," said the enormous man, and the passenger-side door popped open, too. Eli had unbuckled, was trying to push his way out of the car, and the guy on my side reached in and punched me in the left eye.

"Son of a *bitch*," I gasped, and Eli looked like he was about to howl. Eli is not a small man, and even in human form, I couldn't believe the guy on his side was able to keep him in the seat.

"Stay, boy," said the giant on my side of the van. He held up a wicked-looking handgun, pressing it against my temple, and Eli went very still next to me.

"Get her out," ordered the man who'd appeared next to Eli, a weaselly-looking guy in a cheap dark suit.

Eli and I were dragged out of the van and marched around the back. I saw the slick-looking SUV the two men must have brought idling a few feet away. I'd been too involved in my romantic drama to even notice it arrive.

"Cuffs," said the giant, and the smaller man pulled out a glaringly shiny set of handcuffs. It took me a second to realize why they gleamed.

Oh God. "Silver," I breathed.

The giant nodded, looking very smug. "You got it, bitch."

The weaselly guy put the handcuffs on Eli. "So you can't follow," he rumbled, a surprisingly deep voice. Then he kicked Eli viciously in the stomach, and Eli doubled over, gasping. The guy kicked him in the ribs a couple of times for good measure, and I realized that I was screaming. The giant just reached down and picked me up, throwing me over his shoulder and into the back of the SUV, where he scooted in right after me.

The weaselly guy jumped into the driver's seat, and I ignored them both, turning in my seat to look at Eli, who was struggling to his feet. The SUV pulled away, and I felt the tug when he left my radius. Eli dropped like a stone in a pond, writhing on the ground in the parking lot.

"What are you doing?" I yelled at the giant next to me. I lunged across the seat and punched him, which would have been completely ineffectual if he hadn't been taken by surprise. Instead, I got a little weight behind it and hit him straight in the nose.

He cried out in pain, backhanding me across the seat. "You stupid *bitch!*" he hollered.

I was dizzy with pain for a few seconds from where the side of my head had bounced off the window, and when my vision cleared, the big guy was touching his nose, holding his fingers up to see the blood. He did this again and again, fascinated, and I realized that this was a strange experience for him. I closed my eyes and concentrated for a moment, then popped them open. *Vampires.* Which I should have realized a hell of a lot earlier. My fingers scrabbled at the lock on my door, but there must have been some sort of child safety setting on because it didn't budge.

I turned back and said, "I work for Dashiell, you assholes, and he's going to be really pissed."

To my surprise, they both chuckled, and the bloody giant leaned over and leered at me. "Bitch," he said smugly, "who do you think we work for?"

Chapter 11

I stayed quiet for a few minutes, adjusting to both the new information and the pain. If Dashiell had sent these guys to collect me, instead of just calling, he was expecting me to be hostile. To resist.

It'd be a shame to disappoint him. I kicked the back of the driver's seat in front of me. "Hey. Little guy."

The giant next to me snickered, and the weasel reached up and fiddled with the rearview mirror so he could glare at me. "What?" he rumbled.

"Why didn't Dashiell just call me?"

He turned his head to exchange a look with the giant, but neither one of them answered me.

I kicked the seat again. "Hey."

The big guy reached for me, but the driver barked, "Hugo!"

The giant froze.

So the smaller man was in charge. Interesting.

"We're not supposed to hurt her yet."

Fear clenched my heart at the word *yet*, but I pushed forward. "Sit, Hugo. Stay. Roll the fuck over."

"What's one more bruise?" Hugo whined toward the driver. "She's already going to have two."

"Knock it off," he commanded, and Hugo sulked back in his seat.

I waited about thirty seconds, and then I kicked the back of the driver's seat. "Hey. Little guy."

Hugo snarled, but the weasel adjusted the mirror again and looked at me with a flat expression. "One thing you should have learned by now," he said calmly, "Dashiell takes care of his own. Now there's gonna be a reckoning."

He adjusted the mirror back. I kept trying, but no amount of kicking or whining would get him to say anything else, and Hugo followed his cue. I gave up and leaned into my window, as far from them as I could get. A reckoning? First of all, who talks like that? Well, vampires, obviously, but was there actually a point in history where that didn't sound stupid?

Focus, Scarlett, I reminded myself. He'd said that Dashiell takes care of his people. Well, I knew that. It's half the point of having a vampire leader, along with keeping the peace. So Dashiell thought I had done something to hurt his people or disturb the Old World ...

Oh shit.

"He thinks it was *me*?" I sputtered, and yes, it seriously took me that long to put it together. Both vampires flinched but remained silent as we pulled into the long driveway leading to Dashiell's mansion. And for the first time since the giant one had said they worked for Dashiell, I was afraid.

When the car stopped, Hugo dragged me by the arm through the front door and into the room with the patio doors. He had a death grip on my upper arm, but I clenched my teeth and stumbled along, determined not to cry out.

Dashiell was sitting in his usual seat at the far end of the big table, tapping into a cell phone. He looked up when we arrived and gestured to Hugo to bring me closer. Ten or fifteen feet away, I felt the immortality drain from him.

"Sit her down," he ordered, collecting himself.

Hugo shoved me toward the chair next to Dashiell's, and I nearly tripped, catching myself on the chair back. I fought the urge to rub my arm and sat down as calmly as I could.

Dashiell picked up a file folder that had been waiting on the table and removed a thick white envelope. "Albert," he said to the weaselly guy, "please go deliver this to our friend in the department. Hugo, give us some space."

Sneering at me, Hugo retreated a few steps back toward the doors, nodding at Albert as the other vampire went by.

When they had moved, Dashiell leaned forward to place three photographs in front of me. The heads were bloodless and bloated, but I knew without being told that they were the victims from La Brea Park. "Joanna," he said, tapping the photo of the woman. Next was the young man with the punk haircut. "Demetri. And Abraham," he finished, pointing to the photo of the black man, whose face was ashen with blood loss. "Demetri and Joanna were a useless couple, lazy hangers on who required your services on at least one occasion. But Abraham," he continued, picking up the last photo, "he was integral to my financial structure. Losing him is a blow to my business."

I groped for something to say, and finally just blurted, "I didn't kill them."

"No, you're not nearly strong enough. But you certainly helped."

"I didn't," I said, working to keep my voice calm.

"Then who did? Abraham wouldn't have gone without a fight, and you're the only null within three thousand miles. Do you have an alibi for earlier that evening?"

I bit my lip. I had been with Eli, but there was no point in telling Dashiell; he would either think I was lying or assume that the wolves were somehow connected to the murders. In Los Angeles the different factions of the Old World lived in relative peace with each other, but it was an uneasy peace built on top of centuries of fighting. As small as my own place was in the grand scheme of things, I understood what would happen if war broke out in LA.

People would die.

"No. I was home, alone."

"And if I asked Molly, would she say the same thing?" Dashiell shot back.

Oops. Backfire. I didn't know how to respond, so I stayed silent.

Dashiell continued. "Tell me why I should believe you, Scarlett. Tell me why another null would come all the way to Los Angeles, without alerting any of my vampires or the wolves, just to kill three of my people in a public park? It seems far more likely that you were simply paid to be there. Another one of your 'freelance jobs.'"

I leaned forward, too. "Dashiell, with respect, that doesn't make sense, either. Why would I bite the hand that feeds me? If this Abraham—who I've never heard of, by the way—is important to your finances, and your finances pay my bills, why would I help kill him? And if I had helped kill these three, why on earth would I agree to help a police officer investigate their deaths? Why would I still be in this hemisphere?"

"To turn suspicion from yourself."

I leaned back again. All of a sudden, the fear that had been growing since the vampires cuffed Eli just...evaporated. All I felt was tired. "Look, Dashiell, you are scary. The power that you have, vampire or not, is scary to me. If I had crossed you in some way, I would have gotten the hell out of town."

He looked at me for a long minute, considering. The minute turned into two and then three, and I had to work hard not to squirm under his stare. "Hugo," he said finally, without taking his eyes off me, "leave us."

"Boss, you can't be serious—" Hugo started from the back of the room, but Dashiell silenced him with a glance.

The mountainous vampire spun and retreated from the room, and Dashiell turned back to me.

"Ultimately," he said slowly, "I do not care whether or not it was you. I just need a responsible party. Do you understand?"

Dashiell takes care of his own. I knew what that meant now. Dashiell didn't need the right culprit, he just needed to be able to publicly punish—kill—someone to keep the other vampires happy. And I was the obvious choice. I nodded.

"Good. So let's say for a moment that I am willing to consider the possibility that you weren't involved. I will give you until Friday at dawn to bring me the other null, if there really is one, and the person who did the killing. If you don't know by then, I will assume it was you. If you run, if you so much as leave LA County, I will assume it was you."

"You can't possibly expect—" I protested, but he cut me off.

"Of course I can. Dawn is at six thirty-six. I'll expect you here by six, with whoever is responsible."

I thought about that for a moment and chose my words carefully. "If I can't find this person...You're asking me to show up for my own death. Why would I do that?"

"Because you and I both know that you still have people you can lose. Both here and in Esperanza. You don't want anyone else to have to die for you, isn't that right?"

I felt my face turn white. He knew about my brother. How was that possible? I'd been so careful...But it wasn't the moment to figure that out. He had me, and we both knew it. I would be there at dawn, one way or the other.

He saw understanding on my face and made a dismissive motion with his hand. "Go, then. Bring me the killers, or just come yourself. It doesn't matter much to me either way."

My back was straight as I walked out of Dashiell's, but it was an effort. I went to the end of the long driveway, pulled my cell phone out of my jeans pocket, and called for a cab. I was desperate to get back to Van Nuys and get that silver away from Eli, but I'd still turned down Dashiell's offer to have Hugo drive me home. I didn't want to be anywhere near the giant vampire, especially after I'd hit him. I also owed Cruz a call, but my hands started shaking, and I finally just shoved the phone back in my pocket. Tears were blurring my vision. I crouched down to the ground and threw up everything in my stomach. I heaved and heaved until I was empty of everything. Good thing my hair was up.

I scooted a few feet away from the vomit puddle and settled down on the curb to wait for the cab. My insides still churned. Just...goddammit. For a minute there, I'd really thought that Dashiell was going to kill me. And he probably knew about Jack, and maybe Eli, and who knows what else.

Besides, it wasn't just the confrontation with Dashiell. I had always been comfortable in LA, because from a supernatural standpoint, it was so small—I didn't have to work too hard or think too much. Now, in the space of two days, I'd been unable to make it to a job, I'd seen the city's worst crime scene in generations, and my life had been given a short countdown by a very scary guy.

This was not working with my lifestyle at all.

My cell phone rang while I was still calming down. I held it up to see the caller ID—Jack again. I frowned. What the hell? For a brief, dreadful moment I pictured him lying in a hospital bed, dying or in need of a kidney. Jack and I don't talk, but he's the only real family I have left, and the image of something happening to him...I couldn't deal with it just then. I hit *Ignore*. If Jack needed something, he could leave a message. And if I lived through the next thirty hours, I could call him back.

When the cab pulled up, I scrubbed at my mouth with my shirtsleeve one more time and stood up to meet it. The driver was a little Armenian man with surprisingly perfect English. I gave him the address of Artie's studio and leaned back, hoping he wouldn't be too chatty. I hate chatty cabdrivers. He was fairly quiet, though, and I began to organize my plan of attack. First, rescue Eli. Then back to the house to drop him off and call Cruz. I had the vampires' identities now. We could figure out who their human servants were and interview them or whatever. Maybe that could get us somewhere with the investigation. I frowned to myself. Something else was tugging at me, something about the smaller of Dashiell's henchmen. Albert. I'd seen him somewhere before, but where? And did it have any relevancy to the murders? Maybe it was the adrenaline or the stress, but I couldn't place him.

When we were a mile from the studio, I pulled my wallet out of my front pocket. Eyeing the meter through the cab's bulletproof glass, I counted up the cash I had left. I would have just enough to make the fare, although my tip would not be stellar. When the driver stopped in front of Artie's gate, I threw the cash through the slot and ran full-out around the building.

Eli was right where I'd left him, collapsed on the pavement behind my van, only now he wasn't moving. I had a flare of panic. How fast does silver poisoning work? Skin contact isn't as bad as contact with his blood, so it couldn't possibly have killed him this quickly, could it? I pounded across the blacktop, calling Eli's name. I felt it when he hit my radius, and he felt...wrong. Twisted and sick.

I dropped down by his side, looking him over. All the blood had drained from his tanned face, and there were raw, oozing wounds where the silver touched his skin. He had ripped away strips of his shirt, probably trying to get it between his skin and the silver, but had lost consciousness before it could help him. I pulled helplessly at the handcuffs, hearing an anguished sound coming out of my throat. By taking away the werewolf magic, I could make the damage stop, but I couldn't heal anything.

"Eli?" I gently shook his shoulder, but got no response. I scooted a little closer, touching his cheek, and his eyelids fluttered. His hands, still cuffed, moved up to encase mine, and I almost cried with relief.

"Hey," he said wonderingly. "You came back." Slowly, leaning on the van for support, he sat up.

"Of course I came back. Why wouldn't I come back?" I cried, a little too loudly. I cleared my throat.

"I was afraid they'd killed you." He laughed suddenly, with an edge of hysteria, and for a second, I thought the silver had gotten into his brain. "Sorry," he said, seeing my face, "it just...It hurt so much, and then it was gone so fast, like turning off a switch. Thank you."

With no warning, he took my face in his hands and pulled me toward him. Without thinking, I let him kiss me, and then suddenly, I wasn't just letting him, I was participating. And then more than participating. His lips were so warm—it's true that werewolves run hotter than most people—and his long fingers tangled in my hair where it had fallen out of the elastic band. For just a moment, I let go, and the day's frustration and terror dimmed to a background hum. There was only the kiss. We broke just long enough for him to put his handcuffed arms over my head and around me, and then he pulled me into his lap, settling me against his solid chest. My fingers went into his hair, and the kiss went on as we tumbled backward onto the pavement. If it hurt his back, he didn't seem to notice.

This is how it always is between Eli and me—natural and explosive at the same time. When I finally pulled away, we were both breathing hard, and I struggled to put words together in some sort of coherent string. I blurted out the first thing that came to mind, which is more or less how I roll anyway.

"Hey," I panted, "do I smell?"

He gave me a surprised, bewildered grin. "You're a space in the smell. Everything smells but you."

"So I've heard," I said. I ducked under his arms and untangled myself, feeling suddenly awkward. I stood up. "Um, I think I might have something for those handcuffs." I didn't look at him as I opened the back door of the van, climbing in and rummaging around until I found my enormous bolt cutters. When I emerged, he was leaning against the bumper, grinning at me. He still looked pale and worn-out, but miles better than a few minutes ago.

"Why, Scarlett, you're red," he teased.

"Just shut up," I said roughly. "Hold out your arms."

His mouth tightened, but he held out his wrists, and I carefully put the bolt cutters around the chain, leaning into it to snap the heavy silver. Eli pulled his arms apart, flexing his wrists, rubbing at the welts. "Scarlett," he said, and he was looking closely at me. He gently took my chin and turned my face toward the parking lot's lone streetlight. "Who was it?"

I winced, and for the first time since it'd happened, I could feel the bruise where Hugo the vampire had backhanded me in the car. I reached up and touched the opposite eye, which was swollen but still functional. Hugo had pulled that first punch, no doubt. "The big guy. It's fine."

His face hardened, and he was very careful as he let go of my face. I saw his fists clench in their handcuffs. "It's not fine."

"Yeah, well, I may have a bruise, but I broke the asshole's nose. Probably the first time in a hundred years that he's felt pain, and I got to be there. It's good enough for me."

"What did they want with you? How did you get free?"

I told him about Dashiell's suspicion that I was involved in the La Brea Park murders.

"Didn't you tell him you were with me?"

I hesitated. "No."

"God, Scarlett, of all the times to be ashamed of me—"

"It's not like that! Eli, if I use you as my alibi, Dashiell is going to think you're lying for me because we're a couple, and he'll hurt you to get to me. Or he's going to assume you and I killed those vampires together. You're Will's beta, so Dashiell will have to assume we were acting on Will's orders, and there could be a war. Either way, dragging the wolves into this puts more people at risk."

He studied my face for a full minute, until I was starting to itch with the attention. "Maybe not. Maybe he'd just believe us and leave you alone."

"Yes, and then we'll all go adopt newborn puppies and play together in a field of marshmallows and glitter."

He couldn't help but grin at the imagery, tilting his head to acknowledge my point. Then he looked down at the handcuff bracelets on his wrists, jingling them a little. "So I guess I'm kind of attached to you at the moment. Can you pick a lock?"

I shook my head. "Tried to learn once, but I didn't have the feel for it. But...I know someone who has a handcuff key."

He nodded ruefully. "Hey, am I having a great first day or what?"

"Or what," I said seriously.

Chapter 12

The trip to the airport had taken most of the day. First Jesse's identity had to be verified by three different groups; then he had to go around meeting with the individual security teams at all seven of LAX's terminals. And at each new terminal, his identity had to be verified all over again, which must have been a serious pain in the ass for the dispatcher who had to keep taking the calls. As he had expected, no one had seen or knew anything about the three victims. It was all a colossal waste of time, and frustration had itched at the edges of his attention, shortening his patience for each security check.

Jesse hit traffic on the way back to the precinct, of course, and he didn't arrive until after six. He stopped briefly at his desk to type up a report for Miranda. *Yes, I went. No, I didn't find anything. What a fascinating read,* he thought sourly. He sent her the e-mail and packed up to go. This probably wouldn't go a long ways toward convincing her that he was any good as an investigator, but it couldn't be helped. Before he left, he called Scarlett's cell from his desk phone, but she didn't answer. A little annoyed, he left a message for her to call him back. She was probably napping. He considered just going over there, but he was exhausted himself. If Scarlett got to nap, he should get some sleep, too. Jesse's apartment was a hole-in-the-wall studio whose chief attraction was its proximity to the precinct. He slept, ate, and watched television there, but never considered it much of a home. Still, the bed was comfortable, and bed was all he could think about just then.

Jesse got his car and headed east on the freeway, thinking about the case with what was left of his fried brain. Scarlett had said that they'd been looking at the wrong victim pool, that it was probably someone from the Old World…But if he was with Scarlett, that person would just go back to being a regular human suspect, right? It was confusing. He suddenly wished he could be going for a run, or taking his parents' dog to the park, or something. Anything that didn't involve vampires or werewolves or the glare of flashlights on puddles of blood. Was it really only a day and a half since he'd run into that clearing?

At his apartment, Jesse dropped his gun and badge on the table and kicked off his shoes, collapsing on top of the covers. He put his cell phone on the empty pillow next to his. Despite his eagerness to solve the case, he sort of hoped that Scarlett wouldn't call him back until he'd gotten a decent amount of sleep.

But only an hour later, he woke up to the screech of the phone beside his head. "Cruz," he answered, rubbing his eyes. Then he opened them and sat up, fully awake. "You want me to bring what now?"

By 9:30 p.m., traffic had lightened up on the freeway, and Jesse made it from his apartment to Scarlett's West Hollywood home in excellent time. He parked in the big garage where they'd first met—well, for the second time—and hiked up the ramp and down the block. Consulting the house number written on his hand, he rang the bell of a compact, homey Victorian. The door was opened by a twentyish redhead wearing elaborately stitched jeans, a T-shirt that said *Team Edward*, and black toenail polish on her bare feet. "Hi! I'm Molly," she chirped, smiling up at him. "Are you Cruz?"

"Um, yeah…Is Scarlett home?"

"I'm here," Scarlett walked into the entryway, holding a bag of frozen peas to her face with one hand. There was a microwave burrito in the other hand, and she was moving the peas to take a bite of the burrito, then replacing them. When she moved the bag again, he saw the ugly bruise on her cheek, and the opposite eye was darkening under the bag. She leaned against the doorway.

"What the hell happened to you?" He immediately regretted the harshness in his voice, but she just shrugged.

"Got in a fight."

"Are you okay?"

"You should see the other guy."

He suddenly felt *very* awake, for the first time since he'd left his mother's house. "Sounds great. Where can I find him?" he asked, an edge sharpening the words.

But Scarlett didn't answer.

He opened his mouth to press the point, but closed it again. They'd be spending the next few hours together; he could work on her when they weren't with the friend. He turned to the red-haired girl and tried for a pleasant smile. "So you're Scarlett's roommate?"

"Yup. And friend and landlady. Pseudo-employer, too, I guess," Molly said. She turned to Scarlett. "Listen, Scar, I need to head out. I'll talk to you soon."

Molly stepped into sandals, picked up a laptop bag, and was out the door before Jesse could get out a "Nice to meet you."

He turned and looked at Scarlett, raising his eyebrows. "Was it something I don't think I had time to say?"

Scarlett sighed. "It's not you. She's afraid she's going to be ordered to kill me, so she's trying to keep some distance."

Jesse's jaw dropped. "*What?*"

"Get comfortable, Cruz. There are some things I need to fill you in on. But first, there's someone who needs your help. Eli," she called, and a stranger came in from the other room.

He was tall and good-looking, leaning against the doorway and shoving his hands in his pockets. Jesse felt a bewildering sense of jealousy. Why should he care if Scarlett had a boyfriend?

"Cruz, this is my...um...This is Eli. Eli has a little problem." The other man didn't move, and Scarlett prompted, "Go ahead, show him."

Looking reluctant, Eli pulled his hands out of his pockets and held up his wrists. Jesse saw the glint of cuffs, but there was something weird about them.

"Whoa," he said, stepping over to examine them. "Where'd you get these? Tiffany's?" They were just way too shiny. His department-issued handcuffs were stainless steel, but these looked like...White gold? Silver?

"They're silver," Scarlett said briefly, and Jesse looked up, startled. As if she had read his mind. Scarlett glanced at Eli, who gave a very small nod. "Eli is a werewolf," she continued. "Someone put the cuffs on him to incapacitate him. I cut the chain, but I don't have a key to actually remove them. And until we do, he's gotta stay within a few feet of me."

"Um, okay," Jesse said, pulling a little ring of keys out of his pocket. "I stopped at the precinct and signed these out. One of the vice detectives found this ring of handcuff keys years ago in an S and M shop, and the whole department adds to it whenever we find a weird one."

They shifted around awkwardly for a few minutes, but after a little discussion, Eli found a position where he could rest one wrist on the arm of the couch, and Jesse pulled up a straight-backed chair so he could began fitting keys in the lock. It was still kind of uncomfortable, being this close to a guy—another werewolf, he remind himself—he didn't know. It made Jesse talk too fast.

"So the silver thing is true? Poison to werewolves and vampires?"

The blond guy glanced at Scarlett, who gave an *it's up to you* shrug.

"Magic does weird things to silver, or maybe vice versa," he said. His voice was low and gravelly. "I don't know why. Some magics are enhanced by it, some the opposite. For werewolves, it's pretty much our kryptonite, yeah."

"Not for the vampires, though," Scarlett added. "Silver just makes them itch a little, so don't go thinking silver bullets will do the trick there."

Huh. "I meant to ask you about that. Exactly what would do the trick?"

"Oh. Um...sunlight. And fire, of course. Those are classics. Other than that, you have to detach the head or destroy the heart."

"Wooden stakes?"

She held out a flat hand and wiggled it back and forth in a so-so gesture. "Mostly just a superstitious tradition. It technically works, but you have to really squash the shit out of the heart to destroy it. It's a lot harder than it sounds."

Eli glanced at her.

"So I've heard," she added.

Eli said, "I heard once that the vampires spread a lot of rumors themselves, about what would kill them. That way when humans tried to test them, they would always pass."

"I suppose that makes sense." Jesse thought it over for a minute. What else had he heard about? "Crosses and holy water? Garlic?"

"Garlic's also a little itchy," Scarlett said. "No religious stuff, that's a myth. There are also—"

Eli cleared his throat, cutting her off, and Jesse saw the two of them exchange a complicated look.

"Here," Jesse twisted a key in the lock, and the cuff popped open. He unlocked the other and handed both rings to Eli. "Souvenir," he offered.

"Thank you," Eli said, looking very relieved. He quickly dropped both rings on the coffee table, as if they'd burned him.

Which, Jesse realized, seeing the welts on Eli's wrists, they had.

"You're welcome." Jesse turned to Scarlett, who had been sitting on the couch eating her burrito during the exchange. "Now, what the hell's going on?"

The werewolf excused himself to get to a bartending job, and Jesse spent the next half an hour listening as Scarlett explained the call to the dog park, her kidnapping, and the "meeting" with Dashiell.

When she was finished, Jesse was almost in a daze. "That…is a lot to take in."

"Yes."

"The vampire boss, Dashiell—he thinks you're behind it?"

"Yes."

Her eye was already purpling, despite the frozen veggies, and the bruise on her jaw was one of the darkest he'd seen. And that was only from a few hours ago. Jesse felt his teeth grit together. They'd slapped her around for something she hadn't done.

"Dashiell's guys were the ones who did this to you?"

"Yes. To be fair, though, they don't think about this kind of thing"—she gestured to her face—"as all that big of a deal. And I doubt that Dashiell actually ordered Hugo to hit me. I definitely got the feeling that Hugo just really enjoys hitting people. Probably a bad childhood."

Jesse stared at her. He'd been on plenty of domestic abuse calls as a rookie, and most of the abused women tended to be either hopping mad or falling all over themselves making excuses for their piece-of-shit spouse. Scarlett, on the other hand, seemed so…casual. "Why aren't you more upset about this?" he asked.

"About getting hit? Because in the Old World, the favored reaction to getting hit is to hit back. I did that, and now I'm over it. Bigger fish."

She hesitated, and Jesse raised his eyebrows. "What?"

"Actually, there's one other thing you should probably know about. If we can't figure this out by the end of tomorrow night, Dashiell's going to...um...kill me. And you, too, I assume."

"*What?*"

Chapter 13

After my parents' funeral, it took about a week for me to figure out that I had nowhere to go. I hung around Esperanza for a day or two, but the town was too small. Every time I stepped out of the house, I ran into someone wanting to hug me or hold my hands or tell me what wonderful people my parents were. I had been raised to be polite and accommodating, which made me defenseless to what I began to see as attacks of kindness. And every time I was inside the house, I was assaulted by memories, by the holes in the world. To make things even worse, Jack, my goofy, gentle, book-smart big brother, had become a stranger who couldn't look me in the eyes or say anything that wasn't businessy—what to have for dinner, what of Mom and Dad's stuff I wanted, what to do with the house. Eventually, it all built up into a full-blown panic attack, and I threw my clothes into a garbage bag and took off for LA. I still haven't been back to my hometown.

When I returned to the dorms, though, I realized I didn't belong there, either. I didn't go to class, which no one cared about, but my new roommate couldn't look at me, and everything about college seemed so pointless and alien. Frat parties? Free concerts in the quad? A rally to protest some unjust new amendment? I couldn't understand how anyone could expect me to be even a tiny bit interested in college when my mom and dad were rotting in boxes in the ground.

That Sunday night, I got a phone call from Olivia, the woman who'd approached me in the cemetery. With nothing better to do, I agreed to meet her at the Starbucks near campus, and she continued trying to explain what I was, what we were. I still thought she was probably crazy, but I was at least a little more able to listen now.

What I didn't realize until after Olivia died years later was that I had never given her my phone number.

"I'm sorry," I finally had said that day, after she'd gone over it all again, "but you expect me to believe that some wacky branch of evolution created vampires and werewolves, and nulls are people who can neutralize all their powers and basically undo evolution?"

"Not exactly how I would put it, but yes." She took a ladylike sip of her tea. Olivia, I had already realized, was very ladylike. I tried to sit up straighter.

"If even some of what you're saying is true, what makes you think I can do that? That I'm one of them?"

"Scarlett, honey…One of the professors at Santa Monica is a werewolf. Last Monday at exactly eight fifty-four a.m., you learned that your parents died, correct?"

Stunned, I nodded. I remembered the time.

"When you lose control of your emotions, your power intensifies. Your radius, the area in which your power works, widens. Dr. Madchen was almost a mile away, but she felt you, felt herself change back to a human, briefly. She called me to see if I was in the area, and eventually, we…traced the signal, I suppose you could say, back to you." When I said nothing, she went on. "Haven't you ever been in a public place and had a strange feeling brush over you, as though something had pressed against you without touching you?"

I was suddenly frightened, not because I thought she was a crazy person or because I thought she'd been stalking me, but because I realized I was starting to believe her. What she was describing had never happened to me in Esperanza, but whenever I was in LA, I felt it fairly often. And if what she was saying was true, then the world had just become very, very frightening.

"Why did you call me tonight? What is it you want from me?"

She smiled. "Oh, Scarlett, I don't want anything from you. In fact, I'd like to offer you a job. And a place to live, if you need it. The hours are fabulous—you get full-time wages for what amounts to about ten hours per week, give or take. It can be messy, which is unfortunate, but you'll learn quickly, and being what you are, you'll be perfectly safe. I promise. And I'll be with you every step of the way."

It took a little while to calm Cruz down. He was all for having Dashiell arrested or me shipped out of town, and we went back and forth for a while on why both of those plans would end with people getting hurt or killed. Eventually, I managed to convince him that the best thing we could do was just keep working on the case. I tried not to think too hard about what would happen if we hadn't found the killer by Dashiell's deadline. No pun intended. Would I try to run? To fight?

I had very little money, and nowhere to go. How would I possibly stand a chance? Besides, Dashiell knew about Jack. I wasn't going to let anyone else die just for knowing me. Not ever.

Denial, Scarlett, I thought. *Denial is your friend. Focus on the case.* Before I'd left, Dashiell had given me the names of the dead vampires' human servants: Victoria Grottum, Thomas Freedner, and Jason Myles. When I asked him for more information, he'd just waved a hand dismissively. Why would you need the home addresses of your employees' food supply?

Cruz got on my computer and logged in to the LAPD database to check out the names. The news was not good: Grottum and Myles didn't have California driver's licenses, so neither of them had a home address listed with the DMV. That was weird in itself, since LA is a driving city, but maybe they had moved in from other states or something. Neither of them paid taxes or had registered cell phones. They were, for all intents and purposes, off the grid. I guess when a vampire pays all your bills and fills all your needs, so to speak, you don't worry too much about legalities.

Thomas Freedner, the third human servant, *did* have an LA license and an address listed, but when Cruz followed up with the building's landlord, it turned out Freedner had moved two years earlier. No forwarding address, no phone number listed.

So we weren't going to get an easy assist from the LAPD computers. That made things more complicated, but I did actually have a plan. In my job, you learn a lot about where everyone spends their downtime. Werewolves, by and large, hang out at Hair of the Dog when they want to socialize with other wolves. The witches have get-togethers in their homes, like really twisted Tupperware parties. The vampires have their own places to gather, places that are dark and underground and, at best, ethically questionable. But there's another Old World group in LA—the human servants. And they go clubbing.

"So these people are like voluntary food?" Cruz asked me as we drove east on the 10 Freeway toward downtown.

"Yes and no. Human servants belong to a specific vampire. Like going steady, I guess. They're under the vampire's protection, and if another vampire feeds off them, that vamp gets in trouble. But there are plenty of people who offer themselves to the vampires who aren't human servants," I told him. "There's a lot of voluntary food."

"Why would anyone do that?"

I sighed. "Some of them are thrill-seekers; they're in it for the adrenaline rush of playing with fire. Some are the vamparazzi, the groupies who worship vampires and want to become one. They make me sad." I realized that I was speeding and immediately slowed down. What was wrong with me tonight? Oh, right, I'd been kidnapped and slapped around by vampires and might die in like a day. "But the worst ones are the terminally ill. They're hoping to be turned so that they can live forever."

"And how do you get turned again? You drink their blood?"

"Yep. Vampire blood is dead blood; it's infected with the same magic that animates the vampires. In theory, if you drink so much as a drop, you get sick for a couple of days, it kills you, and then you turn. Or the vampire might kill you, and then you turn faster." I could feel Cruz shudder in the seat next to me. "But they don't turn very many people anymore," I added helpfully.

"Why not?"

I sighed. "That's this whole big other thing."

"Can't you just give me the short version?"

I glared over at him, but he just showed me an innocent expression. Ugh. "There's something...wrong with magic," I finally explained. "There are two parts to the transformation—the human crosses the line from living to dead, and the magic bonds with their blood to revive them. But the magic chooses, for lack of a better word, which blood to bond with, and lately, it hasn't been choosing very many people." There have always been failed attempts to create a vampire, but in last century or so, it has become much more likely to fail than to succeed. "Every time it doesn't work, the failure means a human corpse that needs to be dealt with."

"Wait, so magic is...dying?"

I shrugged. That was a question for people a hell of a lot smarter than me. "All I know is, it's gotten a lot harder to make a baby vampire. I think they've mostly stopped trying."

He thought about all that for a few minutes while I drove in silence.

"Scarlett, how did you find out about all this stuff?" Cruz finally asked. "I mean, you neutralize everything, so it's not like you could've experienced any of this firsthand."

"I had a teacher."

"Where is she now?"

"She died," I said shortly. "Cancer."

"I'm sorry."

"Forget about it." I took the exit for downtown, maneuvering the van onto busy Figueroa Street.

"So," Cruz said, ready to change the subject, "how will we know who these people are? I mean, you got their names, but how will we find them?"

For the first time since we'd gotten in the van, I grinned. "We'll just ask," I said cheerfully. "Nobody wants to mess with the bogeyman." Even if she is just a janitor.

The LA night was cool and brisk, clear enough to see miles and miles of city lights. I rolled the windows down when we got off the freeway, and Cruz smiled and closed his eyes. For a second, I thought he was going to hang his head out the window and pant, and I had to smile.

Our first stop was a rooftop club on one of the big downtown skyscrapers.

"Wow," Cruz said, whistling as we got off the elevator. "I was expecting...I don't know, neon strobe lights and techno music. This is actually...nice."

It really was. Aside from the city lights, the only light source on the roof came from paper lanterns that cast a warm glow onto the faces of the partygoers. A DJ played low orchestral music, and some people were dancing. Others sat at tables with white tablecloths, chatting and comparing scars. I noted with some satisfaction that we blended in okay. I was wearing an entire outfit that Molly had lent me—black leather pants and an emerald-green tank top under a soft-gray blazer. I had been afraid to ask her how much any of it cost, so I just promised to return it safely. Cruz, as it turned out, owned a little collection of designer clothes. He was in an Armani suit, no tie, with a dark-sapphire shirt underneath. "Sometimes my parents take me to Hollywood parties," he'd explained sheepishly. I wanted to roll my eyes, but I had to admit, he looked amazing. Well, he'd looked amazing before; now he looked downright criminal. Pun intended.

"This building is owned by one of the vampires. He lets the human servants party here every weekend, and when he feels like it, he and his friends come up, and he's treated like a king—a king at a really big buffet," I said, speaking quietly as we threaded through the crowd. I didn't see any sign of our host. Gregory was nearly three hundred, old enough to have a number of lackey vampires working for him. I'd done business with him a few times, cleaning up their messes. All I really know about Gregory himself is that he works on the international stock exchange, he doesn't keep his own human servant, and he throws these parties. And that he's kind of an ass, but that's often par for the course with vampires. Sometimes I think if you live long enough, anyone will become an asshole.

There was an actual buffet, stocked with vitamin-rich foods. At the end of the table, there were rows of little cups, and Cruz peeked inside. Each one held a condom and an iron tablet.

"Charming," he said, wrinkling his nose in disgust. "So what's our plan?"

"You keep your mouth shut, at least until you get the lay of the land. Don't tell anybody you're with the police. We'll ask around quietly until they start to recognize me. Then we go try somewhere else."

I realized I'd just bossed around a cop about how to, essentially, be a cop. I was glad that it was dark enough to hide my blush. But Cruz only looked amused, not insulted, which was kind of nice. I seem to spend a lot of time around people who take politics and insults *very seriously*. Cruz was kind of refreshing.

We made our way to a table that held only one person, a very young woman in a tight black dress. She was a little overweight, but expensively made up, and someone with enviable skills had pulled her dark-blonde hair into an elaborate fishtail braid. She looked around tentatively and played with an empty water bottle, which showed off the ugly chain of bite marks clustered on each of her wrists. A lot of vampires don't bite at the neck anymore. It's too clichéd, even for them.

I plopped down in the seat next to her, and Cruz sat down on her other side. Her eyes widened with what I thought might be recognition.

"Hi," I said with a smile. "Do you know who I am?"

She was nodding her head before I had finished. Her eyes were huge now.

"What's your name?"

"Stacia Carlson."

"Well, Stacia, do you know any of these people?" I passed her the list of the dead vampires' respective human servants. She started to shake her head no, but then stopped and stabbed at the second name on the list with a long purple nail that matched her dress. "Um, I met this guy at a party once. He has a tattoo here." She gestured to the right side of her neck. "It's weird. It's like one of those dinosaurs from that movie. A T-rex."

Okay, that was a new one.

"Seriously?"

She nodded.

"Okay. Is there anything else you remember about him?"

She shook her head.

"Anything about the other two?"

No again.

I looked at Cruz.

"How old are you, Stacia?" he said gently.

"Nineteen."

Jesse gave me a look, but I just shrugged. There's no law against being vampire food, and I wasn't a save-the-poor-victim kind of gal.

"Stacia, this is my card," he said to her, blatantly ignoring my instruction to not tell anyone he was a cop. "If you ever need any help, you just give me a call, okay?"

She nodded, her eyes fixed on him.

We repeated the process, sans the business card, at three more tables. Cruz and I were falling into a nice interview style, courtesy of his police training and Molly's obsession with *Law & Order*. We learned that Victoria Grottum was African American and that she and Jason Myles had an on-again, off-again relationship. The two of them belonged to the dead vampire couple, Demetri and Joanna. I tried not to think about what double-dating would look like for that crew. The dinosaur guy, Freedner, belonged to Abraham.

"I don't get it," Cruz whispered after the fourth person had stammered and stared as we walked away. We were sitting at an empty table that had quickly been surrounded by more empty tables. "Why are they afraid of you? I mean, vampires I get, but these are humans."

I shrugged. "Olivia thought the vampires tell ghost stories about us. I think maybe it's a fear of the unknown. All I know is, the less powerful vampires and the human servants are scared of me."

"You know, you could be helping these people," Cruz said, a little peevishly.

"Huh?" I said, stopping to look at him.

"None of them seem all that aware of what they're playing with. They're like junkies. Or prostitutes."

Now I felt like Molly. "So?"

"So, hookers are afraid of their pimps, but they still talk to us sometimes because pimps are afraid of the cops. You respect what your boss fears. And if the vampires are afraid of you...All I'm saying is, you could be trying to talk people out of doing this."

I was flabbergasted.

Before I could work up a good response, though, a cultured tenor voice rang out over the music. "Scarlett Bernard!"

I stood up to see the crowd part and the DJ turn down the speakers, as if choreographed. A vampire stepped out of the throng of people, having taken another entrance to the rooftop.

Jeez, did he climb the friggin' fire escape?

"Hello, Gregory," I said evenly.

He made his way toward us, his large, regal nose seeming to lead his entire body through the crowd. That nose always makes Gregory look like a snob, which works out really well with his personality. As did the honest-to-goodness smoking jacket he was wearing over dark slacks and one of those blousy pirate-type shirts.

Cruz had stood up, too. I felt the vampire enter my space and saw his white face come back to life. Gregory is the kind of vampire who makes a fuss about proving he isn't afraid of me, which probably means that he is. He didn't stop strutting toward me, but there were a few gasps around us as he lost his glow and some of his grace. None of his manners, though.

"Darling," he said, kissing my cheek, "you should have let me know you were coming. I would have warned the sheep." He waved a hand toward the human servants milling about the rooftop.

They were whispering among themselves, looking at me jealously. *Talking to the master! Oooh!*

Gregory looked closely at me, examining my bruises. "My dear, what happened to you?"

"I hit one of Dashiell's guys with my face," I said lightly.

Gregory's voice had been calm, but now he looked annoyed to see me. Like being on a hot streak at the roulette table and then having the cooler walk up and bum you out.

"Excuse me, this is my friend, Officer Jesse Cruz. Jesse, this is Gregory. He owns this building."

Cruz stepped forward and offered his hand, which Gregory stared at, probably trying to remember what to do. Vampires don't really go in for friendly touching. He reached out and allowed Cruz to shake, looking as if he'd just seen a talking dog.

"Please, come and sit down for a moment," Gregory said, in a voice that left no room for any other options. Without waiting for a response, he turned and took off toward a far table, away from the crowd. I allowed him to lead us along, shooting Cruz a look first that said, *Tread lightly*. He nodded back at me: *I'll follow your lead*.

"Gregory," I said once we were seated, "Officer Cruz is investigating those murders in La Brea Park."

"Oh?" Gregory delicately raised his eyebrows. "And does Dashiell know about the policeman's activities, or is that what happened to your eye?"

"He knows. I was hoping maybe we could ask you a couple of questions."

"All right, then," he replied, leaning back in his chair and gesturing at me to begin. "Fire away."

"Did you know that the three victims were vampires?"

Despite his current humanity, Gregory gave me a look that had sex and evil and amusement all tied up in it. "I had heard that, Miss Scarlett. Bad news travels fast in our circles, as you well know by now. I had assumed that perhaps you were connected to the murders." He looked pleasantly from me to Cruz. "You didn't come here to kill me, too, did you?"

"No. And I wasn't involved in the La Brea Park thing, either."

"If you say so."

I didn't like that everyone seemed to think I was capable of what had happened in that clearing, but I would worry about that later. I glanced at Cruz, who picked up his cue.

"Did you know the victims?" he asked.

Gregory frowned. "Abraham I knew, of course. Most of the vampires in LA know of Abraham. I'd seen the other two around occasionally, but I don't think we'd ever spoken." He looked disdainful. "Those two were very reckless. Joanna, especially. She liked to drink from children."

Cruz's eyes bugged out, and I saw him struggling not to comment on that. Almost all vampires refrain from feeding off kids. There's no sport or sex to it, unless you're extremely sick in the head, and *those* vampires don't last long in a shadowy society that depends on discretion. But it does happen.

"Can you think of anyone who might want to harm any of them?" I jumped in before Cruz's head exploded.

"I have no idea why someone would want to kill the couple, other than just general annoyance. They fancied themselves a modern-day Sid and Nancy, so perhaps they just irritated the wrong people. I heard that the scene of the crime was quite grisly"—I thought I saw Gregory lick his lips a little—"so perhaps it was witches. Some of their spells require quite the sacrifice."

Hmm. I hadn't even thought of that. I'd never heard of witch magic involving that kind of darkness, but maybe it was worth asking Kirsten.

"And Abraham?" Cruz asked.

Gregory tapped his fingers to his lower lip, looking thoughtful. "Abraham is a different matter. Taking him out of the picture hurts Dashiell, so it could be any one of Dashiell's enemies. Another vampire, wanting to take over some territory. The wolves, if Dashiell's diplomacy has been less than ideal."

I remembered Hugo putting the silver handcuffs on Eli, and thought that Dashiell's diplomacy with the wolves was pretty goddamned far from ideal.

"Gregory, we'd like to talk to the three vampires' human servants. Do you have any idea where we can find them?" I asked.

He looked disgusted for a moment, as if I'd asked him where his hamburger comes from, and then his face stilled as he remembered something. "There is a human servant who organizes things for their little community—he does these parties, and I think he runs some other events as well. His name is James Rucker." Gregory pulled out a cell phone and scrolled through the contact list, leaning over so Cruz could copy down a number. "I believe he also spends quite a bit of time at the Copper Room. Bald, with a beard."

"Thank you, Gregory," I said deferentially, and nodded to Cruz. We stood up. "If you'll excuse us, we'll be on our way."

He stood up, too. "Of course. But, Scarlett?"

I looked back at him, and that same complicated look shadowed his face.

"Next time? Call first."

Chapter 14

The Copper Room is sort of the ugly, unwanted stepchild of the LA vamp hangouts. A lot of the pathetic vamparazzi show up there every night, telling stories and drinking cranberry-vodkas. (Get it?) The actual vampires consider it incredibly uncool—it's in *Long Beach*, for crying out loud—but if they're desperate for a pickup, they occasionally show, one or two a night. If a vamp does work up the courage to show his face at the Copper Room, he'll have his pick of the vampire hangers-on, which isn't saying much, but whatever. Blood is blood, I guess. Suddenly, I wondered if that was true—did different people taste different? It hadn't occurred to me. I'd have to ask Beatrice sometime.

Meanwhile, for everyone else, the food is crappy and the failed actors/waitstaff have all crossed the line into bitter and hostile. On the bright side, I had no trouble finding street parking.

"Whoa," Cruz said under his breath as I led him toward the door. A neon *Bar and Grill* sign flickered unsteadily in the window, and it was hard to avoid the carpet of cigarette butts in the entryway. "This is it? This is...wow."

I shrugged, pulling open the door. "It can't all be glamour and roses, cupcake, even with the fanged set."

We walked into the dim entryway, and I told the bored-looking waitress we'd be in the bar area. It was big and dingy, with those extra-tall tables and stools surrounding a beaten-up pool table and a filmy big-screen TV. There were six or seven people scattered about, and when we walked in, seven pairs of eyes glanced up, hoping for a vampire, before returning to their drinks. Apparently, something about Cruz and me screamed, *Still alive!* When I got a little farther into the room, I understood the desperation. There wasn't a single vampire in the bar.

It was after midnight now, and they were all looking a little defensive and drunk, like the homely girl who's sat on the bleachers for the entire school dance.

"*Díos*," Cruz said under his breath. "You're right. This is depressing."

We sat at one of the too-tall tables, and Cruz gave the barmaid a big grin, which had her hustling right over. I tried very hard not to roll my eyes, but to her credit, when she got a good look at my face, she did a classic double take, then glared over at Cruz. I opened my mouth to correct her assumption, but what was I going to say? Car accident? Doorknob? Anything I came up with—short of "a vampire hit me in the face"—would sound like a lame cover-up. We ordered beer and Diet Coke, and I was pretty sure the barmaid spit in his bottle of Heineken. I chose not to comment.

While she was getting Cruz's change, I scanned the people at the bar.

"There," I said, nudging him and nodding discreetly toward a completely bald, bearded man wearing a ribbed tank top under a khaki button-down shirt. The guy had left the shirt open to display a not-so-small paunch. He was with three others, telling an animated story while they laughed. The ringleader.

"I got this one," Cruz told me under his breath.

I shrugged.

Cruz walked right up to Rucker and pulled out his badge. "Mr. Rucker? Could I have a word with you?"

Rucker's mouth dropped open in the middle of a sentence. When he recovered, his face smoothed back into alpha-geek mode.

"I guess," he said casually, as if he consulted on police cases every day. He nodded to his friends, who retreated to a far corner of the barroom to gossip.

After they'd left, I went up and dropped onto a stool beside Rucker. Cruz took the other side again.

"What do the police want with me?" Rucker asked, a little pompously. "Am I behind on my gas and electric or something?"

"Actually," Cruz replied, putting away his badge, "we're looking into some murders that happened in La Brea Park the other night. Did you hear about that?"

Rucker sobered instantly. "Yes," he said. "We heard. It's terrible."

"We're looking for the three human servants of the vampires that died," I added. I recited their names again. "Do you know any of them?"

But Rucker was peering at my face. "I know who you are," he said, "but who is this guy? How much does he know?" His voice was sharp, suddenly edgy. Human servants are conditioned very hard not to talk about their extracurricular activities. It's the first rule of Vampire Club.

"He's with me, and Dashiell okayed it," I told him, trying to look stern.

I don't think stern is my best look, but his eyes widened when I said the name *Dashiell*, as if I'd said we were on a mission from God. Which probably wasn't far off, from Rucker's point of view. He took a quick gulp of his cranberry-vodka and nodded.

"I know all of them." He pursed his lips, thinking. "But I don't think they can help. Grottum and Myles split town, from what I heard."

"Why?" Cruz asked. "Did they think they were in danger?"

Rucker shrugged. "They didn't know. None of us in the community"—he twirled a finger to include the other vampire freaks in the bar—"know why those guys were killed, so why risk it? Probably, they just wanted to play it safe."

"Do you know where they went?"

"No."

"What about the other one?" I asked. "Freedner."

"He's still around, I think. But I doubt he can tell you anything I can't." There was a note of broken pride in his voice, which Cruz picked up on.

"What makes you say that?" he asked.

Rucker's face blanched, and he huddled into himself a little. "Nothing. Never mind."

Cruz glanced at me. I took the hint.

"James," I said carefully, "were you Abraham's human servant, too?"

And just that quickly, the last traces of bravado vanished and the bald man's eyes began to shine a little. Deflated, he looked down into his drink and made a snuffling noise, mumbling, "Don't tell nobody. I got a wife."

I worked to keep my expression even. I didn't know what a normal human would see in this guy, much less a vampire who could have his pick of the groupies.

"We won't," Cruz promised.

"Me and Freedner talked the day after, you know, the bodies. He was the one who called Dashiell when Abe didn't show up for their plans. But neither of us know a damn thing about why they got killed. Abe wasn't doing anything out of the ordinary—that we knew about—and nobody had threatened him."

"Was there anyone who would have wanted Abraham dead?" I asked. "Anyone who hated him?"

"No. Abe was…He was very calm, you know? Like, a nice guy. I know he was a vamp and all, but it's hard to see anyone wanting to kill him. That's why he did such good work. He kept the peace."

I looked over at Cruz. He had this look on his face like wheels were turning.

"Did you two know about each other?" he asked. "You and Freedner?"

"Oh, sure. There was...ah...a bit of a rivalry for Abe's attention, but it was friendly. Tom works third shift, and I keep daytime hours, so we were able to split up the nights okay. Tom was with Abe in the early evening, and I had the early morning when everyone was asleep."

"James," Cruz said quietly, "where were you two nights ago? Around three a.m.?"

Rucker's eyes narrowed, calculating, and I saw Cruz's hand drift slowly back toward his hip. But then Rucker relaxed. "Hey! That was the night my wife and me, we'd gone down to San Diego to visit our son." He looked at me. "He's a freshman at San Diego State, doing real good."

"Can you prove you were there?" Cruz prompted.

"There will be credit card records and stuff from the trip, and the hotel we stayed at—the Holiday Inn by campus—they might remember me 'cause I chatted with the guy about the free cookies in the lobby." He peered suspiciously at Cruz. "You're not gonna question my wife, are you?"

Cruz had produced a small notebook and was writing down the details. He looked up. "We'll start with the hotel and the cards. But if those fall through, yes, I'll have to ask her."

"Can you tell her something else? Like..." His brow furrowed a moment; then he brightened. "There was something stolen at work, and they're asking everybody, something like that?"

"Let's cross that bridge when we come to it."

Cruz took down both Rucker's and Freedner's addresses and phone numbers, and we headed out. On the street, I stopped and leaned against my car, stretching my stomach muscles, which had gone stagnant. There had been a lot of driving today, which is kind of par for the course in LA, but I was still feeling a little cramped and sore. It was a lovely California night, sixty degrees with a soft breeze, and I closed my eyes, resting for a moment. I was so tired.

I felt Cruz lean against the car next to me. I had about fifteen seconds of peace before the questions started again.

"So, what was that?" Cruz asked. "Vampires have multiple human servants? I thought they only kept one."

I opened my eyes. "Most do. Having a human servant is kind of like having a mistress. They're whiny, they're annoying, they require constant gifts and attention—all just so you can get what you want when you want it. Why would anyone have *two* of those? But some vampires do keep more than one, yes."

"And from the wife comment, I take it there's usually...intercourse?"

I couldn't help it, I laughed. "Dude. Don't say *intercourse*. You sound like my seventh grade health teacher. But yes, there's almost always a sexual component to the human servant thing. And vampires are a lot less picky about sexual preference."

He mulled that over for a while, then asked, "Do they love each other? Are vampires capable of love?"

That woke me up. I looked over at him, but he was just gazing back with calm curiosity. "That," I said finally, "is the big question. Human servants would definitely say yes—they all think they're in a *Twilight* book." Which makes them easy pickings for any vampire willing to style his hair and slouch around looking sour.

"What do *you* think?"

I paused. It had been a long time since anyone at work had asked me that. A few months after I started doing crime scene cleanup with Olivia, I had asked her if vampires had souls. Could they feel? Could they love?

"What do you think?" she'd said.

I had thought it over for a long time. "I think it's kind of like breathing. They don't need to do it, it doesn't come naturally, but they remember the feeling and the need. And they can pretend when they have to."

She'd smiled broadly at me, her star and only pupil, but she never really answered. To this day, I still don't really know. I call them the undead, and they don't need to breathe or eat or have a pulse, but for all I know, they're normal people with a disease that makes them distant and frozen. Who knows?

Cruz was waiting for my answer, looking very serious, and very young, though he had to be at least five years older than me. I realized again how strange and new this all must be for him. I felt the responsibility of it, of teaching him to navigate this world. If I did it wrong, he could get himself killed so easily.

I felt a very brief empathy for Olivia. Then I just wished someone else could be in charge.

"I think it's a lot more complicated than a yes-or-no question. I'm certain that vampires are capable of some kind of love," I said, thinking of Dashiell and Beatrice. "But every human servant I've ever met has been one hundred percent deluded. Human life is rich and desperate and complicated, with all these goals—money, family, power, fame, fortune, happiness, a career. It's different for vampires. They have sort of a culture, a collective identity, but at the end of the day—night—they're after blood and power. That's it."

Cruz's face was very close, and his eyes were fixed so intently on me that, for a second, I pictured kissing him. Sue me. He was beautiful. I tried to imagine being on a date with him, doing something totally normal. He was a human, after all—he wouldn't be using me for my lame ability or to get a leg up in the Old World. We could go to the movies, order pizza, like my dates in high school.

But then I remembered Eli and the tortured little thing we were doing, and how damaged I knew I was. I suspected that my ability to have a real human connection had died with my parents.

Letting the keys jingle in my hand, I took a step back and broke the spell.

"Okay, so what's our working theory here?" I asked.

He frowned. "It sounds like Abraham was the real target, and the other two vampires were just collateral damage."

"But did they actually want to *kill* Abraham, or were they just trying to get to Dashiell?"

"Not sure. I'll check out Rucker's alibi, and we should talk to Freedner. If they were both Abe's human servants, this whole thing could be a love triangle gone wrong. Rucker himself said that there was jealousy."

"He said *rivalry*."

"Same thing."

"I don't know, he didn't sound that...worked up about it."

Cruz shrugged. "Maybe Abraham dumped Freedner, and he decided to off Abe. *If I can't have you, no one can* kind of deal. Rucker might not even know about it."

I thought that over. "Could be, I guess. Getting a null is about the only way a human servant would be able to kill a vampire. But I'm still putting my money on the killer being someone who wants to hurt Dashiell. He's the bigger fish."

"Maybe." He stretched his arms over his head, yawning. "If Freedner works third shift, he won't be home for a few hours yet. In the meantime, we need to know more about Dashiell's enemies."

I thought about that for a second. "Okay," I said. "Come on, let's go."

"Where?" he said, blinking fast.

"We need to know more about Dashiell's enemies, and he doesn't want to talk to us."

We got in the car, and I began to back out of the dingy Copper Room lot.

"So where are we going, then?" Cruz said.

I glanced over at him. "To see his wife."

Chapter 15

We were on the road to Pasadena before Beatrice even answered the phone. I was hopeful like that. To my relief, she agreed to meet me at an all-night coffee shop a few miles away from the mansion, and she reluctantly consented to my bringing Cruz.

The coffee shop, Kalista's Koffee, was sparse and low-key, with concrete floors and unfinished ceilings. Paintings by local artists hung on the whitewashed walls, and flashes of color—a teapot here, a bouquet there—saved the place from sterility. Despite the late hour, there were two college students having a heated academic debate near the front windows and a tired-looking man in his forties typing at a laptop near the counter.

Beatrice was already there, sitting in the far back corner with an untouched glass of water in front of her. She was wearing a dress, as always, but this one was a simple burgundy wrap dress that brought out the auburn in her eyes. She watched us walk up with a calm, even friendly, expression on her face—until I got close enough for her to cross the line into my unique personal bubble. She took a couple of short gasping breaths and then straightened up; her composure returned, if somewhat dimmed by humanity.

"Thank you for meeting with us, Beatrice," I said respectfully. I introduced Cruz, who gave an old-fashioned little bow that somehow worked for him.

Beatrice nodded gracefully and indicated that we should sit. "My husband does not know I'm here, though I will tell him if it becomes necessary," she warned us. She focused on me. "Scarlett, I agreed to see you because I don't think that you are capable of participating in that kind of slaughter."

I have to admit, I was a little surprised she thought so "highly" of me. "Um, thank you."

Her eyes darkened. "And, of course, I am sorry that his employees were a bit...enthusiastic with you."

I touched my face, having forgotten about the bruises on my cheek and eye. As soon as I remembered them, they began to ache. Guess I hadn't been doing much smiling. "It's nothing."

She nodded briskly. "Now, I understand you wish to know more of my husband's enemies."

"Yes, ma'am," Cruz said politely. "We have spoken to the human servants of the vampires who were killed, and they didn't know of any other reason that those three would be killed, except to get to Dashiell."

She looked at him, narrowing her eyes thoughtfully. "You have learned so much in only a few days," she said. "I wonder if it is too much."

He blushed under her stare, and she turned toward me. "Are you certain that it is not the wolves? The carnage—"

"Pretty certain. Will would know if one of his wolves was that twisted, and I just can't see him letting it slide. It doesn't make any sense."

She nodded. "What about Kirsten? I know little of witch magic, but I am told she is very powerful. Is it possible that a spell could cause the same reaction as a null?"

That idea took me by surprise. I thought it over for a second. I didn't know of any spells that could subdue the vampires—surely someone would have told me if that were possible?

"I don't know," I admitted. "I can't see Kirsten causing a massacre like that, but it's something to think about." Unless she'd decided she was tired of the status quo...But Kirsten had sort of established the status quo. I had heard that she was the first to organize the witches, to request an equal share in using a cleaner to keep things under wraps. And she had been very helpful. Before her arrival, there had been too many incidents of witches setting fires or playing with love spells or experimenting with voodoo, of all things. Between my job and hers, there hadn't been a public witchcraft incident in years. Which meant Dashiell didn't have to throw money around to cover anything up.

"Is there anyone else who comes to mind, ma'am?" Cruz asked her.

Her long cream-colored fingernails tapped on the water glass. "There is one who wishes to take Dashiell's place. She has had many names, but she currently calls herself Ariadne." Beatrice's long, regal nose wrinkled with distaste. "She and my husband were involved, many years ago. He ended their affair to be with me, and she was...displeased. When Dashiell became the master of Los Angeles, she was very bitter."

"Can she...?" Cruz began, then paused, looking for words. "Um, can she take him?"

Beatrice smiled benevolently at him, as if he'd just done something adorable. "I do not think so. Definitely not in an even physical match. But a straightforward fight wouldn't be her style. It would be like her to try to cripple him first, take away his wealth, or churn up animosity with the wolves." Her gaze turned toward me.

"Do you know where we could find her?" I asked.

I was expecting her to say that Ariadne had gone underground or that she and some minions had taken over an abandoned warehouse downtown, but I watch too much TV. Beatrice said simply, "Of course. She has a residence in Orange County."

She wrote an address on a napkin, passing it over to me. "If you speak to her, I would appreciate if you did not mention my name. The two of us have"—her lip curled, and though she was currently human, for a moment, I saw the predator beneath—"bad blood."

Five minutes later, Cruz and I were in the coffee shop's parking lot, trying to figure out our next move.

"What are we doing? Are we going to Orange County, or are we going home to bed?" I asked him. I was starting to sway. And not pay attention to my choice of words.

He gave me a bemused look, and I rolled my eyes.

"Our separate homes, idiot."

"I don't want to waste any of your time. Not with that deadline in front of us."

I sighed. "I know. But it's two thirty in the morning, and we're both tired. It might not be the best time to hunt down an ancient jilted vampire." And life on the line or not, I didn't feel like going from downtown to Long Beach to Pasadena to Orange County. That is just waaaaaay more of LA County than any one person should have to see in the same night.

But Cruz's voice was firm when he said, "I don't think we have a choice."

I sighed. "Fine. But you're driving." I tossed him the keys, and he fumbled to catch them as I grabbed the passenger-side door.

When we'd pulled out of the parking lot, he spoke up. "Something doesn't fit with the Dashiell theory."

I tried to stifle a yawn. "Hmm?"

"Look, if this Ariadne person really wanted to hurt Dashiell, and she had access to a null, why wouldn't she just, you know, have the null go stand by Dashiell and then shoot him or whatever? Why go through all the trouble?"

"Maybe she really likes decorative murder." I shrugged. "She *is* a vampire."

He shook his head. "Nah. If she was close enough to those three vampires to kill them, then she'd be too close to the null, too, right? She'd be a human. And unless she's fundamentally a lumberjack, there's just no way a woman could have mutilated those bodies like that."

"Hey," I protested, but it was halfhearted. I was too tired to fight sexism on behalf of female serial killers.

"You know what I mean."

"Maybe she had someone else do it, or maybe she knows someone else who may have wanted to. Or maybe Beatrice is sending us on a wild-goose chase." Beatrice is probably the nicest vampire I've ever known, but my trust in her only extends to questions about as serious as *Do these jeans make me look fat?*

"That doesn't bother you?"

I raised my eyebrows. "Jesse. In the last few days, we've seen a gruesome triple murder, I've been kidnapped, your life has been threatened, *my* life has been threatened, I got punched by a gorilla vampire, and nobody has gotten enough sleep. Why would it shock or offend me that the vampires are playing mind games? Haven't you read Anne Rice? They live for this shit."

"Ugh," he said, frustrated. "You're so..."

"What?" I sat up a little straighter. I was awake now.

He was silent for a moment, then said, "You're, what, twenty-three, twenty-four? You talk like some of the detectives I know who are in their fifties or sixties and think they've seen everything human life has to offer. They're numb from it. But those guys have had thirty years on the force. How are *you* this jaded?"

I didn't answer him, just looked away. I felt my eyes starting to close again before I could come up with a defense.

Chapter 16

Scarlett drifted off for a few minutes, jolting awake when Jesse pulled off the freeway. He followed Beatrice's directions to Ariadne's house, which qualified as at least a mansion, if not a palace. Four stories tall and made of deep-red brick, it stood out even on a street that was lousy with mansions. Every house on that Orange County street had a gate, but Ariadne's was the only one that was standing open.

Jesse stood by, a little amused, while Scarlett rang the bell and then jogged a few steps back. A vampire opened the door, and he tried not to gasp. Beatrice had appeared to be in her late thirties or early forties, which sort of fit with the way Scarlett had described her and Dashiell. But this girl appeared to be twenty at the most, although her outfit may have affected his estimate. She'd gone completely goth: black hair, black lipstick, tiny gold nose ring, and sort of a black layered look, with tights, a short skirt, and at least three shirts. She looked like someone that vice would arrest on Hollywood Boulevard.

She looked them up and down and motioned them closer. "Hello," the vampire said, twitching a bit. Jesse realized after a second that she was switching over to humanity. She turned to look at Scarlett. "I'm Ariadne, as you must know. You must be Scarlett Bernard. Great pants."

"Uh, thanks," Scarlett said, sounding a little nervous. "You've heard of me?"

"Sure." Ariadne shrugged. "They're so rare, your kind. Who's your friend?" She nodded toward Jesse.

"Sorry, this is Officer Jesse Cruz. I'm sort of helping him with a problem."

Jesse stepped forward, unsure if he should reach out for a handshake. He didn't really want to touch this woman, human or not, he decided, so he kept his hands by his side. "Nice to meet you, ma'am. I was wondering if we might have a few minutes of your time?"

"Of course," Ariadne said, smiling genially. "Please come in."

She led them deeper into the house. It was overdecorated, like his parents', but where their house always smelled of spices, lilies, and dog, this one stank of age and decay. It looked like something straight out of Dickens. But although the furnishings were old and uncared-for, Jesse recognized them as very expensive. If Ariadne had this much money, why was she answering the door herself? Shouldn't a vampire who was this rich and powerful have a legion of servants?

The three of them finally reached a Victorian-style sitting room, and Ariadne gestured to two elaborate blue silk armchairs, perching herself on the edge of the opposite matching couch. As if reading Jesse's mind, she said, "You'll have to excuse my lack of proper hospitality. My maid is on an errand, and I'm afraid I'm between butlers right now." She smiled slyly, displaying a mouthful of sharp little teeth.

She was seriously giving Jesse the creeps, and that was as a human. He glanced at Scarlett, but she was just looking at him expectantly. His cue.

"Ma'am," Jesse began, "I'm investigating several murders that took place in La Brea Park a few nights ago. Did you hear about that?"

"Oh, yes, I get all the papers," Ariadne said happily. "I understand that it was quite the bloodbath." She licked her lips, just like Gregory.

Jesse thought of the scene in the park and tried not to shudder. "Did you know the victims?"

Ariadne gazed pensively at the ceiling for a moment, frowning. "Let's see...Joanna and I were friends, of course. I was terribly sad to hear that she had passed." It was such a perfectly normal thing to say about a dead person, but sounded so strange coming out of her black-lipsticked mouth. "I never thought much of her boyfriend, Demetri. Oh, and everyone knew Abraham, of course."

"Can you think of a reason why anyone would want to harm any of them?"

"Why, my dear boy, of course I can. Can't you?" she said demurely, looking up at him through her eyelashes. When Jesse remained stone-faced, she sighed. "Fine. Take all the fun out of it." Her eyes turned to Scarlett. "How much do you know, Miss Bernard, about our internal structure—or lack thereof?"

"Almost nothing," Scarlett answered cautiously.

"As I imagined. Most vampires, including Dashiell"—the name was said with a hint of scornful hissing—"prefer to keep any of our history from the humans, even those in our employ." Ariadne rolled her eyes a little. "But I've always found their need for secrecy a touch excessive. Who on earth would believe you? Besides, it is so easy to control humans' minds. Well, most humans." She licked her lips again and gazed over at Jesse.

He couldn't help a little involuntary shiver, but managed to resist scooting closer to Scarlett, his protection.

"I'm assuming your young man is privy to our world, if he is accompanying you?"

Scarlett nodded.

"Well, then this will be educational for both of you." She smoothed her black layers down as though they were the finest of gowns.

"Once, vampires had a governing council, a consortium, which made important decisions on behalf of all vampires. It was this consortium that decided that we would remain a secret from the humans. When the New World was discovered, however"—she gestured vaguely to the room—"the world became too big for a single source of authority to manage, and the consortium fell. There are now precious few vampires old enough to remember it at all. Without it, we took to governing ourselves." Her eyes darkened. "For decades, vampires fought over territory, both here and in the older countries.

"After dear Mr. Stoker published his book, however, we knew we had to find a more stable way of life or face extinction. When the dust finally settled, each major city was ruled by a cardinal vampire, who was responsible for all the vampires in his territory. Some, like Dashiell, even tried to care for all the needs of the Old World, including the wolves." She wrinkled her nose with distaste.

"What if the cardinal vampire wasn't suited?" Jesse asked, fascinated despite himself. "What if they abused their power, or did things that humans noticed?"

She waved a hand dismissively. "It happens less often than you might think. If you're powerful enough to control a city, you've been around long enough to understand the importance of discretion. Our kind cannot exist without it. But if a cardinal was unfit for some reason, neighboring vampires would group together to help a new candidate usurp the old." She leaned forward, eyes suddenly bright with an intensity that was all her own. "That, you see, became our one rule, besides keeping our existence secret. No petty jostling for position. To maintain order, you didn't just need a leader who would lead, you also had to have followers who were willing to *follow*. If a vampire kills off a master of the city just to gain his power, the vampires in the area will rise up against him."

Scarlett asked, "What kinds of things are grounds for taking over a territory?"

Ariadne leaned back into the couch, her eyes dancing. "I expect you already know that, Miss Bernard. Revealing ourselves to the humans. Inability to keep one's vampires in line. Failure to take care of those vampires."

That rang a bell.

Jesse interrupted. "Ma'am, are you suggesting that the vampires in La Brea Park were killed so someone could take Dashiell's place?"

She smiled at him, her legs dangling from the sofa. "Yes."

Jesse looked at Scarlett, whose face gave away nothing, and back to Ariadne. "Why are you telling us this? You must know you're going to be a suspect."

"Because," Scarlett answered, understanding blooming on her face, "it wasn't her. She didn't kill those people, but is afraid that whoever did will make a play for Dashiell's spot and win. Unless we expose them and stir up enough trouble. In which case, Ariadne could take over instead."

Ariadne said nothing, just smiled her pleased little smile at Jesse. Even as a human, she was very, very frightening.

At that moment, Jesse's cell phone vibrated, and he gave a little jump and pulled the phone out of his pocket. The caller ID was for dispatch, even though he was off duty. Jesse stood up and paced a few steps away from Scarlett and the vampire. "Excuse me, please." He flipped it open. "Cruz."

He was being called in for overtime. As he listened to the dispatcher, he saw Scarlett answer her own phone.

They hung up at nearly the same time, and Jesse glanced at Ariadne, who was holding her hands up and studying them curiously, probably unused to feeling human. He looked at Scarlett. "Let me guess," she said. "Another murder?"

He nodded, and they said in unison, "The comic book shop."

When they were on their way to the van, Ariadne leaned out of the doorway and called after them, "Do give my regards to Dashiell and Beatrice, won't you? Tell him I hope his writing is going better."

Jesse looked at Scarlett questioningly, but she just shrugged and gave Ariadne a wave.

As he drove the van north, Jesse was wide-awake again, thinking about the new murder. He hadn't gotten any details, other than there was a dead body and the officers on scene thought it was related to La Brea Park. Was Ronnie the victim? Was it because he had talked to them? And if so, what exactly had he said that was so important? Jesse replayed the conversation in his head, but other than the thing with the second null, Ronnie hadn't really had anything new to say.

And that was another thing—why kill him *after* he'd talked to the police? If the killer knew Ronnie had been at the site before the police came to interview him, then he should have wanted to kill Ronnie right away. And if Jesse and Scarlett had led the killer to Ronnie, then killing him still didn't make sense. If Ronnie had known something really important about the murder, the cops would have shown up at the killer's door immediately. The fact that they had talked to Ronnie and still hadn't discovered anything should have made the killer feel more comfortable, not less. The whole thing was weird.

"Did you see any video cameras?" Jesse asked suddenly.

"What?"

"At the comic book store. Were there any video cameras?"

"I don't know. But hang on, I can find out." Scarlett fished her cell phone out of her pocket and placed a quick call. She was shaking her head as she flipped the little phone closed. "Will was the one who called me about the murder. He got this weird text about a cleanup. He says no cameras. He's been there a bunch of times to see Ronnie, and the wolves always notice that kind of thing."

"Can we be sure?"

"If Will says so? Definitely."

Okay, so there wouldn't be any footage of Scarlett and him entering the shop to worry about, but there could still be eyewitnesses who remembered the incident from the other day. He hated this. When had Jesse become the kind of person who sneaks around hiding from official police investigations? The second he'd picked up the garbage bag, he realized, and felt a flare of anger.

"Uh, Jesse?"

"What?" he barked, harsher than he'd meant to.

"Um, am I just dropping you off here? I mean, there's no way I'm gonna be allowed at the crime scene, right?"

He tried to focus. "No, I want you to come. You might see something I wouldn't, something related to Ronnie being a werewolf."

"But how am I gonna get that close to him?"

"I've been thinking about that. Do you know anything about photography?"

Chapter 17

My first dead body was a witch case.

It wasn't as gruesome as what I would eventually see, and certainly didn't compare to La Brea Park. I had been working and living with Olivia for about three months, and our days had settled into a routine: each morning we woke up late, ran for three miles, then drank a protein shake and made ourselves brunch. This was the one area where I'd actually shone. Olivia could barely boil eggs, and my mother had loved cooking, especially breakfast. She'd taught me how to do soufflés and perfect omelets. After brunch, we would talk about equipment—mostly what cleaning supplies worked best for what situations, but also what to keep in your vehicle that wouldn't look too suspicious (like the bolt cutters), what to do with dead bodies, that kind of thing. I was already making a little Old World money as an apprentice, but Olivia helped me put a down payment on my van and paid for the custom freezer section to be installed. During dinner, she usually told stories that were funny and sometimes scary, but always instructive, and at night, if we didn't have a job, I was free to do whatever I wanted, as long as I had a cell phone with a full battery and didn't drink. We both stayed up late—most of our work was done at night, after all. I never went out much, though. I had no friends in the city, and I preferred to stay close to Olivia. I was like a scared little girl then, still adjusting to the sudden wrong turn that my life had taken, and Olivia was the only light left in my world.

She spent a lot of evenings trying to teach me about clothes—my mother hadn't been a bad dresser, exactly, but LA and Esperanza standards are very different—and taking me shopping for the kind of clothes she wore: casual tailored dresses with high heels and earrings that matched the necklace. She dressed me up in the brands she liked best: Armani, Burberry, Christian Louboutin. Soon I was her perfect little clone—no, not like a clone. A daughter.

Olivia had inherited money from her husband, a banking consultant who'd died a decade earlier, though she never talked about him. I asked her once why she worked for the Old World if she didn't need the money, and she just shrugged and said she enjoyed the challenge. That never seemed quite enough to me, but I wasn't going to push. I never pushed Olivia, actually. If we got too close to certain subjects—her dead husband, her childhood, her education—she would get this hardness to her, a flashing steeliness that had me backing off quickly. It didn't take very long for me to learn to keep my mouth shut.

That night, I had been planning to read for a while in my room, but Olivia took a call right after supper. She listened to Kirsten for a few seconds, nodded, and hung up, telling me to change and get in the van immediately. I ran to my room and pulled on the coveralls Olivia had given me—just like hers—and was delighted to find that I'd beaten her into the van by a few seconds. She gave me a weird little frown at that but got behind the wheel, driving us to a suburban area in Culver City where a bunch of sensible sedans and SUVs were parked in front of a little split-level house. It just looked like any other party. We backed the van into the driveway and strode through the door near the garage, Olivia in the lead like she owned the place.

There were five witches, plus Kirsten, waiting for us in a small kitchen. I had expected the women inside to look the part of the suburban mommies, but most of them were fairly young, mid-twenties, with a professional look. Like big-business interns who had the night off. There were six of them crowded around the modest kitchen table, which was piled with wads of used tissues. They had all been crying, except for Kirsten, who was leaning against the counter looking furious. Kirsten isn't really pretty, exactly, but with her clear Swedish skin and tranquil blue eyes, you'd never really notice. She has what my high school drama teacher used to call *presence*. In the Old World, though, we just call it *power*.

"Death magics," Kirsten said tersely, her calm eyes flashing now. She had on jeans and a black leather jacket over what appeared to be a pajama top. "They were playing with death magics." She pushed herself off the counter and jerked her head so Olivia and I would follow. Kirsten stalked down the hall to a back bedroom, which looked like the morning after a Wicca-themed slumber party—lights on, used candles and spell books and chalk scattered around next to empty wine cooler bottles and an honest-to-goodness Ouija board. It could have all been fairly innocent, except for the corpse in the middle of the room—a man, stark naked, with no visible injuries, unless you counted the look of terror on his face. He wasn't rotting, didn't even smell yet, but no one would mistake him for alive. I looked away. I wasn't a virgin, but I'd never actually seen a penis in full light before, much less a dead penis. My eyes fell on Olivia, as I waited for her to tell me what to do. She was already opening her black old-fashioned doctor's bag, pulling out some surgical gloves and an extra-strength Hefty bag.

"Put these on," she said, tossing me a pair of gloves. I fumbled the catch and had to pick them up, my hands shaking. The worst thing I'd seen up until then was a severed werewolf ear, but the wolf had grown it back quickly, and the detached ear looked more like a movie prop than anything else. But I wanted so desperately to impress Olivia with my cool.

She unfolded the garbage bag, clearing a space on the floor to spread it next to the body. "You should always know what happened," she told me as she worked. "It might make a difference to the cleanup. Usually the witch who did it—or Kirsten, if it's a bad one like this—will fill you in, but I've seen this before, so she didn't bother." She motioned me to go crouch by the guy's feet. "Death magic usually involves trying to contact the dead. This guy probably knew one of the witches and asked for help to talk to someone." She leaned back for a second, showing me the importance of what she was saying. "A lot of things happen in the Old World, Scarlett, and some witches have a lot of power to manipulate the magic. But magic doesn't like it when someone tries to cross the line between the living and the dead. It takes a very, very powerful coven to control death magic spells. Those witches couldn't do it, and the magic went right back through them and zapped him. Like a lightning strike, but with no marks, which is why we have to take care of the body. No coroner is going to be able to determine cause of death."

"You don't know how lucky you are," Kirsten said, leaning in the doorframe. "Your magic—or lack thereof—costs you nothing." Her eyes were sad. "For the witches, there's always a cost. Some of us can't afford to pay it."

Listening to the two of them talk as if we weren't gathered around a corpse was starting to calm me down. But then Olivia smiled at me, reached down, and wrapped her gloved hands crudely around the guy's head, nodding for me to take his feet and help lift him onto the bag. I had no choice but to look. The guy's feet were on the smallish side, and he'd had a pedicure recently (thank you, LA). I put my hands gingerly around his ankles, sticking my elbows out so his toes wouldn't brush my forearms, and Olivia counted to three. When we lifted him, he felt awful—just *dead*, a dead sack of meat. His sad little penis lolled around with the movement, and the second he hit the bag, I was moving, darting out of the room. Kirsten had already backed into the hallway, pointing at one of the doors with a look of sympathy. I ran by and got the toilet lid up just in time to puke up all of that night's dinner. I lost control of my body, which kept heaving and heaving, ignoring my attempts to calm it down, until at last it allowed me to collapse back against the tub. I stretched out one leg and kicked the handle on the toilet.

"Thanks," I said to Kirsten, who was standing in the doorway.

"Don't worry about it," she said. She gave me a sympathetic smile. "First one, right? It gets easier."

But I don't want it to get easier, I thought. *I'm not supposed to be moving dead bodies; I'm supposed to be a regular person.*

"Scarlett, get back in here," Olivia barked. She sounded furious. "I can't use you if you're going to go to pieces at every little thing."

I froze. I'd never displeased her before. Kirsten frowned, checking my face, but I managed to give her a shaky smile and a shrug. Then I got up and hurried back to Olivia.

We arrived at the comic book store just before 4:00 a.m., and Cruz came around the van to open my door for me, which I thought was incredibly cheesy. We circled around to the back of the building, where a bunch of that yellow crime scene tape segregated the section of the parking lot between the dumpster and the store. Even from thirty feet away, I could see the rust-colored blood still oozing sluggishly down the sides of the dumpster. We weaved through the parked police vehicles and approached the scene.

Before I could worry too much about his plan, Cruz took my hand in his warm brown one and led me straight over to a squat, nerdy-looking guy in his late twenties who was painstakingly cleaning the lens of an enormous camera.

"Hey, Dale? Have you got a second?"

The heavyset guy looked up, wrinkling his nose in a squint at us. "Hey, Jesse. What's up?"

"Dale, this is my girlfriend, Scarlett."

I smiled winningly. Or tried to.

"She's studying photography at the U. I was hoping maybe you could show her around the scene a little, say she's your apprentice."

Dale looked uncomfortable. "I don't know, Jesse. They're pretty careful about who gets across the tape these days."

"Aw, come on, man. Don't make me look bad." He leaned in, and I heard him murmur to Dale, "You know that new Kate Beckinsale movie? How'd you like to go to the premiere?"

Dale's eyes bugged out. "Really? You can do that?"

"My dad's working on the set, man. He can do anything. You think you can help me out?"

"Sure, yeah." Dale nodded his head enthusiastically.

"Thanks, Dale." Cruz squeezed my hand and turned toward me. "You go on home when you're done, baby. I'll have somebody drop me off at my car when I get done. It might be late." He gave me a mischievous grin, then reached over and patted my ass. "Go get 'em."

I glared at him behind Dale's back, but he just smiled sweetly.

He trotted off to join the other cops who were milling around the tape line, and Dale looked me over with interest, taking an extra-close look at Molly's leather pants. *Never borrowing these again*, I thought.

"Wow, you're pretty. Okay, so how far are you in your classes? Have you taken two forty-five with Crawford yet?"

We started walking toward the yellow tape ourselves.

"Um, no. I just declared my major," I said lamely. Undercover is not exactly my thing. I had explained to Cruz that my only understanding of cameras was how to push the big green—sometimes red—button, but he'd just shrugged and told me to fake it. Thanks, Jesse. Very helpful.

"Okay, well, we'll just go over the basics, then. Police photography is straightforward, not much for artistry or technique."

He frowned disapprovingly at the justice system's obvious artistic ignorance, but continued. "The cops drop a numbered marker near anything they think is important, and you take three shots of each marker—close-up, mid-shot, and wide shot." He flashed an ID at the cop guarding the scene and briefly introduced me as his new assistant. The cop nodded, and we ducked under the tape, just like that. Dale kept on talking, but I wasn't listening anymore. I was too busy looking at the dead werewolf.

Ronnie had been tied up with glittery silver chains, bound at the hands and feet. He was tipped over on his side, shoulders against the dumpster, and his mouth and eyes were wide open in a scream. Little white things were scattered across his torn clothing. I resisted the urge to walk over, squat down, and look closer. This was supposed to be my first scene, so I tried to look squeamish.

"Scarlett? Are you hearing me? Oh," Dale said, looking from me to the body. "Yeah, sorry, I probably should have warned you. You have to have a strong stomach for this sort of thing." He patted my shoulder awkwardly. "Just give it a second. I'll grab a few shots."

I followed Dale blindly around to different markers, never taking my eyes off the body. I noticed two things: first, that there were welts under those chains, and second, that all the teeth had been taken out of his mouth. I took one step toward the body. The little white things were teeth, but not human teeth. They were way too long.

I'd cleaned up werewolf teeth after fights, and I knew what I was looking at. It didn't make any sense, though. Why had Ronnie made the change? Why let his teeth get ripped out and then change back?

There was, of course, only one possible answer.

When there was nothing more for me to learn, I made a weak excuse to Dale—"Oh, I'm so nauseous. I'm really not cut out for this at all. I better go,"—and left for the van. As quickly as

I could, I pulled away from the crowd of cops and turned the car back toward home, feeling as if I'd just gotten away with something naughty. One hand on the wheel, I pulled out my phone and speed-dialed Will. I told him what I'd found at the comic book shop.

"Ronnie? Why would anyone kill Ronnie?" He sounded dazed.

"I have no idea. I know this sounds stupid, but did Ronnie have any enemies?"

"No. Well, I don't know. He just joined the pack; I barely knew him."

"Okay, well...um...Give it some thought. I might come around later today with that cop to ask you more about him."

"Yeah. I gotta find his family..." He wasn't really listening anymore, so I said a polite good-bye and hung up.

The sky was getting light by the time I pulled into my parking garage, and Molly would be dead to the world. Pun intended. I decided not to wake her. Maybe I could grab a couple hours of sleep while I waited for Cruz. But when I finally peeled off my clothes and climbed into bed, my mind was spinning too fast for sleep. I was thinking about the clearing in the woods and the dumpster. It had to be the same killer. Aside from the obvious connection— Ronnie had been at the first crime scene and was the victim at the second—both murders had the same feeling of cruelty and anger, and a null had been present at both scenes. I could understand wanting to kill Abraham to hurt Dashiell, and I could even understand killing the other two vamps to throw off the scent. But why kill Ronnie? It served no real purpose. Ronnie wasn't powerful or useful or a good tool to hurt someone. He was just a werewolf, low on the totem pole. Then I realized how Ronnie could be connected to the killings.

Through me.

Chapter 18

As soon as the thought struck me, I was doubtful, figuring it was either paranoia or just self-involvement. But the idea nagged at me. Finally, I put on my bathrobe and went downstairs to make a pot of coffee, sitting down at the table to think. I had been summoned to do the cleanup at both scenes. But in both cases, the police had arrived at the scene very quickly, way too soon for me to do anything except maybe get caught holding the bag. It isn't unheard-of for the cops to simply get to a crime scene before I do—once in a while a crime scene doesn't get reported to my employers, so they can't call me in. At that point, a whole different set of strings has to be pulled by Dashiell, and I'm out of that side of it.

But they'd been too fast. Ronnie's blood had still been all fresh and drippy. Cruz had told me that he happened to be close to La Brea Park when that call came in; otherwise the cops would have been a few minutes later, right when I was up to my elbows in blood. I picked up the phone and dug Cruz's card out of my wallet.

"Cruz."

"Hey, it's Scarlett."

"I'm going to be a while still. We're talking to neighbors—"

"It's fine. Listen, can you find out how the police found the body? I mean, how did you guys know there was a body?"

"Oh, easy. There's an all-night Starbucks a few blocks away. A couple reported hearing screams as they were walking in the door.

Then an anonymous caller also phoned it in fifteen minutes later, must have heard the same thing."

"What time was the first call?"

"Let me check." There was a pause, and I waited. "Three fourteen exactly. Took the cops seven minutes to get there."

I thanked him and hung up, then sent a text to Will: *What time was text from Ronnie, exactly?*

There wasn't an immediate answer, so I used the bathroom and threw on some sweats. I wasn't going to be sleeping anytime soon, and I was determined to go for a run today. After a moment's hesitation, I dug out my old fanny pack and put the Taser inside. Better to be alive than to be fashionable, I always say. When I checked again, the phone was blinking. Will had kept it short and sweet: *3:17.*

I spent a few minutes stretching, then I left Molly's house at a light jog. The sky was overcast, which had made sunrise more or less pointless, but I knew the route and could have run it in a blackout. I pelted down the hill by Molly's house, heading for my usual big loop, but my mind was on the case. Ronnie's murder had happened at 3:14, but the text from Ronnie's phone came three minutes *later*, which meant that it must have been from the killer. He or she had wanted me to get to the scene but hadn't realized that Ronnie's screaming had alerted other people, who called the cops. The killer gave me fifteen minutes to get there and then called the police himself. I felt a quick burst of that escaped-death kind of adrenaline—if the Starbucks couple hadn't called the cops, and I'd been at home on the West Side instead of in Orange County, I would have beat the cops to the scene by just a couple of minutes. Again.

"It's me," I said out loud, panting. Without really deciding to, I had slowed to a walk and then stopped. But why me? Had I pissed someone off so much that they wanted me in jail? Maybe someone wanted to expose the whole Old World and figured I'd sing like a canary if I got arrested? Well, he was wrong there—if the cops ever caught me, I'd make up a story and do my time. Dashiell would never let me breathe a word about the Old World to the cops, Jesse excluded. I thought about how horrible Ronnie had looked, the welts on his skin. Someone wanted to pin that on me?

I leaned forward, resting my hands on my knees. Welts on his skin. Whoever had killed Ronnie—and I was assuming it was a human, because there was no other reason to use a null—must have subdued him with the null, then tied him up with the silver and sent the null away. With that many silver chains, the killer could have basically laid the chains on top of a werewolf in either form and completely immobilized his victim. Ronnie, panicked and desperate, would have made the painful switch back to wolf form, which is what the werewolves tend to do when they get cornered. It must have hurt like hell, especially covered in silver. That's how Ronnie's teeth were pulled out. Then, by command or on his own, the null came back, and Ronnie had switched back to human, where he died. Or, I realized, the null might not have come back, but the bad guy could have killed Ronnie. The thing about werewolves changing back to human when they die, that's actually true. But it takes a *lot* to kill a werewolf, even with silver chains.

People were starting to stare at me, standing dead still in running clothes, panting heavily, so I moved back into a light jog, heading home. I was picturing those chains in my head. They'd been shiny and untarnished, either brand-new or very well taken care of. Where do you *get* chains like that?

As soon as I got home, I called Will—I can never tell whether he's one of those people who can wake up instantly and sound fine on the phone or if he just doesn't sleep, but he answered—and asked him. Not only did he not know, but he was offended that I might think he'd keep that kind of thing around. Will takes pride in not having to beat the crap out of his wolves to maintain his power, the way that some alphas do. I wanted to ask Dashiell the same question—he, unlike Will, would have no qualms with tying up a belligerent werewolf—but it was seven in the morning, and I couldn't wait the entire day to talk to him. I was running out of time.

Back at Molly's, I took a quick shower and put on a T-shirt and underwear. As I was digging through my dresser for clean jeans, I called Cruz and left a simple message for him to call me as soon as possible. Giving up on the jeans—laundry had not been a priority this week—I paced the room a little and plopped down on the bed. I wanted to bounce my idea off someone, but I was pretty much stuck until Cruz finished up at the crime scene.

I didn't mean to close my eyes, but at that point, I'd been awake for almost twenty-four hours for the second time that week, and even all the coffee and the adrenaline couldn't keep my exhausted body conscious. As I drifted off, I felt a muted jolt of fear that I would dream of the clearing. I shouldn't have worried, though; instead, I dreamed of Olivia once again.

It was the smirking, pre-cancer Olivia, as she'd been when we first met. In my dream, she was so real, so present, her chestnut hair drifting loose from its bun and her heavy jewelry clinking on her chest. We walked along the beach, and though we didn't speak, I could feel Olivia radiating that unique sense of purpose. Next to her, I felt ungainly and inexperienced, a colt trying to keep up with its graceful mother. We were heading toward something, two figures in the distance. When we got close, I realized it was my mom and dad, who both rushed to greet Olivia, ignoring me. Olivia pulled out a knife, grinned at me, and in one long swipe, slit both of my parents' throats. Then, with blood covering them, all three danced off into the distance, leaving me behind.

The nightmare woke me up at seven forty-five, less than an hour after I'd drifted off. The first thing I felt as my eyes opened was the loss, all over again, like when you fall and the ground rushes up to meet your face. I curled up into a ball and took a few sobbing gasps. I struggled to get my breathing under control.

"Scarlett?"

I jumped about four feet in the air, leaping off the bed and backing into the corner farthest from the doorway before I realized what I was doing.

Cruz was standing there, a tentative smile dying on his face. "Whoa, sorry. I'm sorry. The door was open, and I saw your van. I got worried when you didn't answer. Are you okay?" He took a step forward, hands lifting to touch me, but stopped.

Good instinct. Anger rushed through me like an electric current—anger and fear and grief, all braided together. I counted to ten, still panting, and as soon as I'd calmed a little, I realized that I was wearing a clingy T-shirt, underwear, and nothing else. *Fantastic.*

He looked down at me at the same time I did, and I heard him take in a breath. "Um, sorry, I—"

"Turn around," I yelped.

He spun. "Sorry! I'm sorry!"

I yanked open the top dresser drawer and pulled out a bra, then scooped a pair of less-than-clean jeans off the floor.

When I was dressed, I said, "Okay. You can look."

"God, Scarlett, I'm sorry, I didn't mean to stare," Cruz said, pivoting. "Are you all right?"

"I'm fine. Please don't sneak up on me again. Breaking and entering is still a crime for cops, you know." My voice came out frosty.

He just said, "Sorry. But I got your message. I thought we should talk."

"Just...Meet me in the kitchen, okay?"

He left, and I took a deep breath, sitting back on the bed. Less than twenty-four hours to deadline. I didn't have time to be rattled.

When I couldn't stall anymore, I jerked my fingers through my hair, pulling it into a ponytail, and went down to the kitchen. Cruz had figured out the coffeemaker and was opening cupboard doors to find a mug. I skirted him to get to the right cupboard, next to the sink, and pulled out two of Molly's kitschy Hollywood souvenir mugs. He didn't ask for cream or sugar, and I didn't offer. We just sat down at the kitchen table, black coffee in front of us, and I began to talk.

I started with the crime scene and what I'd noticed about the silver. Then I told him about the timing of the whole thing, how it almost seemed designed to hurt me. By then I was beginning to doubt myself, wondering again if sleep deprivation had just gotten the better of me, but he looked very thoughtful, nodding. "What about you?" I said finally. "Have you learned anything?"

"I got stuck doing interviews with people in the area, and then I had reports and stuff. I gotta get back to the official investigation, but I did call San Diego to get James Rucker's alibi. He checks out."

I sipped the coffee. "Okay…"

"I also swung by Thomas Freedner's place, but he wasn't home. Guy has a crappy rental in Studio City, and there was no sign of life. I went around, peeked in the windows. Everything was neat as a pin, hardly looked lived-in."

"What does that mean?"

He shrugged. "Might mean nothing. The guy could just be neat. Or maybe he left town, like the other human servants. I'll keep trying, but meanwhile, I also had an idea, along the same line as yours. It's about where those chains came from."

"I told you, I'm on it. But I don't know what else to do until Dashiell wakes up. It'd be different if I had the actual chains, but I don't suppose you want to steal them from police evidence, right?"

"No, no." He waved his hand dismissively. "But I had another idea. There can't be that many people who make restraints out of pure silver."

"No, I wouldn't think so."

"Well, then maybe the chains came from the same place as those handcuffs, the ones that your friend was...um...wearing. Maybe if we figured out where those came from, we could figure out where the chains came from."

"Yeah, but I already know the cuffs were Dashiell's, and he's..." I paused, and an idea sparked in my head. "Okay, you're onto something. What time is it?"

He checked his watch. "Seven forty-five."

"Let me make some calls. If I can get the handcuffs from Eli, I can trace them to their maker."

He looked puzzled. "How?"

"Well, I know a pretty good witch. And she can probably get the morning off."

Chapter 19

Cruz had to get back to the precinct, so I had to go see Kirsten by myself. He'd been unhappy about my going alone, but I'd just scoffed at him. I've been alone with Kirsten many times, and though witches sometimes give me the willies, they can't actually hurt me. Not with spells, anyway. Besides, I didn't have her permission to bring a civilian cop—not an oxymoron here, trust me—over for spell time, and of all the Old World creatures, the witches take that kind of thing the most seriously. Historically, witches and law enforcement have not been good bedfellows.

First, though, I had to go by Eli's and get the handcuffs, which he'd taken home with him, probably to dispose of. I was really hoping he hadn't gotten that far.

Eli's apartment is down in Santa Monica, three blocks from the ocean. It's a ramshackle old adobe building, the kind that's "decorated" with that dingy-seashell look. I parked illegally behind the building's dumpster and climbed three floors of outdoor stairs to knock on Eli's door.

"Hey," he called from below me. I stepped away from the door and peered down the alley. Eli was walking toward his apartment, wearing a wetsuit and carrying a surfboard. He looked as happy and relaxed as I'd ever seen him, at least outside of my radius.

"Hey, yourself," I said back. It was too quiet for humans to hear, but he wasn't human—yet.

He started up the stairs with an easy loping grace that only slowed down as he hit my radius. I'd never really noticed Eli's natural, non-lycanthropic athleticism, which is a shame, since I am the only one who really could.

He climbed the last few stairs and grinned at me, seawater still dripping from his damp hair. "What's the occasion?" he said lightly. "Just here for another quickie?" His voice was teasing, but there was a flicker of hurt on his face, and I felt ashamed again.

Dammit. Eli was the worst three-night stand ever.

"Actually, I'm wondering if I can borrow those handcuffs, the silver ones. They could be helpful for this case."

He frowned at me. "Come in and tell me about it."

I followed him into the small apartment, plopping down on his ancient threadbare sofa and curling my legs up around me. I'd never been there in the daytime—unless you count sneaking out with a hangover in the morning—and I'd never really paid much attention to Eli's habitat. It was kind of messy, which was no surprise, but it was kind of nice, too. There was a lot of ocean stuff on the walls, shells and sand dollars and twists of driftwood. In one corner, a little card table was set up with some carving tools and a big chunk of driftwood. I stood up and wandered over. There was the beginning of a boat carved onto one side of the wood, and it made the wood itself look exactly like waves of the ocean.

"You did this?" I asked.

"Don't sound so surprised, Scarlett," he said wryly. "I can do more than pour drinks."

"Yeah, I know," I said lamely. I put the driftwood down.

"Okay, so explain to me why you want the handcuffs."

I started to tell him about Ronnie and the silver chains. While I talked, Eli stowed his surfboard in the front closet and dried his hair with a towel.

"Ronnie?" he said incredulously, when I had finished. "That's so crazy. Who would do something like that?" He unzipped the back of his wetsuit, pulling it down around his waist.

I tried not to stare. Jesse is prettier, but Eli is no slump, werewolf or not. Muscled chest, just enough hair to not be too much, strong back—

"Uh, Scarlett?"

My eyes flew back to his face, and I blushed like a teenager.

"I'm up here." He touched his right eye, mockingly. "Besides, it's nothing you haven't seen before."

"But now I'm sober," I said without thinking. Then I shook my head to clear it. Jeez, Scarlett. Focus. "Anyway, I'm gonna have Kirsten do a tracking spell with the cuffs, if you just let me borrow them."

"Sure," he said easily, tossing the towel over his shoulder. "But I'm going with you."

My irritation overpowered my fleeting lust, and I scowled up at him.

He just shrugged. "I know you think Kirsten's trustworthy, but there is someone out there who wants to get to you, and what kind of assistant would I be if I let that happen?" I opened my mouth to argue with him, but he shook his head, suddenly serious. "I mean it, Scarlett. I'm coming, or you can't have the handcuffs. Forget... whatever this thing is between you and me. Will would kill me if I let you get hurt."

We stared at each other for a moment while I weighed my options, but it didn't seem as if I had any. Finally, I sighed and nodded.

"Good. So I'm gonna jump in the shower quick, and then we can go," he said, starting toward the bathroom. Then he stopped and looked back at me. Huge grin. "Unless you'd care to join me?"

Oops. My eyes may have wandered again. I turned red again and shook my head.

While Eli was showering, I did a quick search of the living room and kitchen, trying to find the damn cuffs so I could just go. When that didn't work, I plopped back down on the couch and called Kirsten.

If Will is an alpha and Dashiell a king, Kirsten is more like a publicist. The witches used to be completely disorganized, for the simple reason that they're all very different. As I'd told Jesse, witches, vampires, and werewolves are all descended from the same human conduits, but the witches are from a branch that used as little magic as possible, which varied from witch to witch. So some of them have just a little specific magic, and some, like Kirsten, are actually really powerful. With such different talents and personalities, I can guarantee that if you got every single witch in Los Angeles into one huge room, they would not be able to agree on anything, even something as basic as whether magic is good or evil. Of course, the biggest conflict between them is almost always the question of offensive magics. Olivia explained it to me like this: After the vampires, the werewolves, and the witches split off from the same line, they were scattered peacefully across the globe for centuries, each mostly disregarding the others. But in the Middle Ages, the witches, who by nature did the most interacting with normal humans, began to be discovered. And then persecuted, and tortured, and murdered.

Their leaders went to the vampires and the wolves and begged for help, but both groups turned away, the vampires from apathy and the wolves from fear of meeting the same fate. Wolves are pack animals, and look after their pack before anything else. So the witches did the only thing they could: they looked to strengthen their magic. They didn't know about evolution and magical lines back then, but during their research, the witches managed to stumble upon a group of plants that magic had bonded itself to, just like the human conduits. They were known as nightshades: belladonna, mandragora, *Lycium barbarum* (which also became known as wolfberry), tomatillo, cape gooseberry flower, capsicum, and solanum. The entire subspecies was rife with magic. The latter four plants could be used in hundreds of charms and potions, many of which helped the witches to deter the human persecutors. But the former three plants were unique; they interacted with the remaining magical beings in mystifying ways. Belladonna was poisonous to vampires—it took unbelievable amounts to actually kill them, but even a sprinkle of the plant would work as a paralytic. Proximity to wolfberry caused the shifters to lose control, painfully unable to stop from changing, again and again, which was very dangerous to anyone nearby. And mandragora, also called mandrake, was the key ingredient in a spell that could grant a very powerful witch the ability to communicate between living and dead. Which is how I ended up disposing of that naked guy's body in Culver City, all those years ago.

This discovery was your classic Pandora's box scenario. A small group of witches, furious that the vampires and the wolves had abandoned them during their darkest time, began to use wolfberry and belladonna against them—sometimes without much provocation. The balance of power shifted once again, and while the witches' discovery didn't cause a full-out war, it did spawn thousands of skirmishes, minor battles breaking out between the three major factions. Eventually, the use of those herbs was "outlawed" in the Old World, but it was done the way that marijuana has been outlawed in the US—basically, don't get caught. The witches are always arguing about this among themselves; some of them think it should be open season, and others think the ban should be more strictly enforced.

But while they may not be able to pull together a majority vote, in Los Angeles Kirsten has organized the witches into sort of an informal union. I know it sounds crazy, but if actors and directors can have unions in this town, why not witches? As I understand it, the real benefit to joining the union is access: to chat rooms, news-letters, support groups, spell sessions—and me.

The witches' dues pay Kirsten a small salary, and she uses the rest to organize the network and pay me. There are plenty of "non-union" witches in LA, too, ones who either haven't heard about the group or don't want to be a part of it. Kirsten has to deal with their messes, too, because a public witch problem is every witch's problem.

By night, Kirsten Harms-Dickerson is the most powerful known witch in Los Angeles, but by day, she's a chirpy, polite-but-firm receptionist at one of the bigger talent agencies. Well, techni-cally, she's a receptionist, but really, she's more of a gatekeeper, keeping the crazies out and the beautiful people in. She was out for a run when I called, but she picked up the phone anyway. Kirsten always answers. I explained the problem—without mentioning my impending execution—and she said she could easily go into work a few hours late.

Breathless and panting, she said, "Does this have anything to do with that La Brea Park...thing?" That was surprising. Someone was keeping Kirsten in the loop, for once.

"Actually, yeah."

"No problem. I already told Dashiell I would help however I could. Give me half an hour, and come on over."

Eli volunteered his truck, but we took my van, because you never know when you're gonna get called to a crime scene, and because it has GPS. Kirsten's neighborhood is beautiful, if you go for that charming fifties suburbia thing. The lawns are mani-cured, children run from house to house with a secure sense of joint ownership, and cute medium-sized dogs bark playfully from behind honest-to-goodness white picket fences. We drove with the windows down, and I could hear a sharp metallic *crack* coming from the community ballpark on the next street. It's all very Kirsten, who makes Elizabeth Montgomery look like an evil hag.

When Eli and I arrived, I didn't have to do ding-dong-ditch. (There's a *Wizard of Oz* joke in there somewhere.) I only inhibit Kirsten when she's actively opened her connection to magic, so if she's not using it, being near me won't bother her. Although, for whatever reason, I can still feel an inactive witch in my radius, like a soft white noise that's always buzzing.

Kirsten opened the door still in her spotless Nike running clothes, her white-blonde hair pulled into a bun. "Hello, Scarlett. It's nice to see you again, Mr. Glendon. I believe we met at one of the Trials two years ago, but of course, it's been so long."

She held out her hand, and Eli took it, glancing uncertainly at me. I smiled sweetly. Oh, this was going to be fun.

"Please come in, of course." She led us through a Pottery Barn living room and into her spacious kitchen, which was probably the only place in the house that gave away Kirsten's secret identity. Pots of every size and metal hung from a rack on the ceiling, more pots than any TV chef could dream of, and there was an enormous open pantry, a dozen feet high, that was devoted to herbs, preserved in identical spotless Tupperware jars with printed labels. I was tempted to look for the Big Three, but if Kirsten did have any, she wouldn't put them right out in the open.

She did have not one, but two different stone mortar-and-pestle sets on the large granite counter, and there was a small bookshelf above the sink that was crammed with books that had no titles. "Paul, my husband, is playing golf this morning, which leaves the house open for us. May I see the object, please?"

Eli glanced at me and, at my nod, handed over the insulated lunch bag where he'd stashed the cuffs. Given his "allergy," I'd offered to carry them, but he'd insisted on doing it himself. Probably thought I'd ditch him and go see Kirsten alone.

Probably right.

Kirsten peeked inside and bit her lip thoughtfully. "I see what you mean, Scarlett. I've certainly never seen anything like this, although you know we don't have much contact with the wolves." She smiled diplomatically at Eli, who looked as if he'd just taken a bite of a completely new and spicy food. I probably should have told him more about Kirsten, but come on, this was entertaining.

"Can you trace them?" I asked her. "Do you have a spell that will work?"

"I think so." Her eyes drifted to the books above the sink. "It won't go to the last owner, unfortunately, because Eli has had them for too long. But I can get you to their maker. It should take no more than a half hour, I believe, and of course, I'll have to ask you to step outside. Will your friend be staying in here or joining you outside?"

Her eyes looked directly into mine, and I understood the weight behind the question. This was the moment when I had to decide whether or not there was a chance that Kirsten was involved in this mess somehow. If she were on the bad guys' team, she couldn't hit either of us with a spell, not while Eli was close to me, but she could do any number of other things—lie about the cuffs' origins, pull out a gun and shoot us, call some co-bad guys to come kill us. If I said Eli would come with me, it was leaving us vulnerable. But if I left Eli with Kirsten, it was like saying that I didn't trust her, that I thought she was involved. Kirsten would not take that lightly, and she would not forget it.

I hate Old World politics, but I depend on them for my livelihood, so either way, the wrong choice could be terrible. I thought about the crime, about the violence and the use of a null, and I made my decision. "He'll come outside with me, thank you. We'll just wait on the porch."

She nodded as if nothing had happened and started to set out her spell things, which were still mystifying to me. In an effort to curb my ignorance, Kirsten once spent a whole afternoon talking to me about contagion magic and sympathetic magics and hermeticism, and we both finally had to conclude that I have absolutely no aptitude for understanding even the most basic witchcraft. Which makes sense, I guess, since nulls couldn't perform a spell if the *Fantasia* sorcerer himself jumped out of the TV and begged.

Eli and I declined her offer of soft drinks and trooped out to the porch. The only place to sit was the blue porch swing, so there was an awkward moment while I faked like I wanted to stand up, leaning against the side of the house. Eli rolled his eyes and sprawled out on the swing. "She's not what I expected," he said finally. "She's so..."

"Wholesome?"

"Yeah, I guess. I was picturing like a hippie with dreadlocks, or maybe a goth girl with Wiccan tattoos or something."

"I did, too, the first time I met her," I admitted. "She's probably the most powerful witch in the city, but she looks like, I don't know, the exasperated wife on a sitcom." I bit my lip.

Eli looked closely at my face. "Witches scare you a little, huh?"

I shrugged. "Kind of. I guess....Vampires I get, and werewolves. It's transformative magic, it's like a spell that changes you down to your cells, and it's permanent. Okay. But witches, they're human, with all the responsibilities of human society, but they have these powers at the same time. When a witch performs a spell in your presence, you're basically trusting that they're not willing your ears to fall off or your lungs to implode. It's a leap of faith, for most people, to even know a witch. It's not that I'm worried about my safety...But if I were human, I would be."

"What exactly is she doing in there?"

"A variation of a tracking spell. Sort of an origin spell, I guess."

He waved his hand impatiently. "No, I mean what exactly does that entail?"

"Uh, the only thing I really understand about it is that a witch doesn't actually *create* the magic. She pulls it out of the air, out of the energy in the world. The different ingredients in a specific order—the actual spells—they help direct or guide the magic to do what she wants it to."

"So when you're close to witches, it's pretty much the same thing as when you're close to us, right? They become human within your range?"

I nodded.

"But there used to be other things, too, right? Elves and fairies and crap like that? What happens when you get close to them?" I looked at him for a beat, and he shrugged defensively. "Shut up. I know things."

I was swaying on my feet, still exhausted, so I finally gave in and perched next to him on the swing. He moved over to make room, and I tried to relax. "I've heard about them, from Olivia." Her name tasted bad in my mouth. "As far as I know, those things were spirits of magic, the Original beings, and they all died out when conduits—your ancestors—evolved."

I looked over at him, and was surprised at the look on his face. It was...sad and far away, and I could guess what he was thinking about. "Eli...How did you change?"

This was a very personal question, like asking how someone lost their virginity, only bigger, and I regretted it right away. But Eli answered me.

"I was a paramedic, in New York," he said matter-of-factly. "I grew up in Manhattan, my mom and dad were there, and I...I was at the Twin Towers when they fell. I was working to free this woman. She was maybe forty, and she was trapped under a concrete post. She couldn't get an angle to get out, so I was trying to clear some debris. I knew that I wasn't strong enough, and my radio was dead, but I couldn't just walk away. Then the floor above us came down."

His fingers tightened on the porch swing, and as I watched, his face just shut down. He was remembering. "A steel rod pierced me in my torso, and I was dying, right there next to this lady. The collapse had moved the concrete post, though, and she'd actually wriggled out, even with all the crap on top of us. I couldn't believe her strength."

I understood. "She was a werewolf."

"Yes. She felt bad for me, I guess. She bit me, on the shoulder, and pulled out the steel rod, and she left me. I never saw her again." He sat up suddenly in his chair, shrugging. "That's about it."

But it wasn't. It takes about two days to turn into a werewolf— two days of agony. "How long were you trapped, Eli?"

He looked away. "Four days."

"Your parents?"

He shook his head. "Gone."

I struggled for something to say and came up with "You don't look old enough to have been a paramedic that long ago." He looked maybe twenty-eight.

He gave me a little smile. "I was twenty-three then. But you know we age slower than humans."

"Yeah. Are you..." I began, then stopped. This was none of my business.

"Am I what?" he asked. "Am I sorry she bit me?"

I nodded. "I mean, I know you don't like being a werewolf." Werewolves age more slowly than humans—average lifetime is something like one hundred fifty years. He would be stuck this way for a long time.

He looked tired. "I don't. But I'm not sorry to be alive, even if it's like this. Even if it hurts."

We were quiet for a while after that.

By the time Kirsten popped open the front door, I had nodded off on Eli's shoulder, and a little line of drool was making its way down my chin.

"Come on in, guys," Kirsten sang, cheerful. "I've got an address for you." She turned back into the house, leaving the door open behind her.

I stood up unsteadily, wiping my mouth with the back of my hand and blushing like crazy. Eli stretched his arms behind his head, smirking at me. "You're so cute when you sleep. All innocent-like."

"Shut up."

He held up his hand, waving it at me, and I rolled my eyes and reached down to pull him up. He stood up inside my personal space, on purpose, to make me blush even more. God help me, it worked. I met his eyes, only four inches from my own, and he didn't back down one bit. He looked at me, a long, searching look, until I lost my nerve and darted toward the front door.

No witch's supply cabinet is complete without herbs, a cauldron, and...a Thomas guide. Back in her kitchen, Kirsten pulled out the book of Los Angeles street maps and opened it to a section in Van Nuys. "Okay, so the locator spell took me back to where these handcuffs were made—cast? Would we say they were cast?"

Eli and I looked up and shrugged. Not so much with the grammar.

"Okay, well, anyway, they were made here"—she pointed to a tiny pen mark—"in this little block. I copied out the address." She passed over a perfectly formatted Post-it note.

"One more thing," I began, "Olivia mentioned...Well, is it possible that the vampires in La Brea Park were under a spell? Is there a spell that has the same result as being around a null?"

I hadn't realized until that moment how much I hoped she would say yes. If this were all due to some psychotic witch...But Kirsten shook her head, smiling in a patient way that I interpreted as *No hard feelings about accusing my witches of murder.*

"We can't take away magic, Scarlett. We can move it around, funnel it into doing things, but we can't actually take it away."

Couldn't argue with that.

Chapter 20

Jesse was torn. Should he keep his nose down and dig into the grunt work that the scene reconstruction guys had given him, or go pursue leads that he knew were valid and important? Jerry Lexington, the detective in charge of recreating the scene, had given him a stack of files relating to La Brea Park: all previous complaints or crimes committed in the area, the history of the park, the history of the land before it became a park, the biography of the guy who had donated the land, and so on. The stack was three inches of printouts and photos, and Jesse was frustrated and bored just looking at it. Chewing on his lip, he flipped to the middle of the folder on top, smudging the papers around on his desk.

An hour later, Jesse knew he was in trouble the moment he heard his name. Of course, it didn't help that when Miranda called for him, he was half-asleep, his head propped up on his hand. Not a great way to prove that he was working hard.

He took a big chug of the Mountain Dew on his desk, then stood up and trudged toward Miranda's office, wondering how bad this was going to be.

"Sit down, Jesse," she said briskly, waving toward the chair across from her desk.

Miranda's iron-gray hair was a little disheveled, and tiredness and stress had seeped into her face. Jesse sat carefully on the edge of the chair, noting the folded-up *LA Times* on her desk. The head-line screamed, *Park Massacre Baffles LAPD.* He winced.

"We need to have a conversation about your work performance," Miranda said sternly. "You know that this investigation is critical, and the pressure from the media is building every day."

"Yes, ma'am." He did his best to look contrite, but couldn't help feeling a little crushed. He was actually working his ass off on this case, coming up with leads nobody else would dream of, and to everyone on the force, he looked like a slacker. Jesse considered himself a good team player, not at all a glory hound, but come on. If he got demoted over this case, he wouldn't know whether to laugh or cry.

Miranda was just getting started. "I've got everyone working overtime, we're chasing down every stray thought any one of us even has, and even though there's plenty of exhaustion, everyone seems on top of their game—except you. You're distracted and secretive, and the duty officer said she had trouble finding you yesterday. And is it true that you *fell asleep* during the briefing this morning?"

Jesse flinched with guilt. The department was doing twice-daily briefings on the case, and though he'd tried to pay attention, it was just hard to be all that interested when he knew that every lead the police were pursuing was a dead end. There was a mountain of forensics paperwork piling up, all of it saying nothing at all, and theory after theory was being methodically shot down. The department had spent the last two days considering the possibility of gang violence, a serial killer, a crime of passion, everything. They'd been running in circles trying to at least identify the victims and making no progress at all. Jesse, on the other hand, knew all three victims' identities but wasn't able to speak up. It was so *frustrating.*

"Ma'am, I—"

"Stop." Miranda held up a hand. "I don't want to know. Family problems, new girlfriend, new boyfriend, you have a cold, the sun was in your eyes, whatever. I don't care. I just need to know whether or not you're able to perform your job."

"Yes, ma'am."

"Good. Then get your act together, stop dithering about, and do some police work." She picked up a file on her desk, flipping over the top page. "You're supposed to be going through old murder cases, correct?"

"Yes, ma'am. We're trying to determine whether this killing follows the pattern of any established killers, in case it's a repeat performance or a copycat. There's just nothing—so far."

Because the victims were vampires, and the killer was working with a null, and the closest thing to a witness was a werewolf who'd also been murdered. Jesse felt sluggish and stupid, as if he'd been torn in half and all the brain cells had gone to the half that was working in the Old World now. It was a good thing he'd never been chosen for undercover, he thought sourly. A suspicious drug dealer would have shot him in about three minutes.

"Nothing?" she said skeptically, as if he were pulling her leg.

"We've been through all the databases. I'm back to reviewing scene reconstructions and typing up interview reports."

Miranda was silent for a moment, thinking. "Why don't you take a closer look at the park," she said finally. "See if there's a pattern of violence anywhere."

"Yes, ma'am." He stood up to leave.

"And, Jesse?"

He turned back.

"If you can't get your act together, I can't use you."

Chapter 21

I needed to call Cruz and update him on the case, but I felt awkward about doing it in front of Eli. Especially since Eli was pissed about not being invited along to confront the handcuff maker. He did not like that I was going with Jesse instead.

"Who is this guy, anyway? What can he do that I can't?" Eli said hotly.

We were driving back to Eli's, where I would be dropping him off. Traffic had stalled on PCH, and I was working on a grating headache.

"I don't know. Arrest people? Investigate things? How about just carrying a gun?" I didn't mention the fact that I'd never had drunken sleepovers with Cruz, because there's just never a great moment to bring that up.

"That's bullshit. I may not have a badge, but I can protect you just as easily as he can."

I pounded one fist on the steering wheel. "I don't need to be protected, goddammit! I'm not some damsel tied to a railroad track; I can take care of myself. I'm strong and I'm fast, and nothing with claws or fangs can touch me anyway."

"Railroad tracks?"

I threw up my hands, which would have been dangerous if we weren't at a standstill. "Ugh! You know, those old movie serials where the evil guy with the big black mustache would tie up some girl and leave her on the railroad tra—why am I explaining this to you? The point is, I don't need a rescue."

He started to argue again, and with some regret, I pulled out my werewolf card. "Look, Eli, this guy's place is going to be full of silver. If you take one step too far away from me, you could have another horrible reaction and almost die again. Remember how fun that *wasn't*?"

He went silent, but still looked stubborn.

I hammered in my last nail. "If I have to spend the whole time being careful of you," I said, "you'll just slow me down."

Defeated, Eli turned to look out his window. "Fine," he said quietly, to the view of the Pacific Ocean. "The last thing I wanna do is slow you down."

We didn't speak the whole rest of the way to his place. In the silence, I found myself thinking about the first time I'd gone home with him, three months earlier. It had been my mother's birthday, although I never told him or anyone else that. My brother, Jack, hadn't called, and I hadn't gotten up the courage to call him. I couldn't stand the thought of being alone that night, and Molly had gone hunting, so I went out drinking alone. I could have called Jack or tried to rustle up some of my old high school friends, but I hadn't spoken to any of my friends in years, and Jack was the last person I wanted to see. I didn't want to play the happy remembering game with him, especially considering he still didn't know that I was responsible for her death, and my father's.

I had just wanted to drink.

I'd gone to Hair of the Dog by myself. I could have—should have—gone to a normal human bar within cheap cab distance from Molly's, but the truth was, I wanted to punish myself. I wanted the stares, the curiosity, the dirty or eager looks. I wanted to feel what I was, and know what it had cost me. It was a Wednesday night, but Hair of the Dog is always crowded, and it took a while to get a table. After about twenty minutes, some nervous-looking weres got up and scooted away from me, forsaking their little booth in a dark corner of the bar. I swooped in and got it, and crooked a finger at the bartender.

He was tall and blond, with a lot of muscle that was more lean than big, like a swimmer. He was wearing jeans and a Hair of the Dog T-shirt, along with a smudged white bar towel flung over his shoulder. Despite being two whiskeys in, with no food in my stomach, I was paying close attention when he hit my radius. Sure enough, he was a were. He didn't even slow down when he turned human, but a brief look of bliss flew across his face. Ah. One of those.

"We don't usually do table service, Miss Bernard."

"You know who I am?" My voice was still strong and clear, I noted with satisfaction. Although my question was dumb.

"Of course." He gave me a kind of polite *duh* look. I'm like one of those rich society girls—ridiculously famous in certain circles but only for stupid reasons.

"Well, then you know that every time I get up and move around, it makes people nervous. And I am here to serioshly drink." Whoops. Had I just said "serioshly"? "So maybe you could make an exception just this once," I added carefully.

"Fair enough," he said easily. "What are you drinking?"

"Double shot of Irish whiskey. Rocks. Please." It was my mother's drink. My father was something like seven-eighths Irish—his mother had come to America from Galway—but he hated the taste of whiskey. My mother's people were from Eastern Europe, but it was her absolute favorite. They'd met at an Irish pub in LA, and their first conversation was about whiskey.

When Eli brought me my fourth drink, he wouldn't hand it over without getting my keys in exchange. When I asked for my fifth, he brought over a cheeseburger and fries instead and promised me that I could drink more as soon as I ate them. By the time I asked for number six, the bar had emptied out and he was wiping down the tables. I could have walked over to the bar to get it, but I wasn't very confident in my ability to walk straight. So I just yelled across the empty bar. "Barkeep! More whiskey!"

Eli tossed down his towel and went behind the bar, coming back with a big mug of coffee instead. He set it down in front of me and then dropped down into the opposite seat. "Eli. My name is Eli." He pointed to the name tag pinned to his chest, tucking in his chin to see it. "See? It's right here. Eli."

"Eli, this is not what I ordered," I said.

"Drink this instead. Then I'll call you a cab."

"Make you a deal," I said, only slushing the words a little. When I get drunk, the ability to speak is the last skill I retain. Don't ask me why. "I will drink thish coffee if you go pour yourself a whiskey. But it has to be a double, or it don't count."

He looked at me for a long moment, then sighed and scooted out of the booth. He came back with the drink and resumed his post across from me.

"On three," I commanded. I was working pretty hard to get all of the pesky syllables. "One, two, three."

We both stared at each other suspiciously, then took a sip of our respective drinks.

"So," Eli said when we'd set our glasses back down, "do you want to talk about it?"

"About what?"

"Whatever is making you sad."

I thought about that for a second. "What's in it for you?"

"Pardon?" he said, taken aback.

"Are you hoping to hang out in my little circle of peace for a little bit longer, or trying to get laid, or what?"

"No," he said, and there was enough surprise in his voice that I relaxed a little bit. "You just looked like you could use a friend."

"Well, I don't. Friends are for suckers." I took another sip of the coffee and pointed to his drink, which he sipped dutifully. "Tell me about what you did today instead."

So he did. He had slept late, gone surfing, and cooked himself dinner. He talked about surfing with a dreamy look on his face, the way some runners talk about running as though it's the greatest drug the world has ever known. He didn't mention that it helps him tame his inner wolf, too, but I figured that out myself. Then he asked me about what I'd done, which was equally boring, and I told him. Half an hour later, we'd moved to the bar, where he was finishing his second drink, me my second coffee. Since Eli hadn't had alcohol as a human in years—the wolves' tolerance is off the charts, to go with their metabolism, so they mostly don't bother drinking—he misjudged his safe number of drinks, and by the time he finished describing his plans for the weekend, we were more or less on an equal level of drunkenness. Which, on a scale of one to ten, was probably about a seven.

I can't remember who kissed whom first or when we left the bar. In fact, my next clear memory is of being in the back of a cab, kissing Eli with a need and a recklessness that scared even drunken me. We went to his apartment in Santa Monica, stumbling up the outdoor staircase and through the door. The second it was closed, he backed me against it, his lips on my neck, his hands sliding down my back, and I felt my body relax for the first time that day. When he cupped my ass and picked me up, it was the most natural thing in the world to wrap my legs around his waist, and then my memory gets a little fuzzy again.

The next morning, I woke up around five with a bad hangover and no idea where I was. The shower was running, presumably with Eli in it, and so I hastily threw on my clothes and scurried out of there like the coward I was. And I promised myself that I'd stay away from Hair of the Dog for like a year. Minimum.

Seven weeks later, it was my dad's birthday. And we did the same thing all over again.

And then, of course, there was two nights ago, when I had gone to Hair of the Dog specifically for Eli—although let's not kid ourselves; I was there for him the second time, too—who had eventually forgiven me for blowing off his calls (twice) and invited me home with him again. I'd been only a little tipsy that time, and it still scared me that I'd said yes. This time the sex was less frantic and carnal and more...tentative. Exploratory.

When we stopped at a light, I looked over at him and realized—not for the first time—that I barely knew him. Until tonight, I hadn't known that his parents were dead or that he was from New York. Hell, I didn't find out his last name; Kirsten had mentioned it.

What is *wrong* with me?

Eli didn't say anything when I dropped him off, just started climbing the stairs to his apartment. His back was straight, his chin up, but there was a sadness to his face that had me pressing down on the button to lower my window and call out to him. I could still fix this. Then I lifted my hand from the controls. What was I going to say? *I'm sorry? Let's go out on a date?* I sighed and put the van into reverse, backing away down the alley. Eli deserved someone much more stable than me, and dammit, I deserved someone who didn't just need me for my weird effect on the supernatural.

As usual, I ignored the little niggling voice that told me Eli had other reasons to want me.

Chapter 22

Miranda wanted results. Jesse forced himself back to Lexington's La Brea Park file, and managed to make it through about ten pages before he couldn't stand it any longer. He checked his watch, and decided to give himself ten minutes on the Old World side of the investigation.

When he was sure no one was watching, Jesse went back to the computer and ran a search on Thomas Freedner, the human servant of one of the dead vampires. According to Freedner's driver's license photo, the guy was the complete opposite of James Rucker: Freedner was twenty-five, whippet thin, and sported black eyeliner and pierced ears that had been stretched until they were big enough to contain one-inch metal washers. Freedner smirked at the camera, a five-foot-seven, 160-pound kid who seemed bigger because he felt bigger.

Freedner had four arrests, all for smoking or dealing pot. He had served time for the last two incidents and come out of prison with a T-rex tattoo and a massive chip on his shoulder. His last prison sentence—a three-year lockup for dealing pot to an undercover officer—had ended two months ago. Maybe Abraham had hooked up with James Rucker while Freedner was in jail.

The arrest record listed three known associates—two men and one woman. One of the men had been killed in a meth lab explosion two years earlier, and the other was back in prison, serving a ten-year sentence for assault. The woman, Janine Malaka, lived in a West Hollywood apartment. He copied down the address. Glancing around again, he picked up the phone. Scarlett answered on the fourth ring.

"Hey, it's me," he said quietly, trying to look businesslike.

"Cruz. I was just about to call you. I've got an address for the guy who made the specialty cuffs. Do you want to go see him?"

He looked at his watch: 10:15. The whole floor was bustling with cops, most looking tired or discouraged, a few still focused and intent. There was no way he was going to sneak out of there anytime soon.

"Can we wait until about lunchtime? I can get away for about an hour."

"An hour?" She sounded skeptical. "You understand that this is Los Angeles, right? It takes an hour to get out of my parking garage."

"I'll figure something out. Just give me the address."

She read him the address, and he did a reverse search on his computer. "Okay, computer says it's a…bait shop? Are you sure this is right?"

"Look at the map, Cruz. Who would put a bait shop in Van Nuys?"

He MapQuested the area, clicking the little minus button to figure out the context. She was right; the address was miles from the ocean. "Okay. Meet me there at one?"

"Fine." She abruptly hung up the phone, and Jesse wondered what had gotten her all pissed off.

He made a vending machine run and then dug back into the old reports on his desk—hard. If Miranda looked up from her desk, she would see him with his nose to the grindstone. At noon, he bounded down the stairs to forensics, running on Red Bull—he'd switched to the hard stuff—and adrenaline.

"Glory!" he sang, bursting into the lab.

Four different techs looked up, each one annoyed.

"Whoops," he said more quietly.

"Sorry about that, guys. He's like a puppy that won't heel," Glory said tiredly, coming up the lab's main aisle toward the doors. She was usually the night tech, but even forensics was working overtime on this case. Her ash-blonde hair looked wilted, and her makeup did little to hide the dark circles under her eyes. "In my office," she ordered, and Jesse trailed her toward a side door, feeling embarrassed. Her office was a tiny cube, with metal chairs and a cheap fake-wood desk. There were pictures of her children in a little folding frame near her mouse pad. "Sit," she said, and he sat. "Now, what is this about?"

"Can you cover for me for, like, two hours?"

Her face went from indignant to skeptical. "Cover for you? Even if I were willing, how would I pull that off?"

"I don't know. Tell Miranda you need someone to collect more evidence, or that I was down here for the last hour picking your brain and then I went to lunch. Please? You're my only friend in this precinct." He batted his eyelashes at her theatrically.

Glory just shook her head, smiling faintly. "Don't you flirt with me, kid. I'm old enough to be your mother."

"No, you're not—" he protested.

She raised a hand. "Enough. Jesse, what is this about? A girl? That girl with the prints?"

"No. Well, yes, kind of. But it's about the case. I have this lead. I just can't...tell anyone about it." He fidgeted with his shirttail. That sounded lame, even to him.

"That makes absolutely no sense." She stifled a yawn. "Jesse, I'm exhausted. If you've got something, just tell Miranda. I need to get back to work."

"Look, I promised I wouldn't say anything about this lead, and if I go back on it...Well, people could get hurt."

"You're a cop, Jesse. You can't just promise your informants that you won't give information to other cops. That defeats the whole purpose."

Jesse squirmed in his seat. "Glory...It's not an informant thing. I just can't talk about it. Life and death, I promise."

She studied him for a few long minutes, then stood up, walked around her desk, and closed the door, leaning against it. "I'm gonna go out on a limb, here...Does this have anything to do with vampires?"

Despite all the time with Scarlett, the word *vampires* sounded gaudy and ridiculous coming from Glory. But she'd said it all the same.

Jesse's eyes boggled. "Uh...how did...?"

"I'll take that as a yes." Glory sighed, going back to sit down at her desk. "About seven, eight years ago, I was doing evidence on a homicide case where the victim was a teenage boy with two bite marks in his neck. The techs at the scene figured they were superficial; the kid was into playing cowboys and vampires, but the city morgue was backed up and the body came here for autopsy. It happens. They told us it would be hours until the ME could get here, so I happened to be alone here with the body when I got a visitor. Said his name was Dashiell."

Jesse took a sharp breath. "He's a really big deal, apparently."

"Apparently. Anyway, he told me that vampires were real and the teenager was probably going to rise from the dead, and if I didn't want to die, too, I should help him. Naturally, I went to the phone to call security, but he got there first. Just appeared on the other side of the room. He offered me a deal. If I went about my other work for an hour and nothing happened, I could call in the National Guard, for all he cared. But if it did, he said that I would want him there. And twenty minutes later...Well, he was right. I wanted him there."

Glory's chin was trembling, and Jesse reached across the desk to touch her hand. She squeezed his briefly and let go, scooting back in her chair. "I'd never seen anything like it, and I hope I never do again. Anyway, Dashiell said it might be useful to have someone like me know the truth, but I had to stay quiet. Before I could even respond to that, he asked me how Rob and Natalie were doing. He used their *names*, Jesse. He knew that Rob was in fourth grade, and Natalie in kindergarten. That was pretty much all I had to hear."

"What happened to the kid? The teenage vampire?" Jesse asked, caught up in the story.

She gave him a wry smile. "Well, that was the hard part. We figured the easiest thing would be to show that he was still alive. Pretend it was drug-related or something. Dashiell took him out to 'eat,' and then when they came back, I faked a migraine and went home. The kid laid back on the table, and when the ME showed up at four a.m., he was blinking and drooling, like he was shaking the effects of some crazy new street drug. Five people and the ME saw him walk out of this building, and nobody looked at me twice."

"Wow."

"Yeah, wow." Her voice was sarcastic, and Jesse thought of her two kids. It must have been terrifying, worrying that you'd slip and end up losing the people you loved most. "It was one of those urban legend autopsy stories for a few months; then everyone forgot about it."

"Did you ever hear from Dashiell again?"

"Once or twice a year, he calls, even now, asking me to 'accidentally' drop a blood sample on the floor or destroy the log for some piece of evidence. A tooth, once, of all things. He never mentioned Rob and Natalie again, but it's always there, between us. I haven't gotten caught yet, but even if I do, it's still worth it."

"I'm sorry, Glory."

"Yeah." She played with her plastic ID badge, looking unsettled. "Now, what's this about you and vampires?"

Jesse thought for a second. He'd been told very explicitly not to talk abut the Old World, but Glory already knew at least part of it, and he really needed her help. Besides, she'd told him her story. If she trusted him enough to risk her kids by telling him, then it was the least he could do. As quickly as he could, he sketched out the case so far: meeting Scarlett, learning that another null was involved, tracing the silver handcuffs, Freedner. When he got to the part about Dashiell accusing Scarlett of being involved, the color suddenly drained from Glory's face. "Oh, God."

"What? What's the matter?"

Her eyes filled with tears. "I helped him last night; I gave him photos of the victim's faces. I'm so sorry, Jesse, I had no idea..."

It took Jesse a minute to process it, that she was talking about the same photos Dashiell had shown Scarlett. "Oh, Glory, you couldn't have known."

She took a deep breath, trying to settle herself. "You're right, but I feel terrible, anyway. What I did got you guys in trouble with this...man."

"I understand, though," Jesse said, and despite himself, he did understand. He was fond of Rob and Natalie, and really, was what Glory had done any worse than what Scarlett did? *At least Glory has a good reason*, he thought. "Please, don't worry any more about it. If it wasn't you, he would have found out some other way."

She nodded, silently thanking him for the forgiveness. "I've never heard of a null. Well, I never heard of anything besides vampires, really, but I guess it makes sense." She frowned. "It would have been helpful for Dashiell to introduce me to this girl. Maybe we could have worked together."

"I think Dashiell plays his cards pretty close to the vest."

"Yeah, I guess." Glory stood up. "You better get going."

"Will—"

"Yeah. I'll cover." She bit her lip and then added, "But, Jesse? Watch your back. I know you like this girl, but I don't trust anyone from that world. You shouldn't, either."

Chapter 23

With time to kill before meeting Cruz, I had pulled away from Eli's neighborhood and decided to cruise the few miles to the Santa Monica Pier, parking the van in one of the public garages attached to the nearby mall. Three hours of free parking—yippee. I didn't have a towel or swimsuit or anything, but that was okay. I pulled a battered USC baseball cap out of the net pocket behind my seat, smeared a little sunscreen on my face, and began the hike to the pier.

This particular pier is sort of the dingy, sand-covered Disneyland of the Pacific Highway. It's a tourist trap, big-time, and most of the locals who visit are showing off their exaggerated sense of irony. I genuinely love it, though. The first time my parents took me to the city, I was six, and we drove down to the Santa Monica Pier and listened to a reggae band perform a free concert. I sat on my dad's shoulders, giggling and clutching his hair while he danced with my mom. She laughed and twirled in a blue cotton sundress with little pink flowers, her long dark hair swinging along behind her. This one memory has given the pier a free pass from me for life.

I trekked down Colorado Boulevard, onto the pier, and down the metal staircase that led to the beach itself. It was only in the high sixties, and nobody really sunbathes at Santa Monica anyway, so I had a good stretch of beach to myself. I picked my way past the seaweed and snail shells that the ocean had spit up and plopped down on the sand about ten feet from the water's farthest reach. I was wearing jeans and an ancient purple T-shirt that I keep in the back of the van for emergencies. I'd traded my practical sneakers for black flip-flops, and for the first time in days, I felt my body relax. I snuggled my head back into the sand and pulled the bill of my cap over my eyes. Thinking time.

My thoughts returned to Eli, and to males in general. My dating history isn't what you'd call great. My last real, normal boyfriend had been when I was eighteen. Jacob Riley. Jake had had a crush on me all of senior year and finally got up the courage to ask me out on graduation night. We spent the entire summer together, lost our virginities to each other, and by August, I knew that he and I were real, that it was a relationship that could truly go somewhere. My eighteen-year-old mind was dazzled by this revelation: this could be *the guy*.

Maybe there was an alternate universe somewhere where Jake and Scarlett were married and had babies right now. But in reality, our lives had both taken turns. By September, Jake had decided to scrap his college plans and join the air force. He cried when he kissed me good-bye in front of my car as I was packing it for college. We were going to try the long-distance thing for a while, kind of feel out whether or not we could make it. Two weeks later, though, my parents were dead, and Jake didn't exactly step up to the plate, boyfriend-wise. I got a sympathy card in the mail: *Warmest Regards, Jacob Riley.* He called once or twice after that, but I never called him back. By then I knew what I was, and the Scarlett who had loved Jake was as dead as her parents.

Since then, there'd been a sporadic string of one-night stands and dates that never numbered past three. Once a guy plumbed the depths of my trust issues, he never came back for more, and I was more than fine with that. That's what I wanted. But now there was Eli...And, if I were being honest with myself, there was also Jesse.

Yeah, Jesse was growing on me. He was charming and laid-back and had really taken the whole Old World news like a champ. He was great-looking, of course, and kind of bashful about it, which was adorable. And most importantly, something about him was just so genuinely *good*. That's the difference between him and Eli, or for that matter, him and me. Jesse was still untainted, and that was a little bit irresistible. He made me picture a world in which I was someone's normal girlfriend, with movie nights and dinner with his parents and spending the holidays together. And I had to admit, that picture was...nice.

Ugh.

I scrubbed my hands over my face, dislodging my hat. What was I thinking? Eli wanted me for my body, so to speak, and I was already more than halfway to getting Cruz killed. I needed to get this whole park massacre thing over with, get the boys out of my head, and get back to my life before I'd met Cruz. Maybe I had just been going through the motions, but at least no one had gotten killed because of me.

At twelve fifteen, I stood up and dusted myself off, doing my best to shake the sand out of my hair and pockets. Then I climbed the stairs to the pier and hiked back up to the van. Time to go to work.

Van Nuys is kind of the gateway to the San Fernando Valley. Most of LA is in a basin—called, creatively, the Los Angeles Basin—which forms a big backward letter *C*, with the ocean as the open part of the letter. Because there are no mountains between LA and the ocean breeze, it stays cooler than most of the surrounding areas. The Valley is just northwest of the LA Basin, a separate, forward-facing letter *C* that touches Los Angeles. Mountains and foothills form the back of the Valley, so the air from the ocean can't get inside. Which makes it much, much hotter than LA. The people who live in the Valley think of themselves as tougher and hardier than the Hollywood people, and the Los Angeles residents scoff at the poor people who can only afford to live inside an oven. I guess that's probably how the haves and the have-nots cope everywhere.

And Van Nuys is where those two attitudes intersect. Although it's technically a town, it's really just a town-sized strip mall where it's always hot. And where, apparently, you can buy werewolf-proof restraints. I took the Van Nuys Boulevard north exit off the 101, following it almost to the northern border with Panorama City. The GPS directed me to a little block with two sub shops, a tire store, and an appliance repair place. The last business, on the west end of the mall, was called Aaron's Bait Shop and Specialty Metal.

I squinted in the sun, which was blazing down on the Valley with a renewed sense of purpose. Jesse was just getting out of his car as I pulled into the parking spot closest to the road and hopped out of mine.

"You got them?" he asked me, pausing in front of the entrance.

I held up the bag, nodding. "And hello to you, too."

"Sorry," he muttered. "I'm short on time. And sleep."

"Are you okay?" I asked, hesitant. You may have noticed that feelings aren't really my thing.

He looked up, a little surprise in his face. "Yeah, Scarlett. Thanks."

He held the door open, and a blast of air-conditioning welcomed us inside.

I had fished a few times when I was little, but the homemade tackle my dad used had nothing on Aaron's. The store's main feature was the wall to the left of the doorway, which was covered, ceiling to floor, in fake flies, fake minnows, and other little contraptions of feathers and rubber. The room itself was well kept and bright, with wide skylights that spread the sun down onto free-standing shelves filled with all manner of fishing gear.

"Wow," Jesse whispered, still focused on the big wall. "That's a lot of bait."

"Can I help you?"

The guy who approached us was younger than I'd imagined, maybe late twenties, and he was carrying twenty extra pounds on a tall frame that otherwise looked pretty strong. A buzz cut accentuated ears that stuck out a little, and his smile was both friendly and distant, the customer-service smile you find everywhere. He was wearing a baggy polo shirt with a little metal name tag that said, *Aaron*.

I glanced at Jesse, willing him to take the lead. He took the hint.

"Are you the owner, sir?" His tone matched Aaron's for politeness.

"Aaron Sanderson. Yes, I am. Can I help you find something?"

When Jesse reached into his breast pocket for his ID, I caught the little flinch on Aaron's face. "My name is Officer Jesse Cruz. I was wondering if I could ask you a few questions." He looked around the bait shop, which was empty except for us. "Is there somewhere we could speak?"

"Uh, sure. Am I in some kind of trouble?"

"No, sir. We just came across some metal items that may have originated with you. I'd like to talk to you about their owner."

"Oh, okay." Relieved, Aaron stepped past us and reached above the doorframe, pulling down a cardboard sign that said, *Gone fishin'. Back in a few.* He hooked it on the door under the open sign and flipped the lock shut. "This way."

We weaved through the shelves of gear and passed a twelve-foot section of glass coolers filled with live bait. I saw a big aquarium with tiny squid moving around. Aaron took us through a fireproof back door and down a small hallway that led to a modern office with a desk and two sturdy oak chairs.

"Please, have a seat," he said. He lowered himself down onto a wheeled desk chair. "So, what is this about?"

I pulled the small paper bag out of my giant purse and dumped the two halves of the handcuffs on the desk, feeling like a magician's assistant.

"Mr. Sanderson, did you make these handcuffs?" Jesse asked.

"Yes, I did."

Jesse raised his eyebrows. "That's it? You don't even have to pick them up and look at them?"

"I know silver when I see it, Officer. It's not a real practical metal. As far as I know, I'm the only one in Southern California making pure-silver handcuffs."

"To hold werewolves." Jesse's voice had no hint of a question in it, and Aaron Sanderson's face changed. He looked at us with new interest—especially at me.

"I didn't catch your name, Miss...?"

"Bernard. Scarlett Bernard."

"Yes, I thought that was you."

"You've heard of me?" It was my turn to be surprised. This guy hadn't pinged when I got close, so I knew he was human. It must be because Dashiell was his client. Maybe that would make him want to cooperate with us.

Sanderson turned to Jesse. "And as you're here with her, I'd expect you know about this Old World business, too?"

"Yes."

"Okay, good. Now that we've got all that out in the open, yes, I do make items out of silver, for use for and against the werewolves. And I sell things here and there to humans who want stuff that looks good—letter openers, stuff like that. As far as I know, it isn't illegal."

"*For* the wolves? How can this be for the wolves?" I pushed the cuffs a little closer. It was off point, but the image of Eli writhing with pain wasn't vacating my head anytime soon.

"Well, you know, some of the alphas in the Southwest know me, keep some things on hand in case the pack gets out of order. Not Will Carling, who I'd expect you know, but there are some who are interested."

"What about chains?" Jesse leaned forward, trying to get us back on track. "There were silver chains used in a homicide on Pico last night. A werewolf was murdered. Were they yours?"

"Kind of smaller chains, like this one?" He opened a desk drawer and pulled out a foot-long length of small silver chain, with the same hammered oval links as the ones on Ronnie.

"Yes. Do you know who bought them?"

"Nah. The chains are probably my most popular item. People want them for oversized necklaces, ankle bracelets, stuff like that. I get a lot of girls who make their own jewelry wanting a set. There was a lady from a boutique at the Grove here a couple weeks ago, looking at selling them in her store."

"How do these people find you?"

"Word of mouth, mostly."

"What about receipts, records?" I asked.

He shrugged. "Everything is aboveboard. I save receipts here for a month, then send them to my accountant, who shreds them. And I gotta tell you, most of my silver clients pay cash"—he winked at us—"as you can imagine."

Jesse looked frustrated, and I couldn't blame him. "Do you remember anyone, anyone in the last month or so, who might have come in and bought chains? A bigger guy, maybe?"

"Not that I recall." Sanderson grinned at Jesse. "And I don't expect I'd tell you even if I did. Got no reason to."

"What?" Jesse asked, confused.

"You heard me. I'm not interested in helping you with your investigation."

"Mr. Sanderson," Jesse said, getting a little hot, "at least one person has died because of your merchandise. I can get a warrant and—"

"No, you can't," Sanderson cut in, that calm smile still on his face. He folded his arms in his lap and leaned back in his chair. "You're not here in any official capacity, not really. You've got nothing on me."

"You made a weapon that contributed to killing a man; I'd call that something."

"A weapon?" he replied, feigning confusion. "How could silver necklaces be a weapon? Heck, how do you know the dead guy didn't bring them with him? Maybe they were a present for his girl or something." He sat back in his seat, still smiling. "See, Officer, I don't much like werewolves. I've got no problem with them getting killed off; that's why I make the damn stuff in the first place. Oh, and it's *very* lucrative." He glanced over at me. "At any rate, you've got absolutely nothing you can take to a judge or a superior officer, at least not without using the word *werewolf*, which I'm guessing you're not gonna do. And so I think I'd like you to leave my store now. The right to refuse service, and all of that."

My mouth dropped open a little, but I didn't say anything. Jesse's furious look pretty much said it all. There was a long moment while he and Sanderson stared at each other, and then Jesse stood up. "Thank you for your time, Mr. Sanderson. I'll be keeping a real careful eye on your business in the future."

"You do that." Sanderson didn't sound scared one bit, and I followed Jesse as he marched out of the building.

The moment we got outside, Jesse's temper exploded. "I hate this!" He stalked over to his car and kicked at the tires, spitting out a long, angry stream of Spanish. I caught only a couple of words, one of which referred to...uh...lovemaking. I'd never yet seen him lose his cool, so the burst of anger was kind of...fascinating. When he was done, he braced his arms against the car and stared at the ground, defeated.

I leaned against my van. The sun was now taking a breather behind the clouds, and there was a cool breeze riding the September air. "So what's up?" I said lamely.

"What's *up*? Were you in the same interview I was? That guy knows something, but he's not saying anything because he doesn't have to. I can't get a warrant, I can't even write up a report, I'm risking my career and both of our lives, and we've got *nothing*." He turned around and leaned back against his car, sliding down to the ground and putting his head in his hands.

My detachment faded. He was right. We were screwed.

"What about Thomas Freedner?" I asked.

He shook his head. "Same thing. Contacting his known associates got me nowhere, and I can't get a warrant to run his credit cards or search his place. Unless he suddenly just shows up, it's a dead end."

Neither of us said anything for a moment, and then Jesse lifted his head and looked at me. "Scarlett, we might die in the morning. How are you so calm?"

His face was so lost, so defeated, that something stubborn and tight in me just…didn't seem important anymore. I stepped over and sat down next to him, folding my legs and leaning my back on the passenger door with a sigh. "You asked what happened to me."

"Yeah." Jesse raised his eyebrows but let the silence sit there.

"You have to understand, I never had any idea what I was. Once in a while, when I was out in public, I would have these weird sensations, but I just thought everyone had them, the way everyone has headaches or heartburn. I might never have known, even. But when I was eighteen, my mom and dad were killed in a car crash," I said matter-of-factly. "The police said it was an accident, even though no one was drinking and my mom's Jeep had just been inspected. The brake pads were worn down to nothing; the brakes failed, and the car pitched off the freeway during a rainstorm."

"Why were the brake pads worn, if the car had just been inspected?" he said sensibly.

I shrugged. "The police said the mechanic must have missed it, the mechanic said no way, everyone figured the other party was lying. Even me. Because why would anyone want to kill my parents? My mom worked at an animal shelter; my dad taught eighth grade history.

"In any case, right after they died, I met my mentor, Olivia. And Olivia...She stepped into my life and gave me a job, fed me, even let me live with her. I was grateful for it."

Really grateful. My mom and dad had left Jack and me a little money, but so much went into the funerals, and then to the mortgage. Jack, whose grief was so great he could hardly look at me, ended up staying at the house, which was probably a lot easier for him to face than a hysterical teenage girl. None of our distant relatives were interested in housing an eighteen-year-old who should be taking care of herself anyway.

Olivia had taken me in, made me a little family. Gotten me to love her. And if it was a shadow of my old life, well, it was more than nothing. And there was a new world to learn about, and a business, and for a long time, that was all enough to get by.

"Anyway, so a couple years later, Olivia was in the hospital, dying of cancer, and she asked me to go to her house and get a few things. Water the plants and stuff. I knocked over a potted plant in the house, and I felt terrible. I didn't want the plant to die, too, you know?"

He nodded.

"So I went to find some potting soil in this crappy old gardening shed that Olivia had behind her house. I'd never been in there; I hate gardening. But when I went in and poked around, I found something tossed behind a bag of potting soil. It was one of those instruction manuals that comes with your car."

Comprehension spread across his face. "But this one was for your parents' Jeep."

I nodded. "And the thing was, Olivia drove a Saturn. Before that, she'd had a Toyota sedan; she'd told me stories about it. Even so, I probably shouldn't have put anything together, but there was just this...feeling. So I went through her house, found some pictures of me, one in a frame. It was taken at my high school graduation."

Jesse winced. "Ouch."

"Yeah, ouch. There were a couple of other things, and I finally put it together. She'd found me, somehow, months before my parents died. Olivia couldn't have kids, see; for some reason, it's usually hard for nulls. And here I was, this young, impressionable null, perfect for her to take in. She wanted to sort of adopt me, I guess, except I already had parents. So she switched out the brake pads and...*herded* me toward her. Wormed her way into my life and became like a second mother to me." Much, much later, the thought had struck me that I was lucky she hadn't killed Jack, too. I never told him about Olivia, which is just one more reason why we avoid each other.

I pulled my knees up to my chin, hugging my legs to my chest. "She told me once that she'd grown up around cars, but I had no idea..." I trailed off. "Anyway, Will liked me, and he was irate when he found out about Olivia. Dashiell...Well, he'd known about Olivia and my parents, but he didn't care. It made no difference to him that Olivia was the mayor of Crazytown; he was just happy she had found a null apprentice." That still stung. Even then, I hadn't been so naive as to think Dashiell and I were friends, but that level of coldness was still a shock.

"Did you...What did you do?" Jesse asked quietly.

"Nothing. I did nothing. I went to a ratty hotel, and I locked the door and went to bed for ten days. She called my cell, and I didn't answer. Then on the tenth day, it was the hospital calling, and she was dead."

"You didn't confront her?" His voice was shocked.

"No," I said flatly.

That wasn't the whole truth. Two days after I figured it out, I had crept into the hospital late at night, way after visiting hours. The nurses all knew me by then, though, and one of them, a stout older woman with a hundred extra pounds, gave me a little smile and nod to let me know it was all right. "Visiting hours" doesn't always apply on the cancer ward.

Olivia was barely alive by then, almost swallowed up by the machines and tubes keeping her alive. She looked pathetic, her long chestnut hair missing in great patches, her skin yellowed and cracking. Only a few days before, I had been gently rubbing lotion onto her arms, crying over her condition. Now I watched my hand reach toward her, saw it rising up to her mouth. It would be so easy to just plug her nose, cover her mouth. I wouldn't even have to press down hard. There wouldn't be an autopsy.

A strand of long, near-black hair fell in my face, and I froze with my hand in midair. It was my mother's hair. I stepped across the room to the mirror. In the half light, with my hair clouded around my face, I looked just like her. Stricken with shame, I left the room without another glance back at Olivia. It took seven more days for her to stop breathing, but at least it wasn't my hand that did it.

"Anyway," I said, trying to push the memory away, "I did... um..."

"What?"

I winced. "I did sort of burn down her gardening shed." I'd made no effort to conceal my guilt. It had cost Dashiell a lot of money to pull the right strings so I wouldn't go to jail. Mostly, I figure he did it to make sure I'd keep working for him, but he'd never taken any bribe money out of my pay. Sometimes I think it was his apology for not telling me about Olivia.

Jesse gave me a bemused half smile, part reprimand and part approval. He thought for a few moments and finally said, "What was going to be your major?"

Not the question I was expecting. "Um, veterinary science."

He gave me a baffled look.

"What? I like science, and I love animals."

"You do?" He seemed genuinely surprised.

"Yes. The only reason I don't have a bunch is that they're... well, sort of allergic to Molly. Animals can't handle vampires. Their little hearts just can't take the stress of that kind of predator." I rested my head on the car behind me. I missed animals. But even if I survived the week, who knew where I'd be living in a year, two years.

"I didn't know that," he said quietly.

It occurred to me for the first time that Jesse could have known a lot about me. "You know, most of this is public record—my parents' crash, the fire, Olivia's death. You could have looked all this up."

He gave me a heartbreaking grin. "That would be cheating." Jesse reached over and pulled a little piece of feather out of my long hair, a tagalong from the bait shop. It was a pretty suave move, and I could feel the warmth coming off his body. His fingers lingered in my hair, moving toward my cheek, and for the length of a heartbeat, I saw his goodness and I wanted in. In that moment, I wanted, more than anything, to crawl into his arms and make myself a home there. A place to rest, and to let go. All I'd really have to do was be still and let him kiss me.

That's the thing about homes, though; they can just kind of fall out from under you. And I wouldn't be falling again.

"Anyway," I said carefully, turning away so my hair slipped from his hand. "You asked me how I deal with all of this. As bad as it is right now, as bad as it would be even if I were killed, nothing will ever be worse than that for me." I didn't tell him what I really believed—that I was already half-dead anyway. Better to die the rest of the way than let anyone else get hurt because of me. I was just sorry that Jesse's fate was tied to mine.

I was too much of a coward to look at his face, and he finally just said, "So, what do we do now?"

I checked my watch. It was almost 2:00 p.m., which meant I now had about sixteen hours to find the killer and clear my name before Dashiell would come for me. I sighed, letting my head thunk back against the car. "I have no idea."

He looked at me again, but this time it was just thoughtful. "Come on," he said finally. "There's someone I want you to meet."

Chapter 24

Twenty minutes later, Jesse led Scarlett up the walkway to his parents' front door. "Now, you're going to want to stand back," he whispered, with exaggerated seriousness. "Be ready for anything. Remember, it can smell fear."

She'd been game up to a point, but now Scarlett was beginning to look nervous. She touched her hair and tugged her T-shirt down over her jeans. "Jesse, come on, what are we doing?"

"My folks work weird hours, so if I'm in the area, I stop to let him out during the day," he said. She was still processing that when he turned the key in the door. There was a second of frantic scrabbling, and then Jesse pushed the door inward and eighty pounds of taut, hyperactive muscle flew out of the house. With a cursory glance at Jesse, Max beelined for Scarlett, knocking her down onto her ass and licking her face with frantic abandon. Jesse winced—that was a little much, even for Max—but Scarlett was laughing. She'd dropped the guarded look on her face so quickly that he hadn't even seen it happen.

"Scarlett, Max. Max, Scarlett," he called over the sound of Max's excitement and her giggling. "Sorry, my parents are terrible disciplinarians."

She didn't seem to hear him. "Stop, you crazy thing," she was saying, but her fingers were digging into his pelt, scratching enthusiastically. Max took that as confirmation of her love and wagged his tail hard enough to wiggle the whole back half of his body back and forth. Scarlett managed to roll over onto all fours and drop her shoulders into a fake pounce. Max immediately mirrored her, and she attacked, rubbing at his head as he danced around her. Sunlight filtered through the oak tree on his folks' front lawn, and Jesse held his breath as he watched them. For the first time since he'd met her, Scarlett looked happy and unguarded. And young. He felt as if he were in sort of a reverse *It's a Wonderful Life*, looking at what Scarlett Bernard would have been like if one thing in her life had gone differently. Her long hair was slipping out of her ponytail, and her cheeks were flushed. In her ratty T-shirt and old jeans, she was beautiful.

Finally, Max wandered off to pee, and Scarlett returned to Jesse. "Thank you," she said, eyes bright. "He's wonderful."

Jesse was smart enough to be casual about it. "No problem," he said. "Listen, I really do need to get back to the precinct. I'm supposed to be digging through all this paperwork on the history of the park. I know it's a long shot that I'll find anything at this point, but I don't know what else to do."

He winced as Scarlett's face shut back down, and she reached back to redo her ponytail. "That might not be a bad idea," she said finally. Her voice was back to flat professionalism. "Whoever is doing this is obviously trying to say something, with the teeth and the blood and the silver. It could be that the location is important, too."

They made plans to meet up again in a few hours.

Before he went back to work, Jesse decided to take a shot at Thomas Freedner again. He took surface streets the short distance to Janine Malaka's West Hollywood apartment building, a six-floor, pueblo-style walkup that had that LA look of long-expired glory. The halls were a little dingy and the lobby plants were plastic, but many of the residents had made an effort to put out a welcome mat or wreath of dried flowers to spruce up their doors.

Janine Malaka was a Hawaiian woman in her mid-forties, pretty and chunky, wearing a long bright-blue-and-yellow muu-muu. She greeted Jesse with the wary respect that is often borne of a long history with the police department. When he explained that he was asking about Freedner, she shrugged and took the chain off the door, ushering him inside.

"I haven't seen Tom in years," she said, leading him to a worn fabric sofa that had been carefully patched and restuffed. "We was working together at the Stop and Go over on Franklin Street, you know? Just before he got caught dealing that last time? We was just friendly. Used to buy a little pot from him, now and again. What'd he do now?"

"Nothing at all, as far as we know," Jesse assured her. "We just want to ask him some questions about a case. Have you heard from Tom since he was released from prison?"

"Naw. Him and me was never friendly after he went in." She shrugged. "Was more of a work friendship, you know? Never slept with him or nothin'. He was into guys. But I happened to be hangin' with him when the cops came for him the last time, so they took down my name."

"Do you know about his...other activities?"

"You mean the vampire stuff?" She laughed again. "Yeah, he told me once. We was high as kites and I didn't believe him, but then he showed me the scars. I figured him and his friends like to run around and play vampire." She shrugged. "Never bothered me none. All kinds in this town."

Jesse was getting frustrated. He checked his watch—only a few minutes until he had to be back at the precinct. "Do you have any ideas about where Tom might go if he was in trouble?"

She made a show of thinking it over. "You try his friend who plays the vampire? Abe something?"

"Yes, ma'am" Jesse lied. "He wasn't helpful."

Malaka shrugged again. "The thing you need to know about Tom," she said with a new fierceness, as though she'd only just realized she was in the conversation, "is that the vampire stuff was what he lived for. It's all he talked about, like he was in love with vampires the way that some are in love with people."

Jesse frowned. "What do you think would happen if it were taken away? If he couldn't...play vampires anymore?"

Her face lost its dopey relaxation, and the look she gave Jesse was serious and a little scared. "Then I think that boy would flat-out lose his mind."

Chapter 25

Despite my deadline, I was really, really looking forward to getting a few hours of sleep back at Molly's. After forty minutes of traffic, I finally hung my bag and my canvas jacket on the hook that Molly had put up inside the door for me and headed for the kitchen, planning to grab some crackers and a shower and go to bed. Before I'd taken a full step into the room, though, I stumbled and almost went down, grabbing the doorframe for support. There was a bouquet in a vase on Molly's kitchen table: two dozen purple mums. A little white card was folded open on the table, leaning against the vase. Hugging the wall, I moved close enough to see the generic cursive writing: *Just Because.*

Florists don't open until daylight, and Molly hadn't been "awake" all morning.

Someone had been in the house.

I edged around the table as if it might be booby-trapped and picked up a butcher knife from the block next to the fridge. We don't use the knife set much—Molly rarely cooks, for obvious reasons, and I do more assembling than actual cooking—so it was plenty sharp. Keeping my back to a wall, I edged through the house to the staircase, ran up the stairs two at a time, and burst into Molly's room, feeling a vampire presence enter my radius and praying that it was Molly. She had boarded over the windows in her room years ago, so I flipped the light on, holding my breath, and saw her lying on the bed, looking peaceful. I closed and locked the door behind me and went over to shake her shoulder. "Molls? Molly? Are you okay?"

Her eyelids fluttered, and I sighed with relief. She took one look at my face. "Yeah. What's with the knife?" Her voice was perfectly calm. When you're two hundred–odd years old, you've probably been through an emergency or two.

"Someone's been in the house."

We searched the house room by room, me with the butcher knife and Molly wearing her Sailor Moon nightie, and found nothing besides the flowers and a busted knob on the back door. When we were positive that nobody else was there, Molly put on her bathrobe—I waited at the bottom of the stairs to stay in range—and then I returned the knife to the kitchen and started the coffeemaker. There was no way I'd be going to sleep anytime soon.

Molly perched on one of the stools, looking livid, while I filled her in on my suspicion that the La Brea Park murders were somehow connected to me.

"I cannot believe," she spat out when I had finished, "that some asshole was in my house while I was…sleeping." I realized that the Welsh accent had crept back into her voice. Jesus. I'd never seen her this upset. She was still human, of course, but I could see the predator beneath the cheerful exterior. "When I find that fucker, I will rip his goddamned heart out, and I mean that literally."

I said nothing, just huddled around my coffee, waiting for her to wind down. After a few minutes, she looked over at me. "What? What are you thinking?"

"I'm really sorry."

She sputtered a little mid-sip, then put her cup down. "What for?"

"This is my fault. If you hadn't let me move in here, this wouldn't have happened."

Molly looked at me like I'd lost it. "Well...duh."

I blinked. "Huh?"

"Of course this never would have happened if you weren't living here. But, Scarlett, I knew what I was getting into when I signed on. When Dashiell arranged for you to live here, I knew someday something might come looking for you. I just thought it'd be another vampire, because they wanted, you know, your help."

"I don't know what to do. I can't put you at risk."

She thought that over for a few minutes, then shook her head. "Scarlett...He's given you an ultimatum, hasn't he? A deadline?"

I hadn't told her about that. It wasn't paranoia; Molly really had been talking to Dashiell about me. I was hardly in a position to throw stones, though, since I'd just put her at risk. "Yes."

"When is your time up?"

"At dawn."

She winced, nodding. "Okay. There's a Radisson downtown that has two basement floors. Drop me off there; walk me down into the basement. I'll be safe there until all this is over. If you solve it before dawn, you can call me, and I'll come home." She hesitated. "I'm so sorry I can't help you, Scarlett, but..."

"It's okay," I said miserably. "I understand."

And I did.

It took almost an hour for us to get to the hotel, but I finally got her settled in a basement room. Molly paid for two nights in advance, telling the concierge she didn't want to be disturbed, and I helped her duct-tape the *Do Not Disturb* sign on the door, just in case. When I finally got her down to her room, Molly hugged me so tightly that, for a second, I thought she still had vampire strength. "I really, really hope I see you tomorrow. I know you can figure this out."

This one time, I let her hug me as long as she wanted.

As I pulled away from the hotel parking lot, the cell phone in my pocket began the opening chords of "Werewolves of London." I fished the phone out of my pocket. "Hi, Will."

"Scarlett." His voice was grave. "I have this address. You need to get over there right now. It's not a job, but—"

"Will...I can't."

"What do you mean, you can't?" He sounded surprised. "I've never heard you say that."

What did I have to lose? "Dashiell gave me until dawn to solve the La Brea Park thing, or he would assume I was involved. I'm sorry; I have to work on this right now."

There was silence on the line, and I knew Will was thinking about the ultimatum. He could theoretically challenge Dashiell on my behalf, but as much as Will seemed to like me, he knew full well what a war with the vampires would do to this town. If he went to bat for me, there'd be casualties, and plenty of them. Not to mention the fact that the Old World's LA experiment—allowing all three factions control in the same city—would be a resounding and bloody failure. On the other hand, if Dashiell killed me...Well, it'd be sad, but it was just one death, and I wasn't even a werewolf.

I wasn't even mad about it.

Finally, he spoke. "Scarlett, I didn't know. But I think I might have someone who can help you. You need to get to this address as fast as you can."

I rubbed my eyes. I knew Will probably wasn't being deliberately cryptic, but I was all out of patience. "Please, Will, could you just tell me what's going on?"

"I found the second null. Or actually, she found me."

Chapter 26

When I really stopped and thought about it, I realized that, all along, I had assumed that the other null was evil.

Obviously, he or she was a bad guy, a murderer, and when we found him/her, I would call Jesse and he would do some really inspired cop-threatening, and then we'd know everything we needed in order to go to Dashiell.

I certainly hadn't expected her to be a fifteen-year-old rape victim.

Will had sketched in the details for me: Until a few months ago, Corrine Tanger was a cheerful, well-adjusted teenager from an ultra-religious family—her father was a Pentecostal minister, and her mother was the church secretary. Two months earlier, however, Corrine had been attacked by her slimy biology teacher. She hadn't gone into too much detail with Will—understandably—but the impression he'd gotten was that Corrine had been raped. The girl was too ashamed to tell her parents, and then the teacher started hinting about another "get-together" after school. Desperate and haunted, Corrine thought she'd found a way out when a stranger had approached her and offered a deal—if she accompanied him to kill the vampires in the park, he would make the teacher stop. The girl had seen it as the only way out of her own nightmare. She was not exactly the mustache-twirling villain I had been picturing since the case began.

As I drove to Corrine's house in Glendale, I was so nervous that I had to clutch the steering wheel hard to keep my hands from shaking. What had happened to her was twisted and tragic and just so *wrong*, and I had absolutely no idea what to say to her. It wasn't as if I would be showing off a model new life for her to step into. In fact, I realized, there was very little I could even tell her about what we are. My knowledge about nulls as a group is limited to pretty much what I'd told Cruz that night on the way to Dashiell's.

Not for the first time, I deeply wished I had asked Olivia more questions. What would I do when Corrine had questions I couldn't answer? And I'd never really known anyone who had been assaulted like that—should I mention how sorry I was? Avoid the topic all together? I felt a sudden flood of grief. I missed my mom. She always knew the right thing to say in any situation. I never do.

Get out of your head, Scarlett, I told myself sternly. *It's not about you right now.* One thing I knew, beyond hesitation or doubt, was that I had to help this girl. The way Olivia *should* have helped me.

The Tanger family lived in one of those Wisteria Lane–type suburbs, where the houses are all tidy and large and nearly identical. These lots were small, but every single house on her street looked well cared for, like the people who lived there took pride in their homes. It was a lot like Kirsten's neighborhood, actually, but with less money thrown around. I took two wrong turns trying to distinguish the different streets, and finally pulled into the Tangers' driveway a little after seven. When the van was off, I took a deep breath, flexing and unflexing my aching fingers. Will had helped Corrine work up a cover story: I was a math tutor for one of her friends. The friend was sick, so I was picking up her homework and hearing about the day's lesson. Will said the father is pretty overprotective, but I am young, white, and female. Hopefully it would be enough to get a few minutes alone with Corrine. And hopefully no one would ask me anything about math.

As it turned out, I needn't have worried. The woman who answered the door was about fifty and had dark hair shot through with silver and the kind of crinkles around her eyes that meant she smiled all the time. She introduced herself as Mrs. Tanger and invited me into the foyer.

"It's so nice of you to stop by," she said kindly. "I'm sure Amanda will appreciate getting a head start on the work she's missed."

"Um, yeah," I mumbled.

Mrs. Tanger wore a pale-pink J.Crew sweater set and an actual pearl necklace on top of dark tailored pants. I tugged self-consciously at my dark-green hoodie. There were bleach stains on my jeans. I'd been going for "college student," but now I just felt like a homeless person.

"My husband is on an overnight retreat to Palmdale, but Corry's upstairs in her room," she told me. "It's straight up the stairs, second door on the left. I'll be in the kitchen if you girls need anything." She rolled her eyes good-naturedly. "Corry's little brother Jonah needs two dozen cupcakes for the school bake sale tomorrow, and of course he just told me now." She gave me a hurried wave and headed deeper into the house.

Huh. Kind of anticlimactic.

I took a deep breath and climbed the stairs, knocking on the designated door. Just before it opened, I felt an old familiar tug, the water-bending-through-glass feeling of another null in my radius.

Corrine—Corry—must have felt it, too, because her brown eyes were wide when she opened the door. "You feel different," she said breathlessly. "Like them." She was a couple of inches shorter than my five foot seven, with a sweet face, a neat blonde bob, and modest teenager clothes—jeans and a simple long-sleeved purple top. She was pretty in an all-American general way, but her eyes were different. There was something tired and broken about them, as though she had resigned herself to just going through the motions, probably forever.

I swear, it didn't remind me of anyone.

"Uh...Hi, I'm Scarlett. You must be Corrine. Can I come in?"

"Oh, sorry, yeah." She stepped aside, letting me into the bedroom. I don't know what I'd been expecting—maybe posters of boy bands and stuffed animals—but the room's personality seemed to be in transit. There were dark spots on the violet wallpaper where posters had recently been removed, and in the middle of the room, there was a plain cardboard box nearly filled with the kind of junk kids acquire—trophies and battered paperbacks and photo albums. "Everybody calls me Corry."

"Cool...Are you guys moving?"

"What? Oh, no. I'm just putting some stuff in the basement, for storage. Here, you can sit down at my desk." She cleared a stack of binders off the desk chair and perched at the foot of her bed. When we were both seated, there was a long awkward moment while I worked up what to say.

Finally, I said, "Corry...Maybe this would be easiest if you told me how much you know. About what you are and what you can do."

She nodded eagerly, her fingers twisting together in her lap. This girl was just bursting to talk to someone. "Okay, yeah. Um, all I really know is what Jay—that's the guy—told me." She took a deep breath. "He said there are evil things in the world, and I can, like, turn off their evil. Sort of save them. He would kill them when they were like that so they could go to heaven...And he said if I helped him, he'd keep Mr. Herberts from ever hurting me again." Her voice was shaking by the time she finished, and she'd hugged her arms around herself.

I ached for her. "Is there something else?" I asked softly.

"I thought Jay would just, you know, go beat him up, threaten him or something," she blurted. "I didn't know..."

"What happened?" I asked, although I knew the answer.

"Jay killed him," the girl said quietly. "He made it look like an accident in the woodshop classroom, but he died just like all the others." She paused, and I could see her thinking about the people she'd helped Jay kill. "Were they...Were they really evil?" she asked me, with something like hope in her voice.

Corry was trembling now, and I felt completely incompetent. She needed me to tell her that she'd done the right thing, that she'd helped slay the monsters, but it just wasn't that simple. And now I was going to make her a murderer. "Oh, honey...What Jay said isn't exactly right. There are creatures in the world that you maybe didn't know about, but they're not all evil or all good, just like regular people." I was about to say that the vampires were mostly evil, but I thought of Beatrice and held my tongue.

I froze as Corry hugged her knees to her chest and began to cry. My fingers twisted helplessly in my lap. I wanted to touch her but didn't know how she'd take it.

"Jay said we were doing good," she sobbed, "and in the park, I just shut my eyes and stayed still, and he did these things and..." Her voice broke off. "It was so horrible. But the guy in the parking lot, he was even worse. He was crying and...and begging. And I knew something wasn't right, so I ran away." She rolled across the bed, pulling a tissue off her nightstand and blowing her nose. She took a moment to collect herself and then held up a red cell phone with a beat-up Hello Kitty sticker on it. For some reason, the sticker broke my heart. "And like I told Mr. Carling, Jay sent me this text today, and he wants to do it again. When I said no, he...He tried to blackmail me. That's why I called Mr. Carling."

"How did you find him?" I asked, trying to follow the story.

She blushed under her tears. "My parents block a lot of websites, but I can still read the *LA Times* online. I saw the article on the parking lot guy, Ronnie? And it said he had a mother, and I looked her up. I called her and said I worked with Ronnie and I wanted to set up a memorial. She read me the contacts on his cell phone."

"That was very smart," I said. "Back up a second—you said Jay tried to blackmail you. Blackmail you with what?"

"He has a recording that Mr. Herberts made," she said simply. "A DVD."

Aside from Hugo the vampire, I'd never really hurt anyone in my life. But if that teacher weren't already dead, I would have seen to it myself.

When I was sure I was calm, I said, "Look, I need to stop this Jay, and for reasons that are long and complicated, I don't have much time. In fact, I have almost no time. You know how you felt when I came into the room?"

She nodded.

"Well, I'm something different, too—the same thing you are. We're called nulls. And we need to have a very long talk, soon, about what it all means. But right now, I need to find Jay. Can you help me?"

She looked uncertain, and I tried to imagine what she'd been through recently. First the pedophile teacher, and then a man who swooped in and promised to fix everything only to turn out to be just as depraved. No wonder the girl wasn't buzzing with eagerness. I looked around the half-packed room. This was a girl who had lost her inner compass. I took a deep breath. "Corry, what happened to you was wrong. Twice. People have been through a lot less than that and barely survived, so the fact that you're even walking and talking is amazing. And I swear to you that I will help you in every way I can. Do you think you can believe me?"

She hesitated, then nodded, and I prayed that I would have the strength to be everything this girl needed. "Good. Now tell me, what has Jay got planned for tonight?"

She told me about the meeting time and the bus stop while I scribbled down directions on a Hello Kitty pad of paper, which had probably come with the sticker set. When I was sure I knew where I was going, I shoved the Hello Kitty page in my pocket and stood up.

"Okay, Corry, this is really important. I need you to get your family out of here tonight. All night. Right now. Tell them anything you need to—you're in trouble, you saw a ghost, there's asbestos, anything. It doesn't matter. Just get them out of here, and go somewhere safe. Don't tell *anyone* where you're going." She opened her mouth, but I shook my head. "No, not even me, just in case. I just want you to promise me you'll go. Promise?"

She nodded, eyes big and scared.

"Okay." I scribbled on the pad again. "This is my number. You call me if anything goes wrong, okay? And in a couple of days, when my current crisis is over, you and I can have that talk."

Ten minutes later, I was driving toward the Coffee Bean closest to Jesse's precinct. He was sitting in the very back of the shop, blushing furiously while a blonde barista with comically large breasts stood by the table, flirting.

"Sweetheart!" he cried, as I walked up. He stood and kissed my cheek, giving me a begging look that clearly said, *Please, please, please, play along.*

I tried not to roll my eyes. The guy was just too handsome for his own good. "Hi, babe. Sorry I'm late. Oh, hey!" I said to the waitress. "I didn't know they had table service here. I'd like a chai tea latte, please. Skim." I shrugged out of my hoodie and sat down like I owned the place.

The blonde's mouth snapped shut long enough for her to glare at me. She turned and stomped back behind the counter, large breasts wobbling with indignation.

"I'll give her this," I said thoughtfully. "How impressive is it that she can balance upright?"

"Thank you," Jesse muttered under his breath.

"You owe me. There's going to be spit in my tea." He smiled, and I went on. "Listen, I found something."

"Me, too. But you go first."

Without further preamble I said, "I found the second null."

"Really? Excellent!" He said excitedly. "Let's go arrest him— or her."

My jaw dropped. "Wait, for what?"

"Accessory to murder, of course." He sounded pleased. "Finally, the real world can be useful here. The lab picked up tons of fingerprints and DNA at the park scene. A lot of it is probably because it's a public space, but hopefully some of it is the null's. We can use the evidence as leverage to get us to the actual killer."

I drummed my fingers on the table. "I know that was the plan, but...then what?" I asked. "What happens to the null in all of this?"

Jesse stared at me, but I didn't back down. "You're serious? The null...He has to go to jail. He helped kill somebody, remember?"

"It's not that simple, Cruz. The null, well, had good reasons."

"Good reasons for killing four people?" he said, outraged.

I bit my lip. How much could I tell him about Corry? Could I trust him not to arrest her when he got the full story? "Jesse, look, I need you to do something for me. For *me*, you understand? You can't arrest her. The second null."

"Why the hell not?" he demanded.

"She...Please, Jesse. I'm asking you for your trust, just for a little while. I'll explain it all if we get through the next day." When I had Corry's permission to do so.

He looked at me for a long moment. I kept my face even. I'd known Corry Tanger for all of forty minutes, but I'd go to hell and back to get her out of this.

"And if I don't?" he said quietly.

"Then I won't tell you who she is. And since we've already established that, legally, you have nothing on me, the case will stop where it is, and the deadline will pass, and we'll both die."

Jesse went very still. "I can't believe you," he said, studying me. "You're really gonna draw a line in the sand, after everything we've been through?"

"Not if you don't make me," I said, my voice cracking a little. "Jesse, she's...She's like me."

He held my gaze for a long moment, thoughts flickering across his face, and then he nodded grudgingly. "Well...okay. I don't need to know right now. But she can't just get away with murder. This conversation will be back for part two."

I nodded, and the moment passed.

Jesse stared at me as if looking for some kind of reassurance that I could be trusted. Then he lowered his voice. "Listen, I found something, too—maybe. My supervisor's had me going through the reports of all the police incidents that have ever taken place at the park. I thought it was just busywork, but I actually found this one case that I think is...significant." He pulled a folded sheath of paper from his back pocket and slid it over to me.

The top page was a Xeroxed school photo of a young girl. The second page was an adolescent boy, maybe sixteen or so. Their names were handwritten under the photos.

"Jared and Emily Hess," Jesse continued. "Ten years ago, twelve-year-old Emily disappeared from the park. The kids were climbing trees after the park had closed for the night, and Jared fell asleep on a high branch. When he woke up, he claimed that strangers had bitten his sister to death and that a third party had taken the body away. The police came with dogs, forensics, the whole nine yards. They found a little bit of Emily's blood, but no other trace of the girl. Eventually, the cops started looking at Jared."

"Oh no."

"Yeah. His story was crazy, and there were a few other things— kid got into fights at school, a couple pets in the neighborhood had disappeared, that kind of stuff. Nothing solid, but the officers on the case thought Jared was the best suspect. They really gave him the runaround—interrogation, juvie, where the other kids beat the shit out of him, by the way, psychiatric care, anything our guys could think of to try to get him to change his story. Kid never did, though, and eventually, the father sued the department for pushing too hard. They settled out of court."

"Huh." I looked at the photo of Jared. Where Emily's school pose was sweet and simple, this shot had been taken at the police station, and it was obvious that Jared had been badly beaten just before the photo. His face was swollen and unrecognizable, a trickle of blood at his mouth. He must not have been the toughest kid at juvenile detention. There was something familiar about his defiant expression, but I couldn't place it.

"Where is Jared now?"

"That's the thing—nobody knows. All his financial and tax records go up until five years ago, and then they just stop. It's like the guy vanished into thin air. And, Scarlett, that really doesn't happen anymore." He tapped the date at the top of the photocopied police report. "The thing is, there are dozens of reports like this in the La Brea Park file. Other incidents, even a couple of murders. But this one…This was ten years ago *today*."

The blonde marched up and plopped my mug of chai tea in front of me on the table, letting it slosh a little. Okay, now she was starting to piss me off. I dug a five out of my pocket and handed it over. "Thanks so much," I said sweetly. "You can keep the change for your tip." Which amounted to about fifteen cents. I hoped she would put it toward a back brace.

Ignoring her reaction, I reached over to take Jesse's hand. "Baby, what were you saying?"

The blonde huffed away again. The corner of his mouth twitched, but he squeezed my hand gently, giving me an open look that made me wish I hadn't restarted this charade.

"Anyway," he said, a little awkward, "I guess it's possible that Jared Hess really did kill his sister. But the anniversary thing…

This has gotta be it, right? It was really vampires who killed Emily Hess?"

Jared. Jay. "Yes." My voice was firm, and Jesse's face changed with my response.

He carefully removed his hand from mine. "Scarlett...your mentor, the other null..."

Oh crap. I suddenly remembered who I was talking to, and realized what was coming. "Yeah?"

"I know you guys get rid of evidence, but she wouldn't have taken a little girl's *body*, right?"

I flinched. "Yeah, she would have," I said soberly. "If a vampire really killed Emily Hess, and it looked obvious enough, Olivia would have taken the body to an incinerator and had it destroyed. The family would never have found out what had happened." Plenty of bones had gone into Artie's furnace over the years, and not all of them were from adults.

Jesse searched my face. "But you've never done that, right?" His voice sounded just like Corry's had when she asked me if vampires and werewolves were evil. Like he was begging me to tell him it wasn't true.

But I couldn't. Oh, I could have lied, I suppose, but there was a part of me that had been eaten up by this, and that part thought I deserved what was coming to me. "Once. A teenage boy, maybe fourteen." I cringed at the memory. The vampire hadn't actually drained the kid's blood, though just drinking from him was bad enough. Instead, though, the vamp had pushed too hard while he was feeding and broken the fourteen-year-old's neck. Necks are delicate when you have enhanced strength; that's part of why vampires don't usually feed from them anymore.

The puncture marks were enough for Dashiell to call me in for body disposal. Then he had promised me that the vampire would die, too. I'd had nightmares about that one for months.

Jesse was leaning back in his seat, wincing as if I'd just slapped him. "Every time I think I'm getting to know you, it turns out I'm wrong," he said, with quiet, exacting anger laced through his voice. "I've worked cases like that, where a child's body was never found, and it's excruciating." He shook his head. "I just...I never would have thought you'd be capable of something like that."

I said nothing, staring miserably into my tea.

He nodded to himself, as though that were an answer, and stood up, dropping money on the table. "I know we're on a deadline, but I need...I need to take a walk. I'll call you in a little while."

"Jesse, wait—" I said feebly.

He turned and stiffly walked out. I sat there for a full minute without moving. And then I remembered that I hadn't told him about the meeting with Jay.

Shit.

Chapter 27

Ignoring the huffy blonde, who was still glaring in my general direction, I pulled out my phone and hit Jesse's number, but the call didn't even go through to voice mail, which meant he was actively avoiding me. Great. Now what the hell was I supposed to do?

My phone rang in my hand, making me jump, but when I glanced at the caller ID, it wasn't Jesse's name that came up. It was my brother's. Oh, *great*. My thumb automatically slid toward the *Ignore* button, but then stopped. Honestly, what did I have to lose at this point? Without Jesse, there wasn't a hell of a lot I could do, anyway, and if this ended up being my last night on earth...I should probably talk to my brother. I flipped the phone open.

"Scarbo?"

The pet name twisted in my stomach. "Hi, Jack. What's up?" I said with false cheer.

He coughed nervously, and I smiled despite myself, picturing him scrubbing his hand over his hair. "Uh...Wow, I guess I didn't really expect you to answer. It's been a while."

"Yeah, I know. Um, is everything okay?"

His voice perked up. "Oh, yeah, everything's great. Sorry if I, you know, worried you or anything."

There was another awkward pause, and suddenly, I felt ridiculous. Were we really having this conversation? We sounded like strangers, for crying out loud. This was my brother, who'd driven across Esperanza at three in the morning to pick me up from my first drinking party, who'd punched the first boy who'd broken my heart. This was *Jack*.

Do better, I told myself sternly. *Be better at this.* "How are things with you, Jack?"

He laughed nervously. "Good, actually. Really good. That's kind of why I'm calling. I got a job in the city. I'm moving to LA."

For a second there, my heart stopped beating. Jack, coming here? Having an entry point into my life, and therefore my world?

Not. Good.

"That's really great, Jack," I said lamely. "Um...What kind of work is it?"

"Pretty much the same thing I'm doing now, but there's a whole research aspect, too. It's a private company that makes medical equipment, and they want some professional lab techs to put new designs through the specs, try it out with all kinds of testing. But here's the best part," he continued, and his voice was suddenly bursting with excitement, "they're going to help me pay for med school. They want me to get my MD, you know, and then keep working for them. They have a whole bunch of education incentives...." He gushed for a while about 401K benefits and med school, but I wasn't listening anymore. This was terrible.

Unless, of course, I didn't live through the night, in which case it was fine.

"Sorry, Scarbo, I know I'm going on and on. I'm just really excited, you know, and I was hoping maybe you and I could get together soon. It's been too long." I actually heard him swallow. "I know that I wasn't the best big brother or anything after the accident—"

"Jack, you don't—"

"No, hang on, I mean it. I should have done a better job, I know. It was my responsibility to look out for you, and I blew it. And I don't know much about how things are for you now, but...I'd like to. I'm gonna be in the city next week, apartment hunting. Do you think we could get together for coffee?"

Guilt, guilt, guilt. I didn't want Jack to be sorry. I wanted him to ignore me, to be the world's shittiest sibling, because it helped balance out the fact that I'd gotten our parents killed. "I've kind of got a lot going on right now, Jack," I hedged.

"Oh, okay," he said amiably. "Well, listen, you've got my number. You should call me so we can get together. If I don't hear from you in a couple weeks, I'll try again." He sounded so confident and relaxed, and I realized how much I'd missed him. And then, immediately after, that I might be dead really soon.

"Jackie...I love you, you know? And you didn't do anything wrong, after Mom and Dad. I never, ever thought you did. Don't carry that around, okay?"

"Okay, Scarb," he said, surprise in his voice. "Thanks. I'll, um...I'll talk to you soon."

We said good-bye, and I set my phone down on the little table—right next to the pictures of the Hess children, which Jesse had left behind when he'd stormed out.

And suddenly, I knew what to do. I looked at my watch: 8:45. Time to move. I hesitated for a second, considering whether I should run home for my Taser. I like carrying it when I go to big vampire events, but it would add at least forty minutes to my trip, and that was time I just didn't have. Sighing, I headed for the van.

It was quite dark by the time I arrived at Dashiell's house in Pasadena. I got myself buzzed in, parked the van, and performed my quick ding-dong-ditch modification before Beatrice opened the door. She was wearing a midnight-blue cocktail dress with some sort of elaborate weaving on the bodice, reminding me of medieval gowns, even as it clung to her curves. She was stunning, but seemed nervous and agitated when she ushered me in. More than anything, though, Beatrice looked worried.

"Scarlett—"

Without waiting for an invitation, I immediately headed in the direction of Dashiell's office, with Beatrice a step behind me. She was tall, but she was also trotting along in four-inch heels without her usual vampire grace.

"I need to see him, Beatrice."

"I am not sure this is the best time. He has had much trouble with the other vampires; they are so angry about Abraham and the others—" she rushed out, following me closely.

"That's why I'm here, Bea. If I can find the person responsible, everything goes back to normal, right?"

She was silent for a beat too long, and I paused, skidding to a halt on the black-and-white-tiled hallway. I looked back at her. "Right?"

Beatrice shook her head. "I do not know, Scarlett. Yesterday, probably yes, but the situation is quickly growing worse. The powerful vampires in town are saying that Dashiell does not have the strength to hold the city, considering he can't even protect his right hand. Our people say that they have been arguing among themselves about who should challenge Dashiell." Her pale face looked even whiter in the bright hall light. "Scarlett, I know you do not always agree with Dashiell, but there are much, much worse vampires in California. Ariadne is among them."

"She's leading the revolution?"

"Yes."

"And what happens to you if Dash is...overthrown?"

Her jaw tensed as she spoke. "If Ariadne takes control"—she shook her head—"my death will be bad."

I don't know which one of us was more surprised when I threw my arms around Beatrice, hugging her fiercely. "Don't worry," I said quietly.

She leaned back from me, looking shocked, and I stepped back, afraid I had hurt her. But then her hand reached slowly up to her eye, and when it came away, it shone with wetness. She stared in amazement. "I had forgotten."

"Beatrice, listen. I have to help someone tonight, but when I'm done, I'll come back here, and I'll stay with Dashiell, okay? With both of you. I won't let anyone get close enough to challenge. I know that's not a long-term solution, but..." I trailed off. She had the oddest expression on her face. "What?"

"You know that he is ready to kill you for all of this, whether or not you were involved?"

"Yeah. I know."

Her eyes searched mine for a long moment, and then she smiled faintly. "He underestimates you."

Before I could deal with that, steps echoed down the hall in front of us, and I felt Dashiell even before I could see him. He wore the same smooth black suit as always, but with no tie and the top button undone. For the first time, I caught a glimpse of something shiny at his hip, behind the suit jacket. A gun. Dashiell was carrying a gun.

Oh, God. We were all gonna die.

"You," he said, taking that first gasping human breath. "What are you doing here? Have you come to confess? To throw yourself at my mercy?" He raised an amused eyebrow, but his all-too-human voice sounded dead serious. Emphasis on dead.

"Not just yet. But I would like to ask you some questions, if I could." I nodded to his office door. "May I?"

He frowned at me, unmoving.

"Come on, Dashiell. You said I had a few more hours. I'm trying to use them wisely. And I have a lead."

Dashiell glanced at his watch. "Five minutes."

Beatrice squeezed my hand and turned away, walking back toward the front of the house. I was on my own.

I straightened my spine and followed Dash into his colossal office, which didn't match the rest of the house at all. The mansion reflected Beatrice's tastes, which ran toward her native Spain and the Mediterranean. This office, however, was all medieval library—huge ornately carved oak desk, antique everything, oil lamps instead of electric. There was even a pair of white gloves lying out, presumably for the reading of extremely old books. For a moment, I wondered if Dash had seen the Renaissance. He couldn't be *that* old, right? I felt very small, and wished that Jesse were there with me. Or even Eli, as complicated as that was.

Focus, Scarlett.

Dashiell pointed me to the chair opposite his desk, and we both sat down.

It was my turn to open a file of photos in front of him. I took a deep breath and passed over the two shots of the Hess children. "Emily and Jared Hess," I told him, tapping their faces, just as he'd tapped the photos of the dead vampires. "Ten years ago tonight, Emily disappeared from La Brea Park, where she'd been playing with her brother after dark. Jared told the police he saw monsters drinking her blood, but they ignored him—or were paid to ignore him."

Dashiell picked up the photo of Jared and studied it with renewed interest.

"Jared was very angry."

"Go on."

"All this time, we've been focusing on Abraham, figuring that he was the main victim and the other two a distraction. But Gregory told me that Joanna liked to feed from children." I looked up, meeting his eyes. "Someone had to have called Olivia to clean up this scene at the park. Am I getting warm?"

Dashiell leaned back in his chair, looking thoughtful rather than simply angry. I hoped that was a good thing. "I remember this now. You are correct, Scarlett. Joanna went too far, and I sent Olivia in for the cleanup. We didn't know that there was another child on the scene that night. When it made the newspapers, it seemed so perfect—crazy teenage boy kills little sister, hides the body. Joanna was punished—by Abraham, who took care of those things for me." He stared at the ceiling, as if reading text from the tiles. "I believe he had her starved."

I shuddered. Olivia had told me once that Dashiell's punishment for the vampires was to lock them in a basement cell with no access to blood. They would never die, but they could sometimes go insane. Or in Joanna's case, probably more insane. "And you're just telling me this now?" I tried to keep my voice level.

"Scarlett, Joanna has had a handful of these incidents in her centuries of life. She was starved for five years then released, and she hadn't made any trouble since. I had forgotten all about it."

Steady, Scarlett, steady. "You *forgot* about your crazy pet child killer?"

He sighed impatiently, as if that were a foolish question. "Of course, it would have been simpler to just destroy Joanna, but she happened to have powerful friends, Ariadne among them. We don't kill our own lightly, Scarlett. To have her destroyed for harming a few human children would have created certain...tensions."

Created tensions. I clenched my hands together, my fingernails whitening, so I wouldn't punch him. He could easily decide to just shoot me right there and be done with it.

"With respect, Dashiell, I think that might have been a mistake," I said very carefully. "Because Jared Hess is still out there, and I don't think he's done mourning his sister. He killed Joanna and Abraham, he killed the only witness, and since he couldn't kill Olivia, he tried to set up her protégée." I explained the weird timing of the last two murders, how by all odds I should have arrived on scene just in time to get caught. "He's going after everyone involved, Dashiell, and *you* made the call to Olivia. He's gotten information from somewhere; he's going to know that you ordered the setup. If he's cleaning up loose ends...You've gotta be on his list."

There was a long pause while Dashiell stared at the photos. I gazed at him, wondering if his deal was still on the table. Wasn't this enough? Did I still have to find the actual killer? Didn't Dashiell have plenty of thugs to handle that kind of thing? I could just send one of them to Corry's rendezvous, no null included, and—

"I appreciate your efforts, Scarlett, but I'm afraid this changes nothing," he said at last, interrupting my thoughts. "I am tempted to not even let you leave. It would solve so many problems if I made it known that you'd confessed, and I had simply killed you."

My eyes went straight to his hands, which were fidgeting in his lap, altogether too close to his gun. "But Jared Hess—"

He held up a hand, glaring at me, and my mouth snapped shut by itself. "You still do not understand, do you, Scarlett? I don't care a thing for Jared Hess. If I simply kill you, I will remove the only power he has over me, will I not? After all, you still haven't found this so-called second null, have you?"

I swallowed again. Corry couldn't be part of this. She still had a chance. "No."

"So you are still the best suspect, at least from my point of view. I kill you, and even if Hess comes for me, he will not make it so far as the front door before we kill ..im. And my reputation, as it were, will be restored."

As he spoke, he looked more and more thoughtful, and my legs started to go all rubbery with fear. I let the silence linger for a moment, then blurted, "But you're not going to do that, right?"

His attention returned to me, and he tapped his fingers along the antique blotter on his desk. "Not yet. You may thank Beatrice for that; she seems unusually fond of you. I have promised her that I would let you be until our deadline. In, what? Eight hours."

As I left Dashiell's and hurried for my van, I worked to push aside my panic and concentrate. What had I learned? Jesse's theory was probably correct—Jared Hess had to be the killer. But so what?

How did that help me? I glanced at my watch: 10:00. I still had an hour and a half to go before the meeting with Jay at Corry's place. I tried Jesse's phone again, but this time it didn't even ring, which probably meant that the phone was off. So now what was I supposed to do?

I needed Jesse, I decided. If he wouldn't answer his phone, then I would just have to go get him. I would go to the precinct. Just as I started the van, though, my cell phone began to howl "Black Magic Woman." Kirsten. I answered, because even in the middle of the most frightening crisis of my life, Olivia's training still stuck, damn her.

"Hey, Kirsten—"

"Is this Scarlett Bernard?"

I blinked in surprise. The voice was panicked, frightened—and unquestionably male.

"Uh, yeah. I'm sorry, who is this?"

"My name is Paul Dickerson. Kirsten is my wife."

My heart sank through the floor of the van and into the freeway. "Tell me what's happening, Mr. Dickerson."

His voice raised an octave, hysterical. "He took her. He had a thing, a...a stun gun, and he took her. I found your number in her phone. It said, *Emergencies*. This is a fucking emergency. Can you come?"

I suddenly understood. Jared Hess didn't just hate Joanna or the vampires, he hated the Old World. That was why he'd killed Ronnie, who really hadn't seen anything in the clearing. The vampires, the werewolf...And now he had Kirsten. God.

But then I remembered how Hess had used Ronnie's cell phone to text Will, and I hesitated. "Mr. Dickerson, what does Kirsten keep on her kitchen counter? The big granite counter by the sink?"

"What?"

"Please, just answer."

"It's a...What do you call it? A pestle and mortar. She has two."

"I'm on my way."

For the first time since I'd started my new life in the Old World, I was *shattering* my speeding rule.

As I raced toward Kirsten's, I tried calling Corry's cell, but the recorded operator's voice informed me that the voice mailbox was unavailable. I tried Eli, who was working and must not have heard his cell, and Jesse, who still didn't answer. He couldn't be *that* mad at me, could he? With our lives on the line? I pounded the steering wheel in frustration. Where the hell was my backup, dammit! I was not a detective! I did not carry a gun! This was bullshit!

I sped on.

At ten fifteen, nearly all of the lights were off in the houses on Kirsten's street. A single lamp was lit in Kirsten's front window, and I felt a chill as I pulled the van into the driveway. If Paul Dickerson was freaking out, why weren't all the lights blazing? As a matter of fact, why hadn't he called the rest of Kirsten's coven? I would think they'd be in full witch mode, working tracking spells. Unless he didn't know about the coven? I switched off the engine nervously and sat for a moment peering at the house. Then I looked at the clock and shrugged. Fuck it. I did not have time to play Suzy armchair detective. I stepped out of the van, strode up the driveway, and rang the doorbell. Kirsten's door has a little window at eye level in lieu of a peephole, and I saw the curtain behind it move. A man's eye looked me over, and then the eye disappeared and I heard the doorknob turn. As the door opened, I peered into the dark house.

"Mr. Dickerson?"

"Not exactly."

The voice was wrong. I knew right away and took an instinctual step back, turning to run. But before I'd even shifted my weight, a hand shot up and I smelled a harsh chemical like burned cinnamon, and suddenly, I was in terrible, agonizing pain. I gasped, and my overloaded senses put it together—mace.

My eyes were instantly streaming, and I let out a wail of pain, which was the man's cue to seize my arm, dragging me into the house. I kicked wildly in his direction, but it was like fighting in the dark, and he easily evaded me. Amid the burning pain, I felt another—a sharp prick in my arm. By the time I was able to assemble my thoughts around the word *needle*, I was out.

Chapter 28

Jesse Cruz was feeling extremely stupid.

He'd stormed out of the coffee shop like a kid throwing a tantrum, and realized within about ten minutes that he was being ridiculously shortsighted. The revelation that Scarlett was willing to help disappear murdered kids had really thrown him, partly because he really had seen the kind of devastation that unsolved murders wreaked on a family, and, if he was being honest with himself, partly because he was just disappointed that his *crush* would do something like that. That moment in the coffee shop had made him realize, for the first time, just how attracted he was to the damaged girl with the green eyes. And so he'd lost his temper.

Even though it was a much better time to be making sure both of them lived through the night. Back at his desk, Jesse had pulled out his cell to call Scarlett but realized the battery was dead. And, of course, he hadn't actually written down her number, just programmed it into his phone. Sighing, he had trooped downstairs to the parking garage to get the phone charger out of his car, only to realize that he'd left it at his parents' house over the previous weekend. He rolled his eyes. Vampires and werewolves were running amok in the city, and he couldn't remember a cell phone charger.

Jesse had headed back into the building to look up Scarlett's number in the department's computer system, but was detained in the hallway by Miranda, who wanted an update on the files he'd gone through. Thanks to Glory, he'd gotten away with the midday disappearance, but Jesse was still trying to convince Miranda that he could do the job. By the time he had gotten back to his desk, looked up the number, and phoned Scarlett, she wasn't answering. The call went straight to voice mail, which meant she'd turned the phone off. Could *she* be mad at *him*?

If so, it was a damn juvenile time for the silent treatment, he thought, then felt hypocritical. Jesse decided to give her half an hour, then try again. He spent the time trying to reach Freedner again, but the human servant's cell phone also went straight to voice mail. Frustrated, Jesse entered Freedner's name into the department's system again, on the off chance that he'd been given a traffic ticket or picked up by the police in the last day. He was shocked when Freedner's name actually got a hit.

Jesse skimmed the report, made that morning by a uniform in the Downtown division. Thomas Freedner, 30, had been found in a cheap downtown hotel that morning, dead by a self-inflicted gunshot wound. There had been a note, and the ME had confirmed the death as a suicide. The uniform had noted that the room was full of empty whiskey bottles and several vials of Valium. The department had already closed the case.

Jesse leaned back in his seat, stunned. Could Freedner have been the La Brea Park killer? He could have holed up in the hotel after the murders, working up the courage to shoot himself, and then finally followed through. But then why kill Ronnie the werewolf? Even if Freedner thought Ronnie had witnessed something, if he was planning to commit suicide anyway, why would it have mattered? It just didn't fit.

Jesse picked up the phone to try Scarlett, hoping she'd have some insight. When the call went to voice mail again, he started to seriously worry. He left a brief message and then sat at his desk, not even pretending to look busy. Where would she have gone? He thought of the file he'd left with her when he'd stomped out of the shop—it was no big deal, everything had been copies, but had she decided to try to investigate further on her own? Where would she even go? It had to be something Old World, he finally decided. And that meant it was out of his jurisdiction, so to speak.

Jesse tried to find a number for Molly, but she apparently didn't exist. He fretted over trying to call Dashiell, but figured that Scarlett would kill him if it turned out she was just somewhere with a dead phone and he'd pissed Dashiell off for nothing. He found a name and address on his computer for a Jack Bernard in Esperanza, California, but when he called, the phone line had been disconnected. If Scarlett really didn't keep in touch with her brother, Jack was not a great option anyway. Finally, Jesse pulled out the good old-fashioned Yellow Pages and called the werewolf bar.

"Hair of the Dog, this is Eli," a voice shouted over loud punk rock.

"Hey, this is Jesse Cruz. We met the other night at Scarlett Bernard's house?" *When I unlocked silver handcuffs for you in front of the girl I think we both might like,* he thought. "Have you seen her tonight?"

"What? No. Hang on, let me get back to the office." The phone clicked in Jesse's ear, and he sat through a couple of minutes of a Muzak version of "The Rainbow Connection." When Eli picked up the phone again, the bar cacophony had vanished. "Has something happened?" Eli asked, straight to business. Jesse realized the guy reminded him of Scarlett.

"No. Well, maybe. I'm not sure. Did she...um...tell you about her deadline with Dashiell?"

"What deadline?" Eli said, the beginning of alarm in his voice.

Praying he wasn't digging himself or Scarlett into more trouble, Jesse explained about the second null and Dashiell's demand that she either bring him the killer or turn herself in to die by 5:00 a.m. And that now Scarlett was out of contact, and he was afraid she'd gone off on her own to investigate. When he was finished, there was a long, heavy silence on the line.

"She told me Dashiell suspected her, but not that he was planning to kill her," Eli said, his voice just barely above a growl. "Probably because she knew I'd go to Pasadena and rip his goddamned head off."

"Can you really do that? Beat him?" Jesse asked, a little hopeful.

There was a pause, and then Eli sighed into the phone. "No. I'm strong, nearly as strong as our alpha, but I'm not sure even he could take Dashiell. And Dashiell has an awful lot of guys who work for him. Scarlett would even the playing field, but I still couldn't take that many."

"Do you think maybe she ran? Tried to avoid Dashiell entirely?"

"Nah," Eli said after a moment. "It's not really her style. Plus, she has no money, no family that I know of, and Dashiell has a lot of contacts. Scarlett knows she doesn't really have anywhere to go."

Scarlett hadn't told Eli about her brother. Interesting. "So either she's just stranded somewhere with a flat tire and a dead cell battery, or—"

"Not likely. Have you seen how she takes care of that van?"

"Or it's gotta be the killer," Jesse continued grimly. "I don't know much about how you guys handle things. What should we do now?"

"Can't you, like, trace her cell phone?"

"I tried that—illegally, by the way—half an hour ago. The battery is dead or disconnected. She could be anywhere."

"Okay. I got something I can try, but I can't involve you."

"What? What are you talking about?"

"It's better if you don't know, and I don't have permission to out the party in question, anyway. Give me your number."

Jesse recited it, still pissed.

"Okay. Do whatever you can on the cop side of things. I'll call you as soon as I know something."

There was a click, and Jesse found himself staring at a silent phone. "You've got to be kidding me," he told it. Was Eli going to do something illegal, and he didn't want Jesse to know about it? But he'd just confessed to illegally tracing Scarlett's cell phone, so what would that even be? He ground his teeth.

With nothing better to do, he went back to the original copy of the Hess file, flipping through it. Other than the battered arrest photo he'd shown Scarlett, there were no other pictures of Jared Hess, whose identity had been protected as a minor. Jesse dug through the police report until he found the name of Jared's high school—Elm Grove Senior High. Then he logged on to the school's website, searching for online yearbook pages. There were some, but only for the last five years. After some thought, he went to Classmates.com and laboriously went through the school's registered users until he found a few that were still in LA. Jesse looked at the clock: 11:00. *Screw it*, he thought. He picked up the phone.

Thirty minutes and three irritated classmates later, Jesse stood by the floor's ancient fax machine, nervously tapping a beat out on his legs. He'd found a former cheerleader who had been fond enough of her glory days to keep the yearbook handy. The old machine wheezed and sputtered, finally spitting out a scanned page of photos from Elm Grove's yearbook. He ran his finger along the row next to the name *Hess, Jared*, stopping at a grainy shot of a young man with glasses and protruding ears. Jesse stared. Then he leaned his back on the wall and stared a little more, until he was absolutely positive he recognized the face. And he knew Thomas Freedner had nothing to do with the murders.

Now Jesse felt very, very stupid.

Chapter 29

I woke up to a dripping sound.

Plurp...plurp...plurp went the water, and I squeezed my eyes open and shut a few times, trying to clear them. My eyes and nose still hurt, but in a fading way, like when your cold medicine is just beginning to kick in. My head felt like it was full of thick soup, though, and for a few minutes—or maybe a few hours—I couldn't seem to organize myself. Where were my hands again? Was I lying down or sitting up? I shook my head back and forth until my orientation started to return, and then I moved my hands up to rub my eyes, only they stopped halfway to my face. I squeezed my eyes shut again, then opened them and looked around.

Water was dripping from a pipe into a puddle a couple of feet away from me. I was sitting on the floor, my back against the wall and my wrists chained in front of me in handcuffs that connected to an enormous metal ring stuck deep into the concrete floor. The ring was as thick as my ankle, and every link in the chain was thicker than my thumb, but I gave the whole contraption an experimental tug anyway. I could barely get the chain to move, much less the metal ring. I would not be escaping this via strength.

I looked around, squinting into semidarkness. With the concrete floor and windowless walls, I assumed this was a basement, though they're rare in Southern California. The metal ring I was chained to was in the back of the basement, opposite a set of shoddy-looking wooden stairs that presumably lead up to the next floor. The basement's only light spilled down the stairs from the room above, though I wasn't at an angle to see up into it. I squinted toward the darkness, waiting for my eyes to adjust. Fifteen feet away from me, on the left side of the steps, there was a tool bench that looked fully loaded with...something. I squinted even more. I caught a few metal reflections shining here and there, standing out against the gloomy mess. *Silver.* On the other side of the stairs and a little closer to me stood a gleaming metal cage, like a kennel for the world's biggest dog. Or, I realized, a werewolf.

He'd built a cage for werewolves.

I shivered against the dank cold. My canvas jacket had been removed, and I didn't see it anywhere near me, so maybe it was up the stairs. *Or by Kirsten's front door, or anywhere in between,* I thought, fear igniting in my stomach. I had no idea where I was, and worse, no one else had any idea, either.

I don't know how long I just sat there, trying to push away my fear, but after what seemed like hours, I heard a telltale creak and saw a work boot hit the first wooden stair, immediately followed by another boot, a pair of jeans, and a T-shirt. The man flicked a switch at the bottom of the stairs, and light burst into my eyes. When they adjusted, I realized I was looking into the face of Aaron Sanderson, the guy who owned the bait shop.

"You," I said brilliantly.

He smirked. "Me." Aaron Sanderson/Jared Hess made his way across the basement floor, stopping a few feet away from me and folding his arms across his chest. Up close, with only the T-shirt, I realized just how muscled his arms and chest were. How had I not put this together?

"Where's Kirsten?"

He grinned broadly. "On her way to a wedding in Santa Barbara. But damned if she didn't forget her cell." He held up a little blue phone, waving it in front of me like a kid teasing his little sister. "And her keys." He held them up in the other hand.

"What'd you do, steal her purse?"

"Something like that."

"Bad idea," I told him. "Kirsten isn't a great person to mess with."

He snorted. "Whatever. What's she going to do, hex me with warts?" He had dropped the slightly dim, down-home act we'd seen at the bait shop.

"What do you want, Jared?"

He raised an eyebrow. "You know who I am."

"Yes. And I know about Emily."

"You know nothing about Emily," he countered, venom in his voice.

I finally pulled my knees to my chest, putting my cuffed arms around them, and hugging my legs. I didn't want to look weak, but I was freezing. "I know that Joanna killed her and that you killed Joanna, and the vampire who was with her that night, and the vampire who only punished her for a few years instead of ending her. I know that you killed Ronnie, too, although I don't know why."

"Oh, that was for you."

I felt sick. "Just to set me up?"

He rushed toward me then, and I cringed involuntarily, expecting a slap, but he dropped down a few inches from my face and grabbed my ankles, dragging them out so he could sit on my legs. He put one hand around my throat to pin me against the wall. He wasn't strangling me, but I could feel the strength in his hands, how easy it would be. I tried not to move, not to draw any more attention. He looked down at my trapped legs, my stomach, his eyes lingering on my breasts. Holding me there, he leered. "Not *just*. What you do, you and that dead bitch, is a goddamned crime. You deserve to be punished for it. I thought it would be great for you to go to prison for murder; it had a nice ring of irony about it.

But you were just supposed to be a bonus, a little footnote to the plan, and I got tired of you slipping away. I'll settle for just killing you myself."

"Then why don't you?"

He gave me a wicked smile. "I need you first. One more job."

"I won't do it."

He hit me then, a hard backhand that spurted blood into my mouth. I saw stars for a second, and when my vision cleared, he was smiling. "Not so tough now, are you?"

Oh, come on. Stubborn and sullen are my frickin' trademarks. So I spat a glob of dark blood into his face. He screamed in outrage, jumping back a few steps and scrubbing at his face with the tail of his T-shirt.

"Feel better, you spineless son of a bitch? Does it make your tiny penis feel all big and hard to smack around girls? You think that would make Emily happy?"

He bellowed with rage, starting to crouch back down to pounce on me, but just as suddenly, he paused, smiled, and straightened up. "Nope," he said cheerfully, bouncing a little on his toes, "not going to work. I'm not going to kill you just so you don't have to help me. Besides, you *want* to help me." He reached for his back pocket, and I tensed, but he just pulled out an old-fashioned Polaroid picture and flipped it to the ground in front of me.

I reached out my shackled hands and turned it over. It was Corry, with her mom and brother, unloading a suitcase in front of a big Holiday Inn sign. She wore the same jeans and green top I'd seen her in that evening. She was biting her lip, looking worried, but her mom was reaching a reassuring arm toward her daughter's shoulders.

"Remember, you're not the only game in town anymore. Little Corry is all safe and cozy—as long as you do what you're told. If not, I slit your throat and go pick up our girl. I'm not particularly interested in having to kill her *whole* family to take her, but if you insist on making me kill you..." He grinned, and a shiver of fear passed through me.

It was coming to my attention that he was batshit crazy. I turned my head and spit the rest of the blood on the concrete floor. If Hess killed me, maybe Jesse would find my DNA somehow and catch the fucker.

"How did you find her?" I asked.

"Little Corry? Contacts." He leaned back and spread out his arms, grinning. "I've got contacts all over town, on both sides of the Old World."

"Both sides?"

He cocked his head, looking closely at me; then he giggled. "You really don't know? You think there aren't even a few humans who know what's going on, who want to put the animals down?"

I stared. "Like...vampire hunters? You've gotta be kidding."

He smirked at me.

I decided it wasn't important for the moment. "What do you want?"

"I want *him*," he hissed. "Dashiell. The one who makes this all possible. He let that vampire whore kill Emily and did nothing to keep her from doing it again. He hires bottom-feeding twats like you to keep everything covered up and makes sure the police find someone else to blame. Like a grieving sixteen-year-old." He spat out the last few words with an intensity that would have terrified me if I weren't already so numb.

"You want to kill *Dashiell*?" I asked dumbly. I have to admit, for an instant, I thought about just helping him do it. I would probably die anyway, but Corry would be safe. And it wasn't as if I were feeling particularly loyal to Dashiell, who was planning to kill me in a couple of hours, regardless.

But after that instant of consideration, I remembered what Beatrice had said about lesser evils, and I knew she was right. There were other vampires in this town, and not all of them were willing to play nice with the werewolves, or make deals with cops, or keep their minions from killing without prejudice. Like Ariadne, who gave off more than a whiff of batshit crazy herself. Killing Dashiell wouldn't solve my problems. It was just create more, and for everyone.

But it didn't matter; I was wrong about Jared's intentions.

"No, I'm not going to kill him. Another like him would just take his place—it's pointless. But I've been making silver for the vampires for years and years, getting to know all the ins and outs of his little troupe, and I figure there's only one thing that he loves, truly loves, in the entire world. So I'm going to kill her."

My stomach dropped. "Beatrice?" I whispered.

Chapter 30

From the way he'd looked at me, I'd been more than a little afraid that Jared Hess had pre-murder plans for my body, but after his little gloating session, he stomped back upstairs. I twisted my wrist around far enough to peer at my watch. It was midnight. I hoped that Jesse had cooled off enough to worry when he couldn't get a hold of me, but I had little hope for him storming the basement to save me. Kirsten or one of the more powerful witches could have tracked me with an object that belonged to me, but Kirsten was in Santa Barbara, apparently, and Jesse didn't know how to get a hold of anyone. I didn't think he even knew Kirsten's name.

I thought about Corry for a long time. She'd seemed so full of confusion and pain, and despite the direness of my own current situation, I was overwhelmed with sympathy for her. Being a teenager is hard enough without sexual assault and murder staining your soul. Even if I could successfully keep her out of the rest of this ordeal, I wondered if she'd be able to recover from what she'd done, and what had been done to her. There's no therapist for the supernaturally inclined, as far as I know. I hoped she wouldn't lose herself to this.

Then I thought about the two men who had suddenly become so prominent in my life. There was Jesse, of course, who had seemed like he might like me. That moment in the bait shop parking lot came back to me, when he had looked at me as if I were just a girl, a girl that he liked. But I'd also seen the look on his face in the coffee shop. To him, I was tainted. Ethically compromised. And I couldn't really blame him. I had been right when I'd thought that there was something pure about Jesse. I just hadn't realized how little purity there was left in me. No, even if I were...well, not so messed up, Jesse wouldn't be wanting to date me anytime soon.

And Eli. What the hell was I doing with Eli? For starters, I was avoiding letting him get the least bit close to me. I thought about that first night in the bar and the look on his face when I came back for him at Artie's. I reached a couple of conclusions: First, I couldn't let go of the idea that he just wanted me for the calm only I could give him. But at the same time, the way he treated me wasn't the way you treat someone who's just calming. It's the way you are to someone you want. Did I want him back? This was a thought I'd never really considered much, which just goes to show you how deeply messed up I am. It hadn't occurred to me that I might want someone.

Since Olivia died, I had been going through the motions. Clean up crime scenes. Ignore my brother. Watch TV with Molly. Have slightly drunken sex with Eli. Do laundry. Repeat. I might as well have died with Olivia, or with my parents, for all the living I've been doing. But since the moment when I'd decided to push for Jesse to live, it felt as if I were waking up—not that I particularly wanted to. It's so much easier to just think of your life as a giant checklist that has to be worked through. But like it or not, I couldn't sit on the bench anymore. If I made it through the dawn—and really, I had no idea how—I needed to get in the game. Somehow.

Here endeth the pep talk.

Jared Hess had left the light on when he'd gone upstairs, and I was able to twist my wrist around and check my watch, which I did incessantly. At twelve forty-five, Hess came stomping down the stairs, looking very pleased with himself. He was wearing a long black coat, which did little to conceal the two large guns he had under each arm. A bulletproof vest peeked out over his T-shirt, and

I caught a glimpse of a silver knife at his ankle. A wicked-looking dagger was in his hand as he clomped over to me, and he slid it up his coat sleeve, where I assumed there was some kind of a holster.

The big guns. If he was bringing me along, he wouldn't need the knives—Beatrice would go down with one well-placed shot. But clearly, Jared was planning for contingencies. That was not good for me.

"Ready for the field trip?" he said, grinning at me.

He pulled his coat sleeve over the stake and buttoned up the front of his shirt. Then he crouched down in front of me. For once, he was careless about being near my legs, but after a moment's consideration, I decided against kicking him in the face. It would be satisfying, but I wasn't escaping with my hands shackled to the floor, so it'd really only piss him off. And he was stronger than I was; if he hit me again, that would be bad.

"I have to say, you stay in pretty good shape," he said, looking admiringly at my body again.

I tried not to shrink away. I've worked with vampires long enough to know that you don't shrink away from predators.

"God, this is fun, isn't it?" he said happily. "I've been waiting years for this, and now that the night is finally here, I want to celebrate." He reached over to twine a hand in my long hair, then yanked it so I had to tilt my face toward him.

Involuntary tears pooled in my eyes.

"What do you say, little girl?" he whispered, flicking my earlobe with his tongue.

It took everything I had not to shudder away, but I had no room to move, anyway.

Without letting go of my hair, he leaned his weight on my legs and pulled out a tiny key ring, reaching for the cuffs. "You want to celebrate with me?" He was like a little kid, hyper and trying to make everyone else get worked up, too. I knew he just wanted to get a rise out of me, so I stared stubbornly at the floor.

I was in the middle of reevaluating my no-face-kicking decision when the sky fell down.

Okay, it wasn't the actual sky, but it was a damned big piece of the floor above us. With a sudden crash, a six-foot-square chunk of linoleum landed about eight feet to the right of us, with two people riding it down. I squinted past the cloud of dust and made out Kirsten and Eli. Jared yelped and released me, darting to the other side of the room to take cover behind the tool bench. Kirsten, whose powers had vanished the second they dropped through the floor, hopped off the shattered floor section and wisely crouched down behind one of the basement's wooden support columns, keeping it between herself and Jared.

"Hope you have insurance," she yelled toward the tool bench. She was wearing a pretty floral shirt over a simple blue cocktail dress and looked like an angel when she smiled my way. "Hey, Scarlett."

Eli had run straight for me, and I was so glad to see him I choked on my first three attempts at speech. "He's...you...You came," I stammered.

He smiled a sweet, joyful smile that I knew I would remember until my death. "Of course I came. Why wouldn't I come?"

The first bullet hit the wall six inches from my head, and I hissed with surprise. "Keys, keys, keys," I chanted frantically, pointing to where they'd fallen when Jared had bolted. I ducked down, making myself small, and the second shot hit right where my head had been. Jared wasn't just shooting wildly; he was taking the time to aim, which did not bode well for Team Scarlett. Eli scrambled for the keys and then crawled back to me. I was trembling with adrenaline, and my shaking slowed down his attempt to get the key in the lock. I fought to keep still.

All the while, he ducked as silver bullets flew past us to drill into the wall. "Got it," he said breathlessly, and I started to stand, but Eli pushed me back down just in time for the next bullet to bury itself in his back instead of my chest.

"Eli!" I screamed. I looked around frantically for a weapon. I needed to stop Jared Hess and get that bullet out, but if I moved too far from Eli, the silver poisoning would begin. All I had on my side of the basement was a ring of keys, a giant silver cage, and a bunch of stuff that was bolted into the floor. I had nothing.

And then I realized that wasn't true.

Eli tried to push me toward Kirsten and the exit, but I shook him off easily. I gauged the distance and tugged him the other way, to the wooden column opposite her. As the two of us half crawled, half stumbled behind it, I felt the quick slide of power as the witch in the corner came free of my radius.

"Kirsten," I yelled, "you're up!" Then I tried to breathe calmly. The last thing we needed was for me to get all emotional and have my radius expand.

I'd never seen Kirsten work before, so I stared, awestruck, as her hair began to crackle with power and energy. She chanted in something like Latin, and suddenly, the section of ceiling above the tool bench began to rattle and shake, bits of dust and ceiling tile salting the air around where Jared was hiding. He screamed in alarm and bolted away just as a perfect four-foot square of ceiling came crashing down where he'd been crouched. He raced toward Eli and me, pulling out a new gun, but suddenly, he was cut short, bouncing backward as though he'd been swatted. I looked over at Kirsten, who was still chanting. I tried to swallow my shock. I had known that Kirsten was good, but not this good.

Hess screamed with frustration and spun on his heel, cutting his losses. He ran up the stairs, vanishing onto the first floor. As quickly as it had begun, the fight was over.

I barely noticed. Eli had collapsed on the ground, and blood poured freely from the bullet hole in his upper back. There was so much that I could hardly see the entry wound.

"You stupid man," I scolded, trying not to cry into the wound.

I was trying to tear a strip of my shirt to put over the bullet hole. In the movies, they always rip bandages like nobody's business, but with shaking hands, I couldn't even get a tear started.

"Here," Kirsten said, unbuttoning the floral shirt, "take this."

I thanked her and pushed it down hard onto the bullet hole, leaning into it.

"Ow," he protested weakly.

"Shut up," I said. "What were you thinking, charging in here with no weapon? You could have been killed!"

"I brought a weapon," he argued, looking pointedly at Kirsten. "She kicked ass, too."

"Thank you, Eli," Kirsten said, smiling. She looked pale and tired. "I'm not usually a combat kind of witch, so I appreciate it."

"And how did you get here?" I asked her. "I thought you were going to Santa Barbara tonight. Or did he make that up?"

"No, I was there. But Eli knows one of the witches, who knew someone with Paul's cell phone number, and we left the reception. Then it was just a matter of the tracking spell."

"What'd you use?" I asked, my attention still focused on Eli's back. I almost missed the glance the two of them exchanged before Eli answered.

"I had a T-shirt you left at my place once."

I didn't remember doing that, but I didn't care, either. I gently eased Eli onto his side so I could check his chest. "Okay, I'm not a doctor, but I know it didn't go through, which means the bullet is still in there. And it's silver. I can't go after him until we get it out."

"You shouldn't go after him at all—" Eli began.

"Shut up. Concentrate on your bleeding," I told him firmly. I looked at Kirsten. "We have to get the bullet out. Once it's gone, I can move away, and he'll heal fast, but it has to come out first, or the silver will poison him."

"We can try to get it out the old-fashioned way. Hang on." She scuttled over to Jared Hess's workbench, and I heard tools rattling around. When she came back, she had what looked like an enormous pair of iron tweezers. "Do you want to do it?" she asked me.

I shook my head, suddenly afraid.

"Okay. Eli, this is gonna be messy and hurt like hell, but it should get the job done. Ready?"

He looked at me and reached toward me with his good arm. Seeing what he wanted, I dropped down to my side and scooted against him, chest to chest. I wrapped one arm carefully around his back above the bullet hole to hold him still.

"I'm ready," he said to Kirsten, but his eyes never left mine.

The next few minutes were some of the worst of my life, much less Eli's. Apologizing like crazy, Kirsten dug in with the forceps, while Eli made very human whimpering noises right beside me.

"Should we be worrying about infection?" she muttered to me.

I bit my lip. "I don't think so. The wolves never get sick; I don't think they can get infected. I think, when I move away, he should be fine."

Eli snarled at a particularly painful dig, burying his face in my neck, and a second later, Kirsten pulled back the forceps with a little smushed bullet pinioned in between them.

"I got it," she said shakily, then stood up. "Excuse me a minute." She sprinted over to the bottom of the stairs, where I heard her start to retch.

As soon as she moved, I started to get up myself, intending to get as far away as possible so Eli could heal. But he lifted a weak hand to snag my arm before I could fully stand. "Wait," he said, and I crouched back down. "I want to go with you," he said soberly. "You can't face that guy and Dashiell alone. Just give me a minute to heal and—"

"No fucking way," I told him, tears in my throat. "You got *shot*, Eli. With silver. And he's got a ton more silver ammo. I can't let you come."

"But—"

"No," I said, my voice rising. "I can't do it."

He paused and looked at me. "Can't do what?"

"I can't...I can't be responsible for anyone else getting hurt. Not today." In an attempt to ward off tears, I smiled. "And right now, I think I can even outrun you."

He opened his mouth to protest again, but I leaned down and kissed him, not very gently. His good arm rose to touch my face, and when I finally broke the kiss, he was smiling at me.

"I'll accept that as your surrender," I told him.

I let go of his hand and stood up, brushing off my jeans. "Where are we?" I asked Kirsten, who was sitting on the stairs now.

"A little ranch house in Burbank, just off the 101."

"Did you guys drive separately?"

She nodded, and I squatted back down to dig Eli's keys out of his pants pocket.

"Hey!" he said.

"I'm taking your phone, too. I'll bring it back later," I told him. I headed for the stairs before he could answer, feeling the tug as he slid out of my radius. The second he was out, he gave a surprised gasp, and I looked back to see color already returning to his face. Good. I went over to Kirsten and crouched to hug her. "Thank you," I said sincerely.

She gave a shaky laugh. "For the magic, anytime. But no more surgery, please."

"Deal." I ran up the stairs.

Corry.

By the time I got to Eli's truck, I realized I had no idea where to go. Corry and her family were staying at a Holiday Inn, but I didn't know which one. And Hess had a head start, too. I called Will, updated him on Eli, and asked for Corry's phone number, which was still in my cell phone back at Kirsten's. Then I called Corry's cell, which at least rang this time. When it went to voice mail, I punched *End* and immediately redialed. This time she answered on the fourth ring.

"Hello?" Her voice was cautious and hushed, probably trying not to wake her family.

"It's Scarlett. Where are you?" I said abruptly.

"Hi! Um, I thought I wasn't supposed to tell you where—"

"Corry, he got away. I tried to stop him, but he figured out what was going on, and he's coming for you. He knows where you are, do you understand? Tell me and I'll come get you."

"Oh God. It's the Holiday Inn in Burbank, off Colorado Boulevard."

I cursed and started the truck's engine, pulling away from the little house. Dumb fucking luck. If I was in Glendale, that was five minutes away. How long had it taken Kirsten to get the bullet out of Eli's shoulder?

More than five minutes.

"Corry, listen to me. He's gonna be there any second. Get your family up and take them to the lobby, somewhere with a lot of people, okay? Go *now*."

Before she could answer me, I heard a pounding on her end of the phone, and she gave a surprised little yelp. "Scarlett, he's here. He's trying to get in. Oh, God help us—"

"Corry? Corry!" I yelled into the phone, feeling helpless. Then the sounds stopped, and I checked the screen. Disconnected. I called 911 and directed the operator to the Holiday Inn, hanging up when she tried to ask questions. The police would be too late. And Corry and her family would be no match for Jared Hess when he was loaded for bear like that.

I picked a direction and stayed with it until I hit a major street. At a stoplight, I closed my eyes and conjured up my mental map of Los Angeles. I found the freeway and took the east exit toward Pasadena.

Then I called Jesse.

Chapter 31

After about four seconds, Jesse had realized that it wasn't as simple as storming over to Sanderson's bait shop and arresting him. First, he didn't even know whether Sanderson—Hess, he corrected—actually had Scarlett or whether he'd be in a position to kill her if Jesse sent in the cavalry. He'd already asked a police cruiser that had been in the area to drive past the bait shop, and they'd reported that the lights were all out and there were no parked cars in the lot or on the street in front of the building. It was likely that Hess was working from somewhere else, anyway. Jesse knew he had to slow down and think it through, that this was the moment when cops who were emotionally invested made serious mistakes, but he couldn't help the panic.

Think like a cop, he told himself. Even if he did get Hess, what then? Jesse didn't have a speck of evidence linking him to the La Brea Park case. If he really did have Scarlett, then Jesse might be able to get him on kidnapping charges, but that was assuming he could find them. He needed to bring the bad guy to the cops, and he needed Dashiell to know they had the right man in custody.

At midnight, he got sick of waiting and hopped in his car, heading toward the bait shop. On the way, he stopped at an all-night drugstore and bought a new car charger for the cell phone. When the phone booted up, he looked for messages, but there was nothing. He called Scarlett's phone again, but it was still turned off.

The cruiser had been right about the cars—not only was the strip mall's small lot empty, but the street on either side of it as well. Jesse parked in front of the bait shop—screw subtlety—and went right up and knocked on the door. He cupped his hands around his eyes to peer into the shop. Darkness. In the red glow of the emergency exit light, he could barely make out the different stands of merchandise, but that was about it. No lights under closed doors, no signs of life at all. Jesse thought back to his and Scarlett's visit to the shop. There had been only one back door, which led through the fireproof door to the little hallway. The office had been the only other door on the hallway, and then it had led straight to an exit. Jesse got into his car and circled around the building. He found the emergency exit door and checked for lights underneath. Nothing.

Jesse had just gotten back into his car when the phone rang, still plugged into the car charger. He grabbed too fast, fumbled it, and had to rescue it from the floor of the car.

"Cruz," he barked, breathless.

"Jesse, it's me."

He sighed in relief. "Oh, thank God. Where the hell have you been? Listen, I know who did it. Jared Hess became—"

"Aaron Sanderson, I know." Scarlett filled him in on the kidnapping, including her rescue and Jared Hess's plans for Beatrice.

"You're okay, though? Is Eli going to be okay?" Although they both seemed to like the same girl, Jesse didn't want to wish the guy any actual harm. Even with the whole *I can't involve you* bit.

"I am, and he will be."

"I can have the cops at Dashiell's in five minutes," he said.

"No! The police can't handle this, Jesse. You should know that by now. Even if we could get Jared Hess out of there, we can never take him to the cops to talk about the Old World. Most of them will think he's crazy, but a few will start to wonder."

He gestured helplessly with his free hand. "But we can't just—"

"Come on. You know Dash will never let that happen."

Just like that, Jesse saw his dreams of arresting the La Brea Park killer vanish. He rubbed his head, frustrated beyond words. The murders couldn't go unsolved. It would just terrify everyone—

"Jesse!" Scarlett yelled. "Are you listening?"

"Sorry, what?"

"I need you to meet me in Pasadena. Tell me you're somewhere close, please."

Jesse looked up at the bait shop. It was fifteen minutes on the freeway, tops. Less with the siren. "I'm a little closer than usual."

"Good. Bring your gun. We've got to go get Corry."

"Who's Corry?"

"The other null." Her voice grew agitated. "Hess took her, Jesse. She's only fifteen."

Pieces fell into place in his mind. "This is why you didn't want to tell me about her?"

"Yes."

"You could have trusted me, you know." She said nothing, and he put it aside for the moment. "Where should I meet you?"

"Dashiell's."

Jesse sort of remembered how to get there, but he still scribbled down the directions. The second he hung up, he threw the car into drive and put the siren in the window.

Chapter 32

I picked up Jesse at the bottom of Dashiell's long driveway and cruised toward the house with the headlights off, navigating mostly by memory. When I finally parked and turned off the van, I had the door open and one foot outside before Jesse managed to grab my arm.

"Wait," he said. "We need a plan."

After meeting Jared Hess, I was not in the mood for casual touching. "Let go of my arm. Now."

He released me. "What's your plan, Scarlett? You're going to run in there, unarmed, and demand the release of your teenage friend who happens to be co-responsible for the murder that's ruining Dashiell's non-life?"

"I admit that it lacks a certain finesse, but—"

"Stop," Jesse told me, and I closed my mouth, glaring at him. "Okay, look. Where would they be? What's the most likely place where Hess would confront them?"

I thought about it. "Either Dash's office or the patio. That's where Dashiell and Beatrice would have been, if Hess surprised them, and where they would receive guests, if he knocked on the door politely."

"What's the best way to get to those two areas?"

I quickly outlined the interior of the mansion: front door leading to foyer, foyer branching into hallway, hallway leading down to living room, which contained doors to patio area.

"And the office?"

"On the other side of the foyer."

"So basically, we pick left or right the second we get in the door?"

"Yeah."

"Okay." Jesse reached behind himself and took something that had been clipped to his belt. "Do you know how to use this?"

A Taser! I almost did a dance. "Yes, absolutely." He handed it over. It was a slightly more advanced model than my own, but the basics were the same. I should have three crippling jolts before it ran out of power. I felt better.

"Okay, what's your gut instinct? Patio or office?"

"Patio," I said immediately, before I could overthink it.

"All right. Stay close to me, be as quiet as you can, and let's go."

We snuck around the house via the little sidewalk path, and Jesse eased the front door open. Ordinarily, we wouldn't have a chance in hell of keeping our approach from the vampires, but I was hoping that all the vamps in the house were close enough to Corry to be human at the moment. Jesse stuck his head through the door into the dim interior, then looked back at me and inclined his head in the universal symbol for *Let's go*. I nodded.

As soon as we were inside, Jesse gently swung the door closed and motioned that I should lead. In the foyer, I turned right, heading down the long hallway toward the living room. Bizarrely, sneaking around the vampire's lair made me feel like a little kid again, staying up past my bedtime to play Capture the Flag with Jack and the other kids in our neighborhood. I felt the same rush of fear and excitement, and the sense that I was getting away with something.

Until I heard the gunshot.

Jesse and I exchanged a look, and I darted forward into the house, ignoring caution in favor of speed. The second we reached the doorway to the dark living room, however, I felt a gun barrel press against my temple.

"Stop right there," a familiar voice said very softly. In the silence, I could dimly hear muted voices coming from the patio, but I was at the wrong angle to see out the doors.

"Albert?" I ventured.

"Yeah."

"Who is he?" Jesse asked, hand frozen on his own gun.

"Albert is one of Dashiell's men. He's one of the guys who kidnapped me yesterday." Up close, I had the nagging feeling again that I had seen Albert before that. "But I know you from somewhere else, don't I?"

"Shut up."

I snapped my fingers. "The hospital. You were at the hospital visiting Olivia." Why would a vampire visit a dying null?

Next to my head, the sound of the gun's hammer being cocked sounded deafening. "I said," he spat, "shut the hell up."

My knees threatened to collapse. I shut up.

"First he hands me his gun. Then we can have a nice chat."

I was afraid to turn my head to look at Jesse, but at the edge of my vision, I saw him hand over his weapon.

"Okay, turn around," Albert ordered. I did. His small face looked tired and tense, and his rumpled suit looked as if it had seen better days. "What the fuck are you doing here?"

"We're here to help Dashiell."

Albert snorted, a very human sound. "Like hell. Isn't Dash planning to kill you in a few hours?"

"That's in a few hours. Did you see the girl?" I asked bluntly. "The teenager?"

A look of uncertainty flashed across his face. "Yeah, so?"

"Well, she's with me. And if the guy holding her hostage is trying to kill Dashiell, then I'm all about helping him."

"Sort of an 'enemy of my enemy is my friend' kind of thing," Jesse offered.

Albert considered this for a moment. "Then why were you trying to sneak in the door right behind Dashiell, where he couldn't see you coming?" He shook his head. "No, I think you're working with that asshole." He lifted the gun, which had drifted down a few inches. Those things are heavy when you're stuck as a human.

"Wait," I said, confused. "Is there another way onto the patio?"

"Yeah, of course. You think Dashiell would build a patio with only one exit? It's the servants' door, behind the big guy and the little girl."

"May I?" I said, inclining my head toward the patio doors.

He hesitated. "Fine. But he goes, too. Take more than three steps and you're done."

Jesse stuck to my side as I took a few steps into the living room to get a better view of the patio doors. Albert stayed in the doorway, pivoting the gun so it stayed on the two of us as we crept into the room. The living room was dark and the patio was bright with torches, so I wasn't too worried about being spotted. I took the allowed three steps and was able to see the scene outside. Sure enough, Dashiell and Beatrice were closest to the patio doors, with their backs to it. Hugo was on Beatrice's right. I saw Hess and Corry were standing up at the head of the table—and on their left, Ariadne and two men I didn't know were sitting opposite Dash and his people. The guy next to her was short and squat, with Hispanic features and a permanent frown. He wore an expensive black suit with no tie, but didn't wear it well. Next to him, across from Hugo, was a tall, lean man in black jeans and a cowboy hat.

Hess was saying something to Beatrice with a snarky look on his face, while Corry looked miserable and terrified beside him. Her plain green T-shirt was wet at the neck from tears, and— God, was her arm broken? Behind Corry, I could just make out the outline of a door, which had been painted to match the pink stucco of the exterior walls. No wonder I had never noticed it; I was generally scared and distracted whenever I met with Dashiell. There was a very small window in the door, at eye level, which I'd always thought was just a regular window into the house.

I turned back toward Jesse, telling him who was who, with the exception of the men I didn't know. "You see the door?"

"Yeah. Come on." We took the three steps back to the doorway, where Albert waited with the gun.

"Why is Ariadne here? And who is with her?" I hissed.

Albert's face was grim. "She came to make her move against Dashiell. Carlos is the master who's sponsoring her. The guy with them is a werewolf, muscle for hire."

Talk about your bad timing, I thought. I bet Ariadne was wishing she had waited just a bit longer for her hostile takeover.

"Why haven't you burst in there yourself?" Jesse asked Albert. "You could probably get a shot at Hess before he sees you. Isn't that the kind of thing Dashiell pays you for?"

Albert just stared at us nervously.

"He's afraid," I said, understanding. "There's a null out there, and he's scared of getting hurt or killed while she's so close. God, Albert, that really is cowardly."

"Shut up," he growled. "Listen, if you two are so brave, you're welcome to storm out there. I'll take you around to the servant door."

"Give me my gun and we will," Jesse retorted.

"So you can shoot me and then Dashiell? Yeah, right." Albert shook his head. "I may get in trouble for not rushing out there, but I'll definitely get dead if I let Scarlett Bernard waltz past me and take a shot at him. No, you go without a gun." I opened my mouth to protest, but he just glared at me. "Or I could always just shoot you here, see if the sound distracts that guy long enough for Dashiell to jump him. That seems like a good plan, too."

I closed my mouth and looked at Jesse. We didn't have time for this. He nodded at me.

"We'll go," I said to Albert.

"Fine."

As quickly as possible, Albert guided us in a wide circle around the patio, whispering directions in the dark as he held the gun at our backs. We ended up in a large, lavishly equipped kitchen that I had never seen before.

"Why do vampires need a kitchen?" Jesse whispered, but I just shrugged and rolled my eyes.

"Here," Albert said, pointing at the interior side of the servants' door.

I peeked through the little square. The vampire opposite Dashiell, the one closest to Corry, was saying something I couldn't hear.

"Do you have a plan?" Jesse asked me.

"I'll get the girl. You go for Hess."

"And the vampires?" he said, glancing at Albert, who was waiting fifteen feet back, still holding the gun and looking much more comfortable as a vampire.

"Hopefully won't try to kill us the second we get through the door."

"Okay." He took a step toward the door and then looked back. "Hey, I guess you're off the hook for murder."

I made a face at him.

"Ready?" he asked.

"Wait! Jesse?"

"What?" His eyes searched my face.

"Um, I'm just sorry. That you got sucked into this."

He grinned. "Weirdly? I'm not."

And we burst through the door.

Chapter 33

Jesse went straight for Jared Hess as though he had blinders on.
Hess heard the door open and swung the gun around, but by the
time he had it pointed the right way, Jesse had crossed the five
feet between them and tackled Hess around the waist, driving his
shoulder into Hess's wide torso. In his peripheral vision, he saw
Scarlett grab the teenage girl and crouch down in the nearest corner, getting her as far from the action as possible.

Hess went down with an *oomph*, and the gun went flying out of
his hand—and clattered straight down the long oval table, stopping
in front of the lean cowboy-looking guy with the shoulder wound.
The cowboy looked at the giant vampire across from him for a split
second and then dove for the gun, just as the big vamp pulled his
own out of a shoulder holster.

As the cowboy managed to shoot the vampire in the face, Ariadne screamed a terrible, inhuman scream and launched herself
over the big table, straight toward Beatrice. She was still in the
nulls' proximity, so her scramble across was more functional than
graceful, but she dropped into Beatrice's lap within a second, trying to dig black fingernails into the other vampire's eyes. Dashiell
cried out and tried to pry Ariadne off his mate, which caused the
vampire sitting across from him—Carlos—to jump onto the table
himself, trying to protect Ariadne.

Of course, Jesse only barely registered all of this, as he was in the middle of an old-school playground fight with Jared Hess. The two of them made a fairly even match: Jesse had trained in combat at the police academy, but Hess was fifty pounds heavier and fast as anything. Hess recovered from the tackle to pound terrible blows on Jesse's head and shoulders. Jesse jerked his head upward, slamming it into Hess's jaw, which snapped shut with an audible click. Hess released him but clubbed Jesse away with a punch on the ear, forcing him to roll away. For a moment, the world seemed to have lost gravity, and Jesse struggled to get his feet under him.

Hess stood up first and aimed a kick at Jesse's face, which he dodged fairly easily. Hess ducked Jesse's two return punches, driving a fist into his stomach, which forced Jesse to bend in half and take a breath. Hess took advantage of the pause and looked around frantically for the gun, but it was long since out of his reach. When he turned back to Jesse, though, the cop was ready for him, clasping his fists together and driving them up into Jared Hess's nose. Hess screamed with rage as blood flooded down his shirt, then swung blindly in Jesse's direction. Off balance, Jesse stumbled back and couldn't avoid Hess's vicious kick to his left knee. Jesse screamed with pain and shifted his weight as the knee threatened to crumple under him.

Dropping into a roll, Jesse crawled over to Scarlett, Hess right behind him, and she looked up and nodded in a moment of perfect understanding. She thrust the Taser into his hand, and Jesse turned and managed to flick it on just as Hess's hand closed around his throat. Jesse felt the secondary volt run through Hess's fingers and into his own neck, but by the time he registered it, Hess had gone limp, crumbling into a puddle six inches from Scarlett's sneakers.

The girl—Corry—cried out in fear and anger, and clutched at Scarlett with her good hand.

"It's okay, it's okay," Scarlett soothed, and Jesse looked around the patio.

Hugo the vampire was dead, and the cowboy guy was clicking an empty gun at his chest over and over, presumably trying to destroy his heart. The two women had moved to the foot of the long oval table and were wrestling on the ground, paying no attention to either modesty or fairness. They didn't fight like girls in movies—both women had kicked off their shoes and were doing their damnedest to land punches, though there was also more than a little ripping out of long hair. Beatrice had a long line of blood bisecting her face. Next to the patio doors, Dashiell and Carlos were circling each other with wary, fearful eyes. Both of their clothes were torn, and blood dripped from a gash on Carlos's torso. The air was filled with Ariadne's taunts and everyone's heavy, labored breathing. As though they weren't used to it, Jesse thought.

"Why are they still human?" Jesse whispered to Scarlett, nodding down toward the women. "Aren't they out of your range?"

"It's her," she said, looking at Corry. "She's too upset; it's making her perimeter expand."

"Let's get out of here while they're all distracted," Jesse said, moving toward Corry.

She whimpered, clutching Scarlett harder, and he felt like an unspeakable tool. *Yeah, move quickly toward the scared girl with the broken arm*, he scolded himself.

But Scarlett was shaking her head. "I can't go," she said quietly. "You have to take her out of here."

"What? Why?"

"Beatrice," Scarlett said, nodding down toward the other end of the table. "She can't fight Ariadne unless they're both human; Ariadne's way too powerful. I can't let her die."

Jesse cursed in Spanish. "She's a vampire!"

"She's also kind of my friend. And I can save her." She met his eyes. "Get Corry out of here; get her to safety. Check on her family. *Please*, Jesse."

He searched her face for a long moment, then sighed and nodded.

Scarlett saw his acquiescence and bent her head to whisper in
Corry's ear. Jesse heard her say, "He's a good man, honey, and he's
going to get you out of here. He won't hurt you, I swear to God."

Corry sobbed, nodding, and Jesse handed Scarlett the Taser
and gently gathered Corry into his arms.

"Go," Scarlett said, and he gave her one more look and limped
toward the door.

In the kitchen, Jesse staggered toward the interior door and tried
to get his bearings. "Albert!" he hollered impatiently, and he was
surprised to see Albert actually come running. "How do I get out
of here?" he demanded.

"Go down this hallway, take the last left, and the first right
after that puts you in the foyer." Albert pointed.

"Give me my gun."

The vampire hesitated.

"Take the ammo, Albert, just give me the damned gun!"

"Okay, okay." Albert fumbled the clip out of Jesse's police-
issue Glock and handed it over, grip first.

"Thanks. Go help your master. You might get there in time to
look like you're actually trying."

"Fuck you," Albert said, but he took off running back into the
kitchen. Jesse watched him go, said a prayer for Scarlett, and fled
the house with Corry.

Chapter 34

As soon as Jesse was through the door, I bolted across the patio, running parallel to the table on the opposite side from where Dashiell and the vampire I didn't know were still fighting. I pushed hard, putting all my years of running into the sprint. In a snatch of conversation, I heard Dashiell call the other vampire a dishonorable pawn—who talks like that?—but I didn't slow down as I passed the two men. As I hurried toward Beatrice, I saw both of the women jerk suddenly, their faces beginning to glow with power as Corry moved out of range, and I sprinted the last few steps as fast as I've ever run. Just as Ariadne recovered and turned on Beatrice again, I got close enough to get both of them back within my radius. Behind me, I heard the two male vampires cry out as I got far enough away again. They would be finishing their fights as vampires, God help us. I hoped Dashiell was up for it.

As I ran up, Beatrice recovered from becoming human again, a beat faster than Ariadne, and scrambled to her feet. She flashed me a grateful look and jumped back as Ariadne bellowed with fury. The goth girl rose and lowered her head like a bull's, charging straight for Beatrice. Positioned behind her, I saw what Bea couldn't—a long, wicked-looking sliver of glass clutched in Ariadne's hand. The charge was just a distraction. "No!" I yelled, but I was too late. Ariadne tackled Beatrice and drove the long piece of glass into her stomach, angling up to get the heart.

Ariadne's hand was bleeding hard from the edges, but she must have found her mark—Beatrice dropped like a stone in water, a tangled Ariadne falling with her. I realized that I was just standing there, and ran forward, grabbing Ariadne's wrist and dragging her off Beatrice. Ariadne crouched on all fours, panting, as I turned back.

"Bea? Bea!" I yelled, but Beatrice's eyes didn't so much as flutter in response. "Fuck," I groaned, and beside me, Ariadne began to cackle. I heard Dashiell screaming behind me, and the other vampire yelling in response, and then both of their cries were cut off suddenly as my temper flared and I felt the barriers of my power begin to swell. And swell.

The vampires behind me were human again, too, and I heard the sharp pop of a gunshot behind me. I turned and saw Dashiell standing over Hugo's body, holding the dead vamp's gun. It was pointed at the vampire he'd been fighting, who was crumpled on the ground. I could see the blood from this far away.

I didn't register any of that, though, because something was happening inside me. The edges of my aura had grown and grown and still wanted more ground. I felt it all, in that moment—my rage, my guilt, my sorrow for my parents, all of it rose and rose within me, and I poured it into my power, into the circle that had ceased to be a circle at all. Then I looked to Ariadne, who gazed up at me in sudden fear, and I turned that power toward her.

And then something broke inside me, and I felt a warm rush of blood from my nose as the world went dark.

Chapter 35

When I woke up, I could hear rain pattering against the window. *Weird*, I thought sleepily. Then I opened my eyes, squinting them into focus, and realized that I was lying down, that I wasn't wearing my clothes, and that I was in an unfamiliar bed, in that order. As my mind began to clear, I noticed the details—the disinfectant smell, the squeaking of tennis shoes on linoleum, the generic decor—and put together that I was in a hospital room. If it sounds as if I came to this realization very slowly...Well, I did.

"'Lo?" I croaked, my voice hoarse with disuse.

"Scar?" I turned my head left and recognized Eli, his face worried and pleased at the same time. "Are you really awake?"

"God, I hope not."

He laughed, much more than was warranted, and reached over to take my hand. "Oh, man, you had us worried."

"Why?"

"Scarlett, you've been asleep for three days."

"I have?" I tried to sit up in bed, then immediately regretted it. "What happened? Where's Corry? Is Beatrice okay?"

"Whoa, whoa, whoa. Hang on, there. They said you had some kind of seizure or something at Dashiell's and passed out while a bunch of vampires were fighting. Dashiell dragged you away from Beatrice, and she turned vampire again and healed from her wounds.

"Is Dashiell still gonna kill me?"

He frowned. "I don't think so, or he wouldn't have gotten you to the hospital."

"*Dashiell* brought me to the hospital?"

"Yeah."

"Corry?"

"The girl? I talked to your friend the cop—he'll be here after his shift, by the way; we've been trading off—and he said she was fine. She had to get a cast on her arm, but her family was okay. When that guy went to the hotel for them, Corry ran out to meet him so he wouldn't mess with her mom and brother. Pretty ballsy move for a fifteen-year-old, if you ask me." He smiled. "She's a really nice kid, Scar. I can see why you wanted to protect her. Oh"—his brow furrowed a little—"if I talked to you first, Cruz wanted me to tell you that he took care of Corry's tape. He said you would know what that meant."

It took me a second, but I figured it out: Jesse had destroyed the tape that Jared Hess had used to blackmail Corry. Thank God.

"S'wrong with me?"

His eyes flickered with worry. "I'm not sure. The doctors aren't, either, it sounds like. I'll call them in a second, but there's something else you should know first." He took a deep breath, and his face looked...almost nervous.

"What is it?" I asked.

"Uh...What do you feel?"

"What do you—Oh. Oh, wow," I said as I finally noticed that I couldn't feel him in my radius. I closed my eyes and concentrated. My eyelids flew open. "I can't feel anything. You're still a were. Did I...Am I broken?"

He shrugged. "Dashiell says no. He told Will it'll kind of... grow back. I think he's telling the truth—you still don't smell." He smiled, a little shyly. "But without it, you're vulnerable, which is why Cruz and I have been taking turns being here. He fixed his schedule to work days this week, so he's in at night and I'm here now." Eli's face darkened a little. "Dashiell stopped to check on you a couple of times, but Jesse didn't leave him alone with you." He grinned then, remembering something. "He pulled some cop language on the nurses, got them to let him stick around after visiting hours. They were kind of fawning over him."

"Okay, okay," I said, trying to take all that in. What the hell had happened to me?

"Here"—Eli reached over the arm guard and pushed the little red button to call the nurse—"we better tell them that you're awake."

The nurse came in to check on me, and a few minutes later, a balding, fiftyish man in a white coat strode into the room, too. An embroidered patch on his coat read, *Dr. Lipowitz*. I glanced at Eli to make sure we were comfortable with this guy, and he gave me a little nod and slid back in his chair to give the doctor room. Vetted.

"How are we feeling?" Lipowitz asked me, pulling out a little flashlight. He shone it into my eyes while I squinted.

I hate it when doctors use the word *we*. "Hate to speak for you, but I'm doing better."

Eli made a tiny sound like a snort, but Lipowitz frowned. Not a joker. "Any headaches?"

"Just a little one. What happened to me?"

He sat back in the chair, tucking the flashlight back in his coat pocket. "To be honest, Ms. Bernard, we're not really sure. You appear to have had a concussion, but there's no trauma to your head."

"A coma?" I asked, still working on arranging words properly.

He shook his head. "No, not technically. According to your MRI, your brain was simply overwhelmed." I must have looked confused, or maybe he just really liked lecturing. "Think of the brain as sort of an electrical outlet," he went on. "Yours just sort of…shorted out. We'd like to have you sign some forms allowing us to study your MRI further, and possibly even publish our findings."

I thought about that. It would be kind of interesting to know if there was something physically different about my brain, something that caused my nullness. Could I have it removed, like a tumor? But then it occurred to me that if there *was* something really different about my brain, then that could create a lot of fuss and attention that I didn't need.

I shook my head, rather weakly. I felt very tired. "No, thank you," I said.

I'd thought that was pretty polite, but the doctor got a little huffy about it. When his attempts to persuade me failed, and after Eli had started to get upset and suggested where the doc could put his studies, Lipowitz finally left. Which worked out well, because my eyelids were closing anyway. The last thing I was aware of as I drifted off was Eli squeezing my hand.

I didn't dream.

When I woke up again, darkness had fallen outside the window on my left. Jesse was asleep in the uncomfortable-looking armchair by the window. I half smiled. He looked so cute with his head bent all crooked. I slowly turned my head to the right—and saw Dashiell sitting in the chair next to my bed, looking calm and composed.

I may have let out a bit of a squeak. I swallowed and started again. "Are you here to kill me?"

"No, Scarlett." His face softened a little, and I let myself relax. "I owe you a debt of gratitude for saving Beatrice. I know I am not what one would call benevolent. But Beatrice...She is my heart."

I nodded, which hurt way less this time. "And Jesse?" I moved my head back to him as quickly as I could. *He is sleeping, right?* I thought with sudden panic.

"I pressed his mind to sleep for a few hours so we can speak. But yes, he can live, too, for now," Dashiell said seriously. Vampires have no concept of how silly they sound sometimes. "He has not spoken about our world to anyone, as far as we can tell, and he may turn out to be useful. He was certainly helpful in disposing of Mr. Hess."

"Huh?"

His brow furrowed. There was a little bit of a *pull* from his eyes, and I looked away quickly. I had to get used to avoiding vampires' gazes.

"I apologize. I thought you'd been told. Jared Hess's body was found in his bait shop three days ago. Mr. Hess had shot himself after writing out a full confession to the killings in La Brea Park." He smiled wanly. "Your pet policeman picked up the anonymous tip that led the police to the scene."

So squeaky-clean Jesse was willing to let another human being die without getting a trial—granted, a psychotic murderer, but still. Interesting. I would have expected to feel a little smug about that, but I mostly just felt guilty. I was too exhausted to think too much about that right now, so I set it aside for later consideration.

"Dashiell, Eli said you knew I would get better—that my thing would come back. How do you know that?"

He looked at my face thoughtfully for a moment, then reached into his pocket. I tensed, but he just pulled out a sleek little cell phone. The idea that vampires hate or fear new technologies is kind of a myth—you don't live to be hundreds of years old without learning how to adapt. Dashiell pushed a few buttons and held the phone up to me, sideways. It was a little video. I peered at it.

The video was of a nearly naked human woman screaming and throwing herself against the bars of a metal cell. Her face was bruised and swollen, and there were dark mascara streaks under her eyes, which made her look even more terrifying. I looked closer. She was wearing the tatters of a black sheath dress, and her disheveled hair was ink black as well. And then I gasped.

It was Ariadne.

"Is she...?"

"Human?" Dashiell nodded. "There were no nulls anywhere near her when this was taken."

"But that's impossible."

"I'm afraid not," Dashiell said quietly. "I have heard that a turn was possible for some of the very powerful nulls, but I had never known one who could do it. I suspect you are stronger than we knew." He hesitated for a moment. "I was aware that Olivia wasn't entirely forthcoming about some things, and I'm afraid I didn't help."

It was sort of an apology, but my brain was still foggy enough that I didn't get it. "Wait, what do you mean, a turn?"

"Scarlett," he said patiently, "you turned Ariadne into a human. Permanently."

My mouth dropped open in absolute shock. "You're kidding."

We were quiet for a moment while the implications of that sunk in.

"Dashiell, I would never turn you back," I said hurriedly, tears rushing to my eyes, "I promise. I wouldn't do that to you. I couldn't—"

He held up a hand to silence me. "I know." His eyes may have twinkled a little at me. "If you wanted me dead, Scarlett, you had plenty of chances that night at the mansion. But I must admit, this changes things."

"How?"

"I am not sure yet."

Another thought occurred to me. "What about your status with the other vampires? Is everything...okay now?"

"You mean, do I still have to find a scapegoat? No, I do not." He smiled at me again, but this smile was deeply unsettling. "My vampires now believe that Ariadne was behind the killings, and I let the mystery go on so long so I could flush out those who were faithful to her. My status is more secure than ever."

"And Ariadne?"

"She is no longer with us. I retained this video to show you, but I am not ready to let my people know about what it is you can do. Perhaps later." He gave me a thoughtful look, and despite my blankets, a shiver slid up my spine. He wanted to use me to scare his enemies in the Old World.

He wanted me to be a weapon.

I almost opened my mouth to threaten Dashiell, but my slow-moving brain managed to stop me in time. This was not the time to plant my feet and take a stand. Especially since a) my power was currently gone, and b) I literally couldn't stand.

"What happens now?" I said carefully.

"Now...I am very interested in your young friend, Scarlett. Have you considered taking her on as your apprentice?"

I admit, for a second, I thought about it. I pictured bringing Corry on jobs, teaching her about crime scenes and the Old World and how to survive. We could be a team, and I could be there for her, but not at all in the way Olivia was for me. I could do it right. And Corry could have a whole new future. A job, a friend, an entire new world.

The only problem was, it would be just like mine.

"No. That's not happening." Although I'd just promised myself not to antagonize Dashiell, my tone came out harsh and final.

He raised an eyebrow at me. I looked away quickly again. I felt suddenly cold. It's very scary, I realized, being around actual vampires. I had never appreciated being a null more than I did at that moment.

"We could make her a very nice offer, Scarlett." His voice was soft and dangerous.

"No. She's out of this." This time there was definite belligerence in my voice, and I glanced back at him, waiting for him to slap me or scream or something. Instead, when I looked over, he was calmly playing with his little silver phone. Then he held it up to me again, showing me a new video.

"Scarbo!" Jack's tinny voice was cheerful and filled with excitement. "Can you believe this? You and I work for the same guy!" My stomach churned with horror, and I felt my hands begin to shake. In the little video, Jack was standing outside of some sort of office building, talking right to the camera. His red hair had grown out a little, and it looked as if he'd been working out, too. He looked good. "Dash owns the company I'm working for now, and I was talking about you today, and it turns out that he uses your cleaning service. How cool is that? Anyway, he told me you were out of town for a couple of days, but he was going to see you soon, so we thought it'd be fun to make a video." His smile grew a little embarrassed, as though he didn't know how to sign off, so he just waved and winked at the little camera. "Call you soon, Scar!"

Oh God. Dashiell didn't just know about my brother, he'd taken steps to get Jack under his thumb. That's what Jack's whole move to LA had been about—Dashiell wanting to have better leverage over me, in case I got too uppity.

"You son of a bitch," I hissed. "He's my family. My only family."

Dashiell's vampire glow hummed as he gave me a mild smile and tucked the phone away, too quickly for my eyes to follow it. "Come, Scarlett, you must have realized I would have to take some measures to keep you...content with your place, let's say."

"But Jack...You started this with him way before we knew that I could do this!"

"Yes, wasn't that lucky of me?"

I stared. Had he anticipated my new ability? It was entirely possible, even likely, that he knew way more about my power than I did. And I was pretty frickin' sick of it. *That will have to change,* I thought grimly.

"Now, I have absolutely no intention of harming Jack. He's quite a good researcher, or so I'm told. Lots of promise to go to medical school as well."

My mouth snapped shut. Message received. Scarlett has to play well with others. I fully intended to do...*something* about this, but now wasn't the time for that, either.

"Now, because you were so helpful to Beatrice and me," Dashiell continued, "I will drop the issue of your young null friend—for the moment. You will spend a little time recovering, and then you'll be back to work. For now, things will continue as they have been." He looked at my face, his eyes narrowing, and I looked away. "But remember who you are, and who you work for, or things could become much less pleasant."

I said nothing. The first thing I would do when I recovered, I promised myself, was go track down one of the other nulls.

After a moment, Dashiell stood up from his seat. "You are tiring, Scarlett. I will let you rest."

"Wait," I said, and he turned to face me. "Ariadne, she said something when Jesse and I talked to her..."

He frowned. "Beatrice told me she sent the two of you down to see her. What did she say?"

"She said to tell you..." I began and paused for breath. I really was tiring. "She hoped your writing was going better. What did that mean?"

Dashiell just stared at me until I started to feel uncomfortable. Finally, he sat back down in his chair. "All right, Scarlett. You saved Beatrice. I suppose I owe you a story. Do I need to go into why this must remain between us?"

I tried to shake my head, but it hurt. "No," I whispered. I could have stopped him then—I didn't really need to know—but now I was curious.

"I'm not as old as I may seem, Scarlett. With most vampires, power comes from age, but I was turned only two hundred years ago. Do you know anything about English literature from that time?"

"Not really," I admitted. "Nothing past the average public school education."

He allowed me a faint smile. "Let's just say that while many vampires will boast about a relationship with a celebrity in their long lives, mine came before I was turned. In eighteen sixteen, I was a personal physician to the famous poet Lord Byron. That summer, he and I rented a house in Lake Geneva with some friends—Percy Shelley; Mary Godwin, his bride; and Mary's stepsister, Claire."

"*Frankenstein*," I whispered.

"That's right. The weather was horrible, and we were stuck indoors. One night, Byron read aloud from a book of horror stories and suggested we each write one. Mary started writing *The Modern Prometheus—Frankenstein*—on that trip. Percy wrote a number of short ghost stories, and Byron started a story, which came to be called *Fragment of a Novel*, about a vampire. Something spooked him, however, and shortly after the trip, he abandoned it."

"What did you write?"

He waved a hand. "Claire and I, we were just what you'd call hangers-on. Neither of us had much talent for writing, but we wanted to be around the three of them so badly, we were determined to...play in their league, I suppose would be the phrase. Claire decided to throw herself at Byron, which started a great deal of anguish. And I...Well, I was foolish." He leaned back in the chair. "I picked up Byron's discarded story and tried to make it my own. I added every detail I could think of, from every silly vampire story I could find. Back then, vampires did what they wanted— Stoker's book wouldn't come out for nearly a century, and vampires were just folklore. When I tried to get the book published, however, I was visited by three of them."

My eyes widened, and he smiled. "Oh, yes, they threatened me. I suspect they pressed my mind as well, because I awoke the next morning with no desire to be a published author whatsoever. But in a stupid twist of fate, one of my servants passed a manuscript to someone, and the story was published without my permission. *The Vampyre*. They came for me that very night."

"That's how you were turned," I said quietly.

"Yes. I believe they only did it so they could torment me further, but something strange happened. When I was 'born,' for the second time, I was more powerful than I should have been, with more control over myself. It happens that way every now and then. A few years later, after her affair with Byron had gone wrong and their young daughter had died, Claire came to me begging to be turned as well. Claire was always trying to find a cure for her restlessness, her endless search for self, and she had decided that being a vampire would solve all her problems. After two years of begging, I relented. She decided she was in love with me, which caused more anguish…" He lifted a shoulder in an elegant half shrug.

"Ariadne."

"Yes."

"Did it work? Did it make her happy?"

He frowned. "No. In fact, a few dozen years later, I met Beatrice and realized what love really felt like. And Claire was furious. So furious that she acted rashly, once again. She went to a young theater manager and failed novelist named Abraham Stoker, determined to give away secrets that would lead to the destruction of vampires. Luckily, Stoker was smart enough to do some…What would you call it? Fictionalizing."

My jaw dropped open.

He saw it and smiled. "I won't go any further into this particular drama. Suffice it to say that when you turned Ariadne—Claire—you did me a great favor. She was a thorn in my side for nearly two hundred years."

He stood up again, straightening out his clothes. "Of course, if you tell anyone that story, I will shoot you in the chest." He touched his forelock, as though tipping a hat, and just that quickly, he was gone again.

My jaw hung open.

I spent two more days in the hospital, sleeping and getting CT scans. I never asked who was in charge of supernatural cleanup while I was out, and Eli was in my hospital room every day. Maybe Kirsten, Dashiell, and Will were taking care of things themselves, or maybe they just ordered everyone to be cool for a week or so. I didn't really care either way. I was more concerned with getting better. By the morning after Dashiell's visit, I was starting to feel short, tingling bursts where the edges of my radius had been, like an electric fence struggling to turn itself on. I had also finally caught up on sleep, and was getting bored with the hospital.

Corry and her mother came to visit me on Thursday afternoon. Corry's arm was in a neon-green cast, and there were dark circles under her eyes, but she looked calm.

Her mother trembled as she took my hand. "Corry has explained some things to me," she said tearfully, "but I still have a few questions. Perhaps you could come for coffee sometime when you feel better?"

"Yeah, maybe," I said, glancing at Corry.

She nodded happily and turned to her mother. "Mom, could I have a second alone with Scarlett, please?"

Her mom hesitated, with: as if she might object but couldn't come up with an excuse.

"You'll be right outside the door, Mom," she said softly. "We'll leave the door open."

Mrs. Tanger finally nodded and turned away. This was a very different woman from the one I had met only a few days before. This woman knew that her children could be hurt, that she could become powerless to save them. It was a terrible thing to know, and the weight of it seemed to pull on her. I hoped she'd recover.

When she was gone, Corry took the chair on my right and dragged it close to the bed. "So...um...I guess thanks for saving my life and stuff," she said, smiling hesitantly.

I laughed a little. "You're welcome." I pushed the button to raise my bed up, trying to get a better angle for talking to her. "How much are you telling your mom?"

"Not a lot, so far. She knows that I can do something that's valuable to certain...I think the term I used was 'criminal elements.' She isn't asking a whole lot of questions. I think she doesn't want to know."

"And your dad?"

Her smile was sad and wistful. "He's just pretending the whole thing never happened—that we had a botched robbery or something."

We were silent for a moment, thinking about that.

Then I said softly, "Have you told them about your teacher?"

"No."

I nodded. "Look, Corry, I'm not exactly the poster child for mental health, but you really should tell someone. A counselor, a therapist, your mom. You need to be able to talk about it."

She didn't answer me, and I didn't push. We were silent for a long moment, and then she reached into her jeans pocket and pulled out a black Magic Marker. "Um, do you want to sign my cast?"

She held out the marker, and her eyes were full of something—hope. I took the marker, uncapped it, and turned the cast over very gently with my free hand. She already had signatures and little notes from her parents, her brother, a couple of friends, even a teacher. I paused. Then, with guilt and sorrow roiling in my stomach, I put the cap back on the marker.

She looked puzzled. "What?"

"Corry...I don't think you and I should spend time together."

Her face changed immediately, beginning to shut down, and I held up a hand.

"Wait, wait, hear me out. The things that we can do, Corry, they're really valuable to some people. I'm 'out of the closet,' or whatever, but nobody knows what you can do except for a very few people, who I trust not to say anything." At least for now. And I hadn't forgotten that someone had given Corry away to Jared Hess, but there wasn't much I could do about that now. "You can still walk away, and I think you should."

"Why?" she cried, hurt in her eyes. "Why should I bother trying to hide?"

"Because it's safer, honey," I said gently. "You were right, what you told your parents. You can do something that some very bad people would love to have at their disposal." That was a lesson that we'd all learned the hard way. "And as long as you're spending time with me, those people won't have to look very hard to find you."

"But you do it! Everyone knows what you can do, and you're fine!"

I gestured to the bed. "Look at me. Do I look fine? My situation is complicated, Corry. And you deserve a chance to finish growing up before you choose how complicated you want your life to be."

"That's not fair!" she cried. "You're the only one who...who knows..."

"I'm sorry, Corry. I swear I am."

Without another word, she stood up, her back perfectly straight, and marched out of the room. I bit my lip hard enough to leave marks. Had I just done the right thing? Or was leaving her out of Dashiell's protection even worse than having her free? I wished there were someone who would tell me the right thing to do.

That same afternoon, Kirsten came by with a big basket of organic fruit and a plate of cookies. She seemed completely recovered from the whole rescue/surgery trauma and wore a sunny smile on top of her pretty sundress and Grecian sandals. Since I hadn't had a shower in about five days, this was not healthy for my self-esteem. I nodded at Eli, who kissed my forehead and told me he'd run out for some food. He gave Kirsten a peck on the cheek as he passed her, and she smiled in return. Battling Hess together had definitely built up some trust between the two of them.

I gestured for Kirsten to sit, and she perched in the rocking chair. "They're chocolate chip," she said, handing me the cookies.

I took a cookie and bit into it. "Thank you, it's delicious."

"You're welcome," Kirsten said.

When I had swallowed the bite, I asked, "Did you...Are you okay, after everything that happened?"

Her face turned serious. "I am. I've been getting more calls from Dashiell lately. I think he's starting to see me as a...a player, I suppose. I'm not sure if that's a good thing or a bad thing."

"Neither am I."

"Listen," Kirsten said, "there's a meeting that I need to get to, unfortunately, but I wanted to stop by to tell you something."

"Oh?" I said, munching.

"The tracking spell? The one I used to find you in that basement? Eli didn't really have one of your T-shirts."

I stilled, my mouth full of cookie. I'd completely forgotten. Had I left something more embarrassing at Eli's? A bra? Panties? Wouldn't I remember not having panties? "What did you use?"

She looked uncomfortable. "This is awkward...I still thought you should know. We couldn't find anything and were in such a hurry...So I used Eli. Himself."

"For a tracking spell? I thought you needed a belonging."

"I do," she said quietly, then looked at me as if I were missing something obvious.

"Wait...I'm sorry, are you saying that Eli *belongs* to me?"

"Sort of." Her fingers twined in the air as she struggled for an explanation. "It's more like...his heart does. He considers himself yours, and so in the eyes of the spell, so to speak, he is." She winced. "Was I right to tell you?"

"Yeah, no...I mean, yes, it's good to know. Thank you," I managed.

She nodded and squeezed my hand, rising to leave.

Eli belonged to me?

I had a few other visitors in the hospital. Caroline brought me a huge stack of trashy magazines and romance novels. Will came by with an apologetic smile and a beaten-up checkers board. We didn't talk about how close I'd come to dying, but he made a point to tell me that I was welcome in his bar anytime I wanted, null or not. He ruffled my hair when he left, and I knew things were okay between us.

Since she couldn't come out during visiting hours—and apparently didn't want to sneak in, like Dashiell—Molly called to check on me every night. Beatrice and I had a long phone conversation, too, during which she thanked me profusely and I managed to cajole her into sharing some stories about famous people she'd known. She didn't mention the story that Dashiell had told me, so I didn't, either. Dashiell stopped by one last time to tell me that they had finally figured out how Jared Hess had gotten the three vampires into the clearing. Hess had approached Joanna and Demetri through his silver business contacts and gotten the couple interested in buying some silver chains for use against the werewolves. They had arranged for him to meet with Abraham, the money guy, to talk about the specifics of the deal. Dashiell still didn't know about how they all got to the park that night, but it looked like we might never find out. That was fine with me.

During the day, Eli and I played cards and watched TV in between my naps. At night, Jesse would arrive, kiss my head, and collapse in the armchair. The two of them were never together very long, and there was a wariness between them that I found a little amusing. But they were always polite and cordial, at least in front of me.

Jesse was pissed that Dashiell had pressed his mind, and was determined not to miss anything else. He scooted the armchair to within four inches of the bed and woke up every time the nurses came to check on me, though he wouldn't make eye contact with anyone but me. He seemed exhausted all the time, and on my last night in the hospital, I finally asked him how things were at work.

"Um, okay," he said cautiously. "I got a lot of credit for the Hess thing, and since none of the La Brea Park victims had families to put up a big fuss, we were able to close the whole case pretty quickly. It ended well, public relations–wise. And"—he smiled shyly and pulled a new-looking leather wallet out of his pocket, flipping it open—"I got promoted."

I looked at the shiny new detective badge. "Oh, Jesse, that's awesome."

"Thanks. Not how I wanted to get it, but…"

"But you still deserve it."

We were quiet for a moment, and I watched him fidgeting.

"There's something you're still not telling me, isn't there?"

He sighed, leaning back in the chair. "My boss has been looking at me funny," he admitted. "She wasn't all that impressed with my performance during the investigation, and then I get this miraculous tip and solve the whole thing…I think she's not even sure what she suspects me of doing, but she's definitely suspicious. I've been busting my ass to appear competent so she'll relax."

"Is it working?"

"I don't know."

He was quiet after that, and we played falling-asleep chicken for a minute. Then he leaned forward and looked at me very seriously. My hands were folded on my stomach, and for a moment, he reached over and pressed his fingers against mine. "Scarlett, about that day at the bait shop, when we were in the parking lot—"

I shook my head, withdrawing my fingers gently. "Jesse, I can't. I just can't even think about...um...relationship stuff right now." Especially since I apparently owned another man.

"I understand, and I'm not pushing you," he said quietly. "But we almost kissed, Scarlett. And I wanted to let you know that if you ever wanted to almost kiss again, or even actually kiss...Well, I wanted to throw my hat in the ring."

I blinked, surprised. "I thought after you found out what I did..."

He gave a little nod, conceding a point I hadn't been able to make. "I still have...strong feelings about your job. But I almost lost you, and that definitely made an impression."

Happily, before I had to respond, a nurse—and my new favorite person in the world—bustled in to get my blood pressure, and when she left, we started talking about something else.

Dammit, I thought a little while later, when Jesse had fallen asleep again. I had pretty much written off Jesse as a romantic option, and then he goes and says something like that. No matter how things turned out later, he and Eli had both been incredible to me in the hospital. Better than I deserved. What I'd said was true, though—now that Jack was under Dashiell's thumb and I apparently had this crazy new ability, my thoughts had to be elsewhere. I hadn't told anyone about what I'd done to Ariadne, and I didn't plan to. The fewer people who knew about that, the better. And, if I were being honest with myself, I particularly didn't want Eli to know. Eli did not like being a were, and I was very afraid he'd ask me to change him back. Until I knew more about what I could do, I didn't want that between us.

By Friday afternoon, I was ready to check out of the hospital. My body was recovering nicely—I could stay awake for the whole day again—and although it was very weak, my radius was defined again. I could tell Eli was inside it, but it wasn't changing him back into a human, which was okay for the time being. I was just relieved that it was coming back. It's scary being vulnerable.

It took hours to get through the last-minute exams and paperwork—I was starting to think one nurse in particular was dragging everything out—and it was getting dark by the time everything was done. I was practically bouncing in the wheelchair as the nurse drove it down to the emergency room entrance. I was sick of hospital food and bad cable, and to my own surprise, I missed running and work and the rest of my life. I even missed watching romantic comedies with Molly, who had told me she was planning a Brat Pack marathon for when I got back.

When we got down to the lobby, Eli went ahead to bring his car around. The nurse who had driven the wheelchair was looking nervous and fidgety, so I finally told her I could wait on the bench outside the hospital entrance by myself. As soon as I was settled down, she hustled back for the door. My thoughts were elsewhere, thinking about how I could get time off work to go learn about being a null—not to mention Eli and Jesse.

It's right when you're distracted by boys that the powers of evil will come for you.

I idly watched a little boy with a blue balloon walk into the hospital, and when I turned my head back toward the street, a vampire sat on the bench next to me, looking smug and dangerous in a tailored red dress. She grabbed my arm, digging her fingernails in, and tossed back waves of chestnut hair to smirk at me.

And the bottom dropped out of the world.

"Hello, Scar-bear. Did you get my flowers?"

"No," I breathed. "That's not possible." I shook my head frantically. "It's not possible!"

"Oh, but it is possible," Olivia cooed at me. I tried to pull away, but she just dug her nails in deeper. "No, honey, you're not going anywhere. You and I just have so much to talk about." Blood began to drip from my arm where her nails had pierced it, and she licked her lips. "I came to the hospital to see you, even though you stopped coming for me. And why was that? Did you find out something you shouldn't?" Her voice was syrupy sweet, and silent tears began to run down my cheeks. "Why *did* you have to go digging up the past, Scar-bear?"

I heard the squeal of tires and saw Eli's truck careen out of the parking garage, bearing down on us.

"Oh, darn, looks like your ride is here already. To be continued, honey." She released my arm and licked blood off her fingers, giving me her old, serene look. Then she was gone.

I began to scream.

Acknowledgments

Like Scarlett's, my life once took a surprising sudden turn away from the path I had planned for myself. Unlike Scarlett, however, I had quite the heavy-duty support system to help me adjust, and this book happened because of them. A huge thank-you to everyone who had my back as I started writing, especially my aunts and uncles, and my laid-back husband, who was always willing to help by brainstorming or taking over parenting duties, and who read the first draft and delivered (still) the best compliment I've gotten: "I kept forgetting it was you."

Thank you to my crack team of beta readers Nicole Rosario, Kay Basler, Jason Martell, Brieta Bejin, Stephanie Olson, Megan Lane, Linda Crossett, Lisa Mysker, Tracy Tong, and Elizabeth Kraft—and to Carrie Welch, who was gracious enough to watch my daughter so I could work on *Dead Spots*. This book wouldn't have been what it is without all of you. I also want to thank Scarlett's namesake, Scarlett Welch, still the most terrifying toddler I have ever encountered. Please don't read this book until you're much older.

Much gratitude also goes to my mentor-heroes, author Alex Bledsoe and my graduate advisor Liam Callanan. You guys were always willing to entertain mundane questions about publishing and plotting, far beyond the call of friendship or duty.

Thank you, of course, to the "official" team: my agent, Jacquie Flynn; my wonderful development editor, Jeff VanderMeer; and Alex Carr, who saw *Dead Spots* the way I had hoped someone would. If I'm forgetting anyone, please forgive me. I'm new at this.

A big thanks to the Madison Writers Institute folks at the UW-School of Continuing Education, who provide wonderfully valuable classes and conferences in my very own town. In particular, I want to thank Madison-area author and retired teacher Marshall Cook, who probably doesn't even remember my face, but who took the time to encourage me the first time I tried to write fiction, and then wrote a lovely letter of recommendation to help get me into grad school. Your generosity for a student you'd just met made a big impression on me, and gave me a much-needed boost of confidence when I had none. Every student you've worked with has been truly lucky to have you, me especially.

Finally, thank you again to my mom and dad. As far as I'm concerned, I've won every "who has the best parents" contest, real or imagined, in my lifetime. I love you guys.

About the Author

Photograph © Tyler Lane, 2011

Melissa F. Olson was born and raised in Chippewa Falls, Wisconsin, and studied film and literature at the University of Southern California in Los Angeles. After graduation, and a brief stint bouncing around the Hollywood studio system, she moved to Madison, Wisconsin, where she eventually acquired a master's degree from the University of Wisconsin–Milwaukee, a husband, a mortgage, two kids, and two comically oversized dogs—not at all in that order. *Dead Spots* is her first novel.

18947706R00174

Printed in Poland
by Amazon Fulfillment
Poland Sp. z o.o., Wrocław